CARGO OF EAGLES

Margery Allingham was born in London in 1904. She attended the Perse School in Cambridge before returning to London to the Regent Street Polytechnic. Her father – author H. J. Allingham – encouraged her to write, and was delighted when she contributed to her aunt's cinematic magazine, *The Picture Show*, at the age of eight.

Her first novel was published when she was seventeen. In 1928 she published her first detective story, *The White Cottage Mystery*, which had been serialised in the *Daily Express*. The following year, in *The Crime at Black Dudley*, she introduced the character who was to become the hallmark of her writing – Albert Campion. Her novels heralded the more sophisticated suspense genre: characterised by her intuitive intelligence, extraordinary energy and accurate observation, they vary from the grave to the openly satirical, whilst never losing sight of the basic rules of the classics detective tale. Famous for her London thrillers, she has been compared to Dickens in her evocation of the city's shady underworld.

In 1927 she married the artist, journalist and editor Philip Youngman Carter. They divided their time between their Bloomsbury flat and an old house in the village of Tolleshunt D'Arcy in Essex. Margery Allingham died in 1966.

ALSO BY MARGERY ALLINGHAM

MARGERY ALLINGHAM

Cargo of Eagles

VINTAGE BOOKS
London

Published by Vintage 2008

4 6 8 10 9 7 5

First published in Great Britain in 1968 by
Chatto & Windus

Vintage
Random House, 20 Vauxhall Bridge Road,
London SW1V 2SA

www.vintage-books.co.uk

Addresses for companies within The Random House Group Limited
can be found at: www.randomhouse.co.uk/offices.htm

The Random House Group Limited Reg. No. 954009

A CIP catalogue record for this book
is available from the British Library

ISBN 9780099513285

The Random House Group Limited supports The Forest Stewardship
Council® (FSC®), the leading international forest-certification organisation.
Our books carrying the FSC label are printed on FSC®-certified paper.
FSC is the only forest-certification scheme supported by the leading
environmental organisations, including Greenpeace. Our
paper procurement policy can be found at
www.randomhouse.co.uk/environment

MIX
Paper from
responsible sources
FSC® C016897

Printed and bound in Great Britain by Clays Ltd, St Ives plc

Contents

This book was left unfinished by Margery Allingham at the time of her death in June 1966. It has been completed by her husband Youngman Carter who had been her partner for nearly forty years and had helped to hatch many of her plots. The whole fabric of this story had been mapped out long before her death and the book has been finished by him at her specific request.

All the characters are fictitious and no reference to any person, living or dead, is intended.

The estuary, the village of Saltey, the Rattey river and the 'back road' to London will not be found on any official map.

'By this time the road was full of passengers, everyone furnish'd with no small appetite. Citizens in crowd, upon pads, hackneys and hunters, all upon the titup, as if he who rid not at a gallop was to forfeit his horse. Some spurred on with speed and cheerfulness, as if they never intended to come back again. Some rode double, some single. Every now and then a lady drop'd from her pillion, and another from her side-saddle, some showing the milky way to bliss to the company, which, tho' it made them blush, made us merry.

'Horses, coaches, carts, waggons and tumbrils fill'd the road, as if the whole town had been going to encamp; all occupy'd by men, women and children, rich, poor, gentle and simple, having all travelling conveniences suitable to their quality. In this order did we march, like Aaron's proselytes to worship the calf, till we came to the new-rais'd fabric call'd Mobs Hole, in Wanstead Parish, where the beast was to be eaten.'

The London Spy by Ned Ward

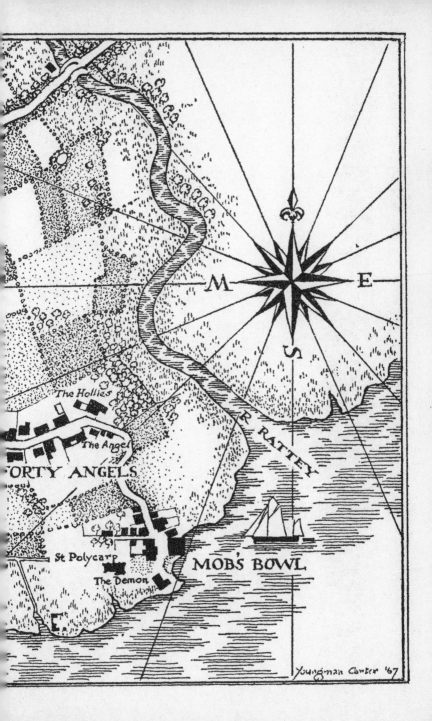

The Hollies

The Angel

FORTY ANGELS

St Polycarp

The Demon

MOB'S BOWL

R. RATTEY

M E

S

Youngman Carter '67

Back Door to London

T HE rain was falling in a sweet relentless fashion as it does in spring in London and it was all very peaceful and pleasant if uncompromisingly wet. The voice in the car echoed the unhurried pace of the afternoon.

'I found this absurd place Saltey, you're so interested in, perfectly enchanting in an off-beat sort of way but I'm damned if I can tell you quite why.'

It was a young man talking to a middle-aged one. He was not being completely disingenuous, for subsequent generations seldom are with each other, but at least he was playing scrupulously fair.

'I realise that the whole township—or as you'd say, village—pretends to be deeply and secretly wicked, which is naïve and kind of endearing. I wish I had more to report on it,' he went on, 'but unfortunately its modern life appears to be almost entirely vegetable. If you were interested in its history I could do better. I'm very sure a full scale archaeological dig there would pay off, for one thing. But the living inhabitants are not exactly go ahead except for the couple at the pub who are working like hell—or at least the woman is—to get a little tourist trade.'

'Is she having any luck?'

The lighter voice of Mr Albert Campion betrayed interest. He had curled his long body in the passenger seat of the Lotus Elan and seemed anxious to talk.

The driver shook his head. 'A little—at weekends. The natives themselves don't respond to anything which looks new or difficult, however profitable. Their great interest is the contents of each other's wills. They sit around speculating for hours and there's a grand frustration scene every time one gets published.'

'An end will come to that, in due course,' said Mr Campion. 'Mark my words.'

'You're telling me!' The driver laughed and slid down behind the wheel in an attempt to get a better view through the railings of the public gardens beside which they were parked. 'Are we sitting here in the middle of London waiting for someone? Or do you just feel that this is the quietest place to talk?'

'It has its advantages.' Campion surveyed the deserted scene with satisfaction. Lunch time was over and the streams of office workers had been sucked back into the tall buildings for another few hours before the next mass exodus. Although the Lotus was in one of the busiest parts of the town, between the University and the Oxford Street shopping centre, there was for the moment hardly a pedestrian in sight and the other cars parked regimentally at their meters were empty.

Mortimer Kelsey, Morty to his friends and the other members of his faculty at Vere University, Constance, New Jersey, appeared a happy man. A great deal about Britain struck him as funny after nearly a year's residence, but he was also deeply attracted by its ancient spell. Both the elegant car body and his casual clothes, conscious efforts in understatement without dullness, were custom built. His haircut was long for one country and short for the other and managed to make him look mildly distinguished. This was fair, for he was already a marked man among the newest crop of historians and he was one of that army of Western scholars who have discovered so much more about the cities of the old world than their inhabitants dream there is to know. He was in his mid-twenties, a good looking youngster with well shaped, compact bones, a deeply scored face which already showed signs of the notable scholar he would appear in later years.

He was lucky not to appear offensively intellectual—which is to say not at all—and he was not conceited although the pundits expected interesting results from the piece of original research on which he was now engaged. His father was American, his mother English: both families unfashionably well endowed. Mr Campion had met him through his own son Rupert who was now working for an honours degree at Harvard.

The two men although very different in age had a good deal in common. Albert Campion, too, was tall and fair but he was over-thin and the careful veil of affable vacuity which had begun, like his large spectacles, as a protection and had become a second skin, had robbed him of good looks, whereas Morty's thick light brown hair had a wave in it and there was nothing bleak or colourless about his grey eyes.

In his own apologetic way Mr Campion was a celebrated figure. In his time he had performed a number of services for a great many causes. He was a negotiator and an unraveller of knots and there were still people who suspected, because of his war time activities, that he had a cloak and a dagger somewhere concealed. Those who disliked him complained that he seemed negligible until it was just too late.

At the moment he was looking out at the patch of rain-soaked London green which formed the centre of Killowen Square. The downpour which had persisted all morning was getting lighter but the air was soft as if there might be more rain to come.

'If I should want you to go back to Saltey for a while, could you manage it?' he asked suddenly.

'I was hoping you'd say that. When will you know?' Morty's eagerness seemed a little surprising, even to himself, for he coloured faintly. 'It's got something,' he said defensively.

The older man continued to look out at the garden. The prospect was not imposing. Four wet asphalt paths met in the centre of a roundel of grass and the dripping plane trees in their scant shrouds of new green looked sparse and sodden. The only ornamental feature of the place was a tiny Victorian bandstand perched among regimented tulips. Constructed of florid cast iron work, it was white painted, gay as a sunshade and just as silly on a rainy day. Mr Campion glanced over the empty garden to the immense wall of the buildings beyond.

'That over-stuffed contraption squatting under the new sky-scraper is Lugg's favourite hotel,' he remarked. 'You saw him down there, of course? He considers the old Ottoman is "quite the article", which is his highest praise. In my father's day the valets there always ironed the laces when they cleaned the boots and a rope ladder was kept under every bed in case of fire. How is Lugg?'

'Very impressive. He shoots the most magnificent line ever. I've heard him on the well pressed bootlace. *Was* he ever in Royal service?'

Mr Campion controlled his amusement. 'He's looked after me for quite a few years as a sort of housekeeper,' he began cautiously.

'I know, but he says this was when he was younger. He was telling one of the architects he did a spell for the Monarch before he lost his figure.'

The thin man relaxed. 'That was only for six months,' he said. 'It was the—er—Palace of Wormwood Scrubs, I believe. Which architects are these?'

'The people who are gunning for the job of building his bungalow.' Morty spoke with authority. 'He's retiring to Saltey to take up archaeology, or so he says. Didn't he tell you? He could choose a worse place.'

'Oh, what is there?'

'I'm not sure, yet.' The distinctive young face had become earnest. 'As you know, the paper I'm doing is on London's approaches in the seventeenth and eighteenth centuries and when you asked me to investigate that crazy damn story there, I was genuinely looking for something else.'

'Saltey: gateway to the East End?'

'You're not so far out, and it's my own beautiful discovery.' Morty's grin was joyful. 'There's not a breath of it in any of the authorities but I think I've got proof that the little harbour

14

there, which is practically silted up now, is all that is left of the ancient bolt hole, old London's eastern emergency exit. As a matter of fact, Saltey is the other end of Mob's Hole. I'm sure of it now. The lower half of the village where the best pub stands is called Mob's Bowl today and that's hardly a distortion, is it? There it is, written on the survey maps and the signposts.' He paused in sudden doubt. 'You have heard of Mob's Hole?'

'Should I?'

'Perhaps not. I'm quite besotted with my subject. Anyway, you can take it from me that it existed in Wanstead about seventeen ten or so. It was a rakehelly dive, a kind of roadhouse where the "mobility"—that's the joke name of the period for the tarts and townees who had transport—used to ride out of the city for a feed, what we'd call a barbecue, and a punch-up. There is a fine fruity account of it in *The London Spy*.'

'Do the present day people of Saltey subscribe to this?'

'Gosh, no. They've never heard of it. They think, if they think at all, that the Bowl is derived from the silted up tidal basin by the quay and that it could be a relic of a prehistoric salt panning industry. One old biddy told me it was "Mab" and not "Mob" and was a direct reference to the Fairy Queen.'

'How old is Saltey?'

'Oh, dateless. In prehistoric times it was at the edge of the single great river mouth. Then it became a delta as the mud banks shifted and finally it grew into the marsh and plough we know. Since its heyday, which was probably pre-Saxon, it must have grown more and more inefficient as the clay took over. I'm certain there's an early fortress by the highest part of the sea wall just waiting to be uncovered.' He sighed and laughed at himself for it. 'That's not my period and so is not my province, which is the infuriating thing about history. It does keep repeating itself but only in its untidy way. New names get attached to old happenings and vice versa. If I don't stick to my own period I'll be lost in a morass of extra information. But it's a honey of a find. Do you know what the upper or respectable end of the place is called? *Forty Angels.*'

'Really?' Mr Campion so far forgot himself as to take his eyes off the garden he had been watching so steadfastly. 'Come to think of it, I did know that one. It's later than the other end and the name was given it as a safeguard against slander. Call a gathering The Forty Thieves and it could mean trouble, but say Forty Angels and no one wants to black your eye. Yes, your meaning is clear. Isn't that right?'

Morty wagged his head.

'It looks pretty damned odd on the Ordnance Survey,' he said. 'It's a crazy name for a village district, even in England. Saltey was on the end of an escape route. It was the funnel through which secret goods or people were smuggled in or out of East London. It's remote even now. Not in miles of course—it's just cut off. The approach is terrible.'

'Through that maze of lanes lying beyond the Southend road, I suppose?'

'Oh yes, it's still a Cinderella. Today there's a bungalow dormitory two miles wide but before that one has to pass a waste of worked out clay pits which have been turned into a wilderness by various army training courses and old defence works. Long before they were as much as thought of, that was where the Great Dump was.'

In the back of Mr Campion's mind a faint bell rang. 'Was that "The Trough"?'

'That's right!' Morty was delighted. 'It was a swamp really. The little Rattey River rose in it and drained out to reach the sea at Saltey. It first appears as a place of ill omen in the Middle Ages, when for a time it was thought to be the source of the Plague. For generations it was a no-man's land, an Alsatia worse than any shanty town. Bands of diseased beggars wandered around. Indestructible rubbish was shot there. Rats and wild dogs bred there and I believe there were ferocious wild

16

pig as late as eighteen hundred. No one in his senses took a path through the place and there are some hair-raising tales of kidnappings, murdered coachmen, wandering lunatics and even cannibalism. On the far side of it, nearer the coast, there was woodland, an arm of the old forest which covered the whole country at one time. Then there is a strip of twitchy heath, some of which isn't enclosed even now, and after that the mouth of the tiny Rattey River estuary and Saltey. You can drive through it all now, but it's still not easy to find. No industry you see. Not suitable land for development. Just the saltings and Saltey. When you do reach it, there it sits, smug and deserted and not very pleased to see you.'

'You say there are no new residents?'

'None that I've heard of.' He turned and glanced across the garden. 'Its only claim to fame is that a peculiarly revolting mother-figure was found in a field at Firestone, four miles away, in nineteen hundred. That's in the British Museum now —in the horror comic room. Hey!'

He leaned forward. A solitary figure had appeared on the path approaching the bandstand. He was some distance away and was making for the distant gate in front of the skyscraper and the baroque hotel.

'See who that is?' he demanded in some excitement as he took a small gunmetal cylinder from the open map compartment in front of him. 'I think I'm right, though I've only seen him once before. He's almost commonplace close to, but utterly distinctive from a distance. It's the thing I particularly noticed about him. Hang on, I'll give you the bird-watching glass in a moment.' He put the little telescope to his eye and crowed.

'I'm right! That's L. C. Corkran, head of Intelligence and Security or whatever you call it over here. My, my! He looks pretty sour, doesn't he?'

Mr Campion, who had stiffened involuntarily at the mention of the name, recovered himself and accepted the little instrument.

'He's retiring, I believe,' said Morty, his ingenuousness un-questionable, 'at the end of the year.'

His passenger grunted. 'About time too, if he's as well known as that.'

'Oh, it's not general knowledge. One of our attachés pointed him out to me at a Test Match when I first came over. I re-membered him because I was told he was quite somebody years ago.' He spoke regretfully. 'Burn-before-reading top secrets are dead ducks nowadays. It must be tough on these old boys to have their hush-hush departments degenerating into tatting houses all round them. They're all full of old ladies sticking little silver knives into each other's backs now. Or so they say.' He shook his head and changed the subject.' You know, I can easily imagine this town teeming with sedan .chairs and stink-ing bullies in silk coats, but I'm darned if I can see it as the gaping ruin it must have been only twenty odd years ago. It doesn't seem possible. It's so elderly and permanent and—I won't say pompous—urbane, perhaps.'

Mr Campion let him chatter. Through the 'escape and evasion' glass, an instrument with which he had once been uncomfortably familiar but had now become a mere 'war surplus store', he was watching the grim features of one of his oldest and closest friends. He and L. C. Corkran, 'Elsie' to his familiars, met seldom nowadays but there had been a time when each had been content to know that his life was in the other's hands. Morty was right. The old man looked bitter. Mr Campion knew that expression and he kept the glass on him as he came up with the bandstand. He shot a glance at it from force of habit, because of its memories and strode on, his heavy chin thrust out, his shoulders sagging and his eyes down. There was defeat written all over him. As he turned and his face was hidden, Mr Campion raised the glass to the new skyscraper beside the old hotel. Of the nest of windows on the ninth and tenth floors, two had curtains looped back by cautious hands. They dropped into place as the solitary figure advanced.

Old ladies with silver knives? More accurately dry grey serpents with shiny duct-fed teeth. The thin man shivered and returned the little telescope to its locker.

'How soon can you get back to Saltey?' he enquired.

'You've made up your mind already? Wonderful. I thought you'd have to have a conference or something. I can go down there today, as a matter of fact. Am I still to be investigating the great Saltey Demon? I'm afraid that's going to turn out to be a dead loss, by the way.'

'I thought it might. What is it? A rustic joke?'

'Sort of. The lady at the pub has been casting round for something to attract visitors ever since she took over the place. She had a yen for one of those God-awful wishing-wells you find all over the West Country. You know the sort of thing. Fling your dime into the water and the local pixies will reward you with a lucky pebble and a picture postcard of the waterfront. She kept worrying to know if Saltey had such a sprite and eventually someone—her husband perhaps, for he's a local—came forward with this unlikely devil. They tell the tale on Friday nights in walnut time when the moon is full. Or something like that.'

Mr Campion laughed.

'She must have sold the idea to the local papers because the nationals picked it up a year or two back. I read it somewhere. A coloured Sunday, I think.'

'You told me. Anyway, the legend provides me with a fairly reasonable excuse for hanging round. At the moment I'm the poor young Yankee professor, good for a free pint and folksy tale any day.'

'And no one new has arrived in the village in the past year or so?'

'Only the pub people, or rather the woman. A couple called Wishart. Her name is Dixie and she's not exactly an intellectual but she means well and she's a worker. Her husband is not. He's a man of culture in his odd way—quite a different background, anyhow, I'd say. I think he lived around those parts as a boy. He writes poetry and gets it published or used to.'

'Not H. O. Wishart?'

'That's the man. He's about sixty-five now and not the best of value, but he's in the anthologies. She keeps a Georgian Poetry under the bar counter and trots it out on the least provocation.'

'*Beware of me: I cast no shadow when I pass,*' quoted Mr Campion. 'That's the chap, isn't it? A genuine minor poet and a white hope at one time. I didn't know he was at the inn. Did you say it was called "The Demon"?'

'That's very recent. Dixie got the brewers to change it. Partly because the other pub is called The Angel, and partly on account of the old joke about the Demon. It used to be called "The Foliage", which she was mistaken enough to think dull.'

Morty met the other man's raised eyebrows and laughed. 'I know. It can only be a contraction of "The Foliate Man", can't it? I tell you the place is full of good things. Add that to the Fertility Venus and one or two other items and the shenanigans the wilder teenage gangs get up to along the sea wall don't seem half as modern as they might.'

'Tearaways? You get them down there?' The thin man looked interested but Morty shrugged.

'They're everywhere. They don't stay. They just swoop down on motor bikes—ton-up types. They tear off their space-man rig-outs and jump in the sea. Then they eat the shop out of cake, drain the pub of shandy and mock champagne and rush off again. That and the occasional orgy.'

'It sound promising.'

'Not really, as it turned out.' He was a thought sulky as if something still rankled. 'Little tramps,' he said suddenly. 'I went round to the sea wall only a week ago to watch some saddleback gulls and I sat down out of the wind and went to sleep. It was quite early and pretty nippy weather. When I woke up there were some of these kids—they were sixteen or seventeen I suppose—screaming and dancing almost on top of

20

me, dressed in crash helmets and boots and damn all else as far as I could see. Not that I blame them for the boots, the saltings are infested with grass snakes they say, but the point is—they wanted to shock me.'

He paused. 'Little tramp,' he repeated.

'One in particular?'

'As a matter of fact, yes. The ringleader, I think. She was skipping round me like Salome without much in the way of veils, just waiting for the laugh when I opened my eyes. It was all unnatural and wild because it was so early in the year for that sort of thing. I scuttled back to the village and in a minute or two they came roaring past and rode me into a dyke. Seven or eight of them, all scruffy ringlets and black leather, and as high as kites, I'd say. Full of pep pills or worse. Perhaps I'm growing old. Anyhow, they didn't stay and I haven't seen a sign of them since. I take it you're interested in something a little less fancy?'

His passenger took out his wallet and extracted a photograph.

'That's someone I'd like you to look for. He'll be quite a bit older than he is there. His name by the way is Teague—James Teague.'

Morty studied the picture. It was a head only: the man had been caught by a press photographer, looking over his shoulder. It was a distinctive face, handsome and swarthy in the white-toothed fashion of the early film stars and crowned with sweeping curls of black hair. He could have been in his mid-thirties, but the outstanding impresson he gave was of youth and that superabundant energy and vivacity which go to make the powerful visual personality. He looked both dangerous and exciting. A violent, magnetic, unpredictable animal.

'Quite a guy.' The younger man handed back the print. 'I'll know him if I see him. It's not a face you'd miss anywhere, let alone in my little Saltey.'

His grin held a remembered pleasure and Campion spoke on impulse.

'What is it that attracts you so down there? A woman?'

A guilty colour suffused Morty's cheeks.

'Not really,' he said with dignity. 'And certainly not that little tramp.' He paused, amused at himself, before continuing. 'But in a way you're right. I did happen to encounter a dazzler down there the other day. She could become one of your new residents in time, but that's almost too much to hope for. She's just inherited a house in the respectable part of the village and there's some sort of trouble packaged in with the deal. She certainly has something, that one.' He was staring into the greenery ahead of him and his wide smile twisted.

'I'm crazy,' he said with the tolerance of a man who cannot quite credit his own absurdity. 'I've only seen her for a few minutes. She came into The Demon with someone who was showing her round. In fact she was only . . .'

'Passing by?' suggested Mr Campion.

Morty laughed at himself. 'And across a crowded room, same like the other song says. Forget it, I'll recover. I'm to look for the picturesque guy in the photograph. Is that all?'

'Not quite. I'm also interested in a man with a glass eye. If he should appear, get on to me at once.'

'O.K. Any other distinguishing marks? I mean that sort of thing is very well made these days. I could miss it.'

'I don't think so. Not this one. He is a tall man with a protuberant real eye and the unequal effect is noticeable—or used to be. That's what I'm told. Also his own eye is that very bright clear Nordic blue which you find on your own east coast. Difficult to match, you know. The tendency is to get the false one too electric. Should this lad appear Lugg will go to ground, so it will be up to you to keep him in your sights. I take it you're treating Lugg as a stranger?'

'Oh, yes. We fraternise as man to man in the pub but everyone thinks we met down there. May I ask what we're supposed to be up to?'

'I'd much rather you didn't. It may be safer that way. Do you mind?'

'Not at all.' Morty was polite but astonished. 'Who am I working for?'

'Me,' said Mr Campion promptly. 'Me alone, I'm afraid. And as for me, I'm working for a lady.'

'Her Majesty?' Morty was a royalist by nature.

The thin man appeared momentarily embarrassed. 'Well, no, as a matter of fact,' he said with uncharacteristic awkwardness. '*Au contraire*, now I come to think of it.'

2

The Old Pal's Act

MR CAMPION had been a member of Puffins, one of
the least publicised of London Clubs, for many years and
never expected to find himself embarrassed by the fact, but as
he hurried down St James's towards the Georgian portico he
felt an unfamiliar discomfort. He passed the place at speed and
his sidestep into the alcove which concealed the service entrance to Fitzherbert's, the Club next door, was furtive.

He was keeping an appointment with Stanislaus Oates, a
retired Assistant Commissioner of Police famous in his day,
and the choice of rendezvous was typical of that ingenious old
man's latest phase. Membership of Fitzherbert's was said still
to be decided by heredity and it certainly remained a last
stronghold of unregenerate class consciousness and the kind of
prejudice which is on the direct route to embalmment.

On the other hand old Oates, who had risen from the ranks
and never suffered from fear of heights, appreciated service,
privacy and comfort when he saw them. Fitzherbert's appealed
to him strongly and nowadays, when he came to town from his
retreat in the suburbs, he made a point of looking up one of his
erstwhile sergeants who had a job in charge of security in the
basement there. Often he stayed the whole afternoon and
evening, during which time people were liable to drop in to
see him. Mr Campion was one of many who were highly
dubious of the ethics of such an expedient, but then, as was the
case with most other callers, it was he who was seeking help.

Today he went quickly down the area steps, restrained himself from pulling up his collar, scuttled past cellar and kitchen
doors and turned into a third entrance. This was as uninviting
as he had been warned to expect and as he came to the end he

found himself in a small hall containing six service doors. They were all blank save for one which bore a hand-lettered ticket with the inspired instruction: *'Try next door'*.

He tapped softly and lifted the card to reveal a metal grille with an interior shutter. It opened at once and a pair of suspicious eyes looked out at him. He murmured his name, the eyes defrosted and he was shown at once into a small butler's pantry where silver cleaning was in process. A man who was clearly an ex-sergeant, superb in a crested baize apron, motioned him towards an inner room.

'Mr Oates will see you now, sir.'

But for the fancy dress he could have been back at the Yard again. Mr Campion stepped into a snug apartment whose walls were lined with glass fronted steel grilled cupboards. These were kept lit perpetually for security's sake and upon their shelves in limpid glory the old Club's fabled collection of George II silver glittered like a fairy tale, proclaiming without contradiction that it was worth a fortune of anybody's money. A mahogany table filled the centre of the room and there was a shabby green leather armchair on either side of a garrulous gas fire.

Oates was dozing in one of these and he opened an eye as Campion appeared. He was growing frail and the discovery hit the newcomer who had not seen him for a year or two. For so long he had regarded that grey man with the mournful bloodhound face and the thick stomach as the finest policeman of them all. To find him grown old at this of all times was a blow he had not envisaged.

Meanwhile the ex-A.C. was permitting himself a sly little grin at his own cleverness which in his early days he would certainly have kept hidden.

'How do you like my office? I spotted its value as soon as I saw that peephole in the outer door,' he said proudly. 'It makes the perfect interview room, don't it? Just the spot for a quiet jaw. We're much more comfortable down here than we would be upstairs, you know.'

Mr Campion could not have agreed with him more, if only in view of the fact that neither of them were members, and he said so with mild reproof.

Oates grunted. 'Move with the times, my boy. The Old Pal's Act isn't confined to you public school types above stairs now. You've taught the rest of us the drill. Jessop and I are a cell of our own down here. If I'm caught, by the way, I'm an insurance man come to see no one has hocked the trophies. That ought to cover me, don't you think?'

His visitor regarded him in astonishment. The recklessness inherent in age had unleashed an unsuspected impish streak in his old friend.

'I don't know what you'll be, Albert.'

'I do,' said Mr Campion with feeling. 'Now, any news of James Teague?'

To his relief the mischief in Oates' eyes faded and his frown grew cold.

'They've still not found him. It's not Luke's fault. There's so much efficiency at the old place today that a routine job like keeping an eye on a released prisoner is almost too simple for the clever beggars.'

Mr Campion who had brightened a little at the mention of Superintendent Charles Luke, whom he admired, relapsed into anxiety.

'I couldn't believe it of them,' he said. 'They knew it was important. To lose him within a matter of hours seems inept. I made certain the press would have got on to it.'

'Would you? I think they've forgotten him. Remember that paper was very short at the time, so he didn't quite make his fair share of headlines. He's been inside a long time and he earned no remission. A bad prisoner in his early days and a trouble maker—two attempted escapes and a warder beaten up.'

'I gathered that.' Mr Campion sat down in the other armchair. 'I was out of the country at the time, so I've been looking it up. There doesn't seem to have been an appeal.'

is one of those larger than life characters who resent any events which don't match up to their own idea of themselves. He got under a thousand pounds in cash from the safe, two pictures from the owner's state room, a few valuable odds and ends and a parcel of booze still crated which must have been hell's delight to transfer in mid-ocean.'

He paused and lay back in the chair, his eyes half closed. 'I've been sitting here and thinking about you,' he said presently.

'Oh, yes? With what in view?'

'I was wondering what the devil you could be up to. I had one idea.'

'Does it matter?' Campion made the request very gently but Oates had grown old enough to be openly disappointed.

'I don't want to know your blasted business,' he said. 'I've known you for close on thirty years. I'll tell you what I thought, though. It couldn't have been hard cash or we'd have heard all about it. But suppose some of those cases of champagne contained something equally heavy but potentially much more valuable . . . paper, for instance?'

'Paper?' His visitor might never have heard of the material.

'Files,' said the ex-A.C. firmly. 'Their contents would be wartime secrets, long out of date by now. Scandalous international stuff, perhaps. But secrets, like H.E., keep their destructive power for longer than one would expect. I notice that they are at a premium these days. Newspapers publish extraordinary libels and pay the fines cheerfully and eminent old blokes such as me, who ought to know a darn sight better, go and write highly sensational memoirs. Cast iron evidence on one or two subjects I can think of could be well worth hawking and that might not suit . . . ?'

He let the sentence trail away in a query and his visitor smiled at him.

'It's a great gift,' he said admiringly. 'Being able to romanticise one's own past, I mean.'

Oates ignored him. 'It was during that spring—'46, wasn't

it?—before the *Lily Marina* crime that you and Elsie Corkran were closing down that extraordinary set-up you had in the mountains behind Cassis,' he said. 'I remember very well who your boss in London was at the time and if I know him, you must have had to keep records and documents just like any other department. Now if Christoff's yacht happened to be re-fitting down the coast near Marseilles just then—and it was, you know—then it could well have been just the sort of transport to appeal to you two. There she lay, a safe conveyance belonging to a man of no official allegiance, who probably owed you a kindness. If you used her you'd be asking no favours from any other service, signing no chits, spending no money ... am I embarrassing you?'

'Not in the least.' Mr Campion was affable. 'The one thing I enjoy is a good spy story. Have you heard the one about the Russian, the Chinese and the American who suddenly found out they were an Englishman, an Irishman and a Scots-man ... ?'

Oates waved him silent.

'Never mind,' he said. 'Forget it. I merely thought that since we are here, two old friends in Lodge, that you might care to come across. However, security was always security and I want to oblige. You asked me to give you a hand and I've spent the morning getting all I can for you.'

'My dear chap, I can't tell you how grateful I am. Don't you think yourself that Burrows is bound to be looking for Teague, or Teague for Burrows? They were thought to be on a barge together, weren't they? In that last dash before Teague was picked up in Harwich?'

'We really don't know.' Oates was shedding his years. 'But that was what we made of it. All we are sure of is that, at a time when half the world's shipping was looking out for her, the *Lily Marina* put into the Hamble River in fog and was there abandoned. That was on March 20th in misty weather with spring tides running. On the same night two of her crew of four, small villains called Goddard and Hunter, were killed outright in a crash on the Portsmouth road. They were in a stolen car and on the back seat were a couple of oil paintings. There was a case of Krug in the boot and each man had just under two hundred pounds in notes. The paintings were valuable and Christoff identified them as his. Meantime Teague and Burrows had vanished and there was no sign of them until Teague alone was picked up in a street in Harwich five days later. If there was a woman around we never found her. He had nothing incriminating on him and he wouldn't talk. It wasn't for want of persuading.'

Mr Campion appeared puzzled.

'I thought there was a barge in the story?' he said. 'The newspaper accounts at the time mention it. It was found in the estuary near the mouth of the Rattey on the east coast.'

'So it was. The barge *Blossom*,' Oates agreed irritatingly. 'But there was no hard evidence to connect her with Teague. She was a Thames craft that had been on a trip to Gossingham which is not too far from the Hamble. She'd unloaded there and her master and mate were in the town. This was on the night of the 20th when the *Lily Marina* crept in. Either *Blossom* broke away, which is highly unlikely, or she was stolen. She was seen by a Coastal Command plane not far from the Owers light vessel at about seven the following morning and then lost in the mist. As you say, she turned up eventually, high on the mud in the estuary.'

'And only Teague could have got her there?'

'That was the professional view at the time. He was highly thought of as a sailor in those parts. Two experienced men could have done it. Also of course the place isn't too far from Harwich where he was caught.'

'Anything on board to connect her with the piracy?'

'One empty champagne bottle.' Oates was unsmiling. 'The right year and the right brand and it hadn't a print on it.'

'What happened to Target?'

'There again we never really knew.' He shook his head over

31

past shortcomings. 'Some time after Teague had been sent down, Yeo got word that Burrows had been seen in Liverpool. The Lancashire police co-operated but we'd lost him. It was the time of the infamous two-way traffic with Ireland ... rationed food coming into this country, men on the run going out of it. That damn barge gave us no end of trouble. Our men were mud-larking down there in Essex for weeks. It was a wild goose chase.'

'In wild goose country by all accounts. There's a village down there called Saltey....'

'You can say that again!' Oates was suddenly wrathful. 'Contrary hole! I shall never forget that name or the trouble our people had as long as I live. My chaps took detailed statements from every man, woman and child and got precisely nothing except colds in the head and a vague sensation of doubt. A population of smiling savages playing stupid. Teague knew the place well before the war, probably as a smuggler of some sort, and Yeo made certain he'd gone ashore there, but either they were all lying, which isn't impossible if you knew them, or he went the other way. The *Blossom* went aground on the far side of the estuary, and there is a road of sorts which he could have taken. Saltey is up to its tricks again now—did you know that?'

Mr Campion sat up. 'I sent a youngster down there and Lugg is about somewhere,' he said cautiously. 'I thought some of the brotherhood might be gathering in those parts.'

'Waiting for Teague? I wonder. No, this is a native mischief —the natural evil of the locality.' Oates was unamused. 'It's the element of coincidence which captures me every time,' he confessed. 'Coincidences aren't natural. But how about this for a likely tale? At the back of St Botolph's Hospital, down in Antrim Street, there's a small café called The Swallow. The hospital staff use it, so do a group of kids and it has a second string amongst the coffee drinkers at night. I'm going to send you down there in a minute to see a young doctor whom I think you ought to look at. Actually she's going to meet Detective Sergeant Throstle, but I've fixed it so that you can get in.'

'Why?'

'Wait for it. She has inherited a property from a senile ex-patient of the hospital and got herself into the centre of a fine old poison pen storm. . . .'

'All from Saltey?'

'The house is there but the letters seem to be coming from anywhere. The hospital secretary has had three from three separate places, London and two towns in East Anglia.'

'Unpleasant.'

'That was my attitude. It's the natural reaction. Throstle was very sniffy until he discovered that the whole hospital thought it was the most natural thing in the world.'

'That a junior medico should inherit from a grateful inmate?'

'Better than that. The old lady *wasn't* her patient. She hardly knew her. The girl had only been in the ward a few times to attend to somebody else. The old thing "did but see her passing by" in fact. And no one was astonished when she left her home and its contents. What are you looking at me like that for? Remembered something?'

'In a way.' Campion was laughing. 'At least, someone else used the phrase about a girl this afternoon. Come to think of it, it could have been the same woman ... which is utterly absurd. What is your coincidence?'

'Mine?' Oates seemed taken aback by this welter of circumstance. 'Oh, mine concerns Teague, which is why I'm telling you. Late last night when the waitresses at The Swallow Café were clearing up, they found a wallet containing three out of date pound notes, a few other significant items, a press cutting and so on, hidden in one of the majolica jars they keep on the ledges.

'On their way home they handed it in to a police station and a bright lad there spotted what it was and reported it. Whilst I was at head office this morning positive identification came through from the prison. It was Teague's all right. It had been given back to him along with his other personal possessions when he came out, just a week ago.' He paused. 'There's no real connection, except for the bequest and the village.'

Mr Campion blinked.

'I don't see it,' he said. 'None of it fits anywhere at all, does it? Is the inference that the wallet was a plant? Some sort of come hither gesture?'

Oates shrugged his shoulders. 'Maybe. Or it could have been pinched by someone in the normal way and ditched there because the hiding place happened to be convenient. Dippers often do that. The café staff don't remember anyone remotely resembling Teague coming in and women usually recall him. These say they haven't had anyone but their regulars for weeks. That means the hospital staff and the usual young crowd.'

'Did you gather how Teague managed to fade out so effectively? No one was asked to keep an eye on him, I suppose?'

'Not at all.' The old eyes were very thoughtful. 'There's something not quite right about the whole business. Teague was released, as such chaps are, into the arms of the good people who give up their lives to take care of long term prisoners. Apart from sending them out on a dog lead they couldn't be in safer hands. Teague appeared very quiet and was thought to be quite as shaken by the speed of life as any other newly released long term man. He was taken along by the social worker to one of their best addresses, in Lewisham. That means motherly lodgings where there's a man and a wife interested and experienced. This particular couple knew what they were taking on. They've been doing the same for other lifers for years. It's a better system than the routine ex-prisoners' institute where the men are inclined to feel that they're better off inside.'

'Did he go to them without protest?'

'Oh, yes. His "stunned" act was very convincing. He spent the morning sitting in the old girl's kitchen and not talking, just reading the newspaper. Whilst she was getting the meal, her husband Tom Blower took him down to the local for a pint. Tom is an ex-constable, very steady and knowledgeable. This is his hobby and he's a good, kindly sort of chap. They went down to the Bunch of Grapes, a biggish house in the Gresham Road. It's quiet and almost deserted in the mornings as a rule, at any rate until the dinner hooter goes. There was only one stranger in the bar, a woman whom Blower says he thinks was on the game. She spoke to Teague but she was civil and he encouraged it, for as he says, a man has to get used to talking to a tart again some time.

'Then suddenly the place filled up with a great swarm of people from some local factory, works people who use it regularly it seems. In the flurry Teague and the woman vanished. Blower thought very little of it at first but he reported it by mid-afternoon, which was lucky because Teague hasn't been seen since. Not a word of him, until the wallet turned up here in the West End.'

'It seems a trifle elaborate if it was engineered.'

'That's what I thought. It's a romantic story book idea, I said to Throstle.' Oates hesitated. 'There was one item about the evidence which struck me. When Blower was describing this woman he said she was dressed up "old fashioned". Our man took him up on that and he explained that she looked more like the 1930s than the late 60s, though she couldn't have been more than forty years old, if that.'

Mr Campion stared at him. 'How disconcerting!'

Oates laughed. 'I thought so. I don't know why. Is there something sinister in being out of period?'

'No,' said Mr Campion. 'Just phoney. And that's perfectly idiotic in the circumstances. Why dissemble? By the way, what about Teague's background? Who wrote to him in prison? Who came to see him?'

The old man consulted his mental notes and spoke as if he was giving formal evidence. 'His correspondence seems to have been sparse, mostly from sailors who had wartime experiences to share. Very rarely from the same address. The officer who vetted them recently says he *thinks* several of them might have been from the same man using different names, but he can't swear to it. Teague isn't a great writer, but if a correspondent said *"Charlie Brown, who's now at such and such an address, would like to hear from you,"* then Teague used his once-a-month letter to write to that man. No rule against it. But it's suggestive. If he used a code it was of the unbreakable variety: *"Remember the lark we played on old Bubblegum and the row there was about the match-sticks?"* You know the sort of thing. Only the man at the receiving end can tell if it's a joke or has a double meaning. But there was nothing to make anyone really suspicious. Of course messages can be smuggled both ways. We can't rule that out, and it's a possibility. As to visitors, there was a woman who was a regular at one time whom they checked on, but found nothing exceptionable, though her address changed several times. The padre thinks she may have died because the visits suddenly stopped, but he never got a murmur out of Teague. There's nothing helpful there, I'm afraid.'

'Too bad,' said Campion regretfully. 'Now about this girl doctor. What's the idea of my joining the tea party?'

The old man cocked an eyebrow at his guest. 'You're getting slow,' he said. 'I've told Throstle that you know more about analysing the contents of anonymous letters than any other practitioner alive. That's harmless, plausible and possibly true. I thought if you went in under that banner you could slide into the Teague business and into Saltey without giving yourself away.'

'That was very kind and civil of you.'

'Wasn't it?' Oates was smiling sardonically. 'I realise that you can't confide in me but I happen to know that you need a bit of help just now, whatever you think you're up to. You had a set-back today. I don't believe you know that yet?'

'Really? "Fly. All is discovered." That sort of bad news?' enquired Campion blandly.

'Not quite. But just as I was leaving the old place this morning I heard a murmur of what you might call above stairs gossip. Today Corkran was expecting to lunch very privately, not to say magnificently, in Westminster. Did you know that?'

'He's always eating.'

'Very likely. But this was unusual. When a man in Corkran's position takes a step which is reserved for extreme emergency and risks irritating the "machine" by exercising his peculiar prerogative and going to his supreme boss direct, even a silly old copper like me knows he has something on his mind. Then when he gets fobbed off yet again with some young P.S. all gas and no authority, I'm bound to put two and two together.' He laughed. 'Corkran doesn't have to "come in from the cold". It's gone out to meet him. That's real news to you, isn't it?'

His companion did not reply but looked down his nose.

Presently the old man snorted. 'Damn it. You *had* heard. How the hell did you know?'

'I have second sight,' said Mr Campion, cheerfully. 'I must show it to you. It's about four inches long, virtually a telescope and...'

'Put a sock in it,' said Oates. 'It's time you learnt to be your age. And don't play the fool in front of Throstle, either. He's a young man and he'll take a dislike to you. He thinks everyone older than himself is Victorian and ought to behave like it. Besides, he's stretching a point at my request in letting you see the letters at all. Now you'd best be getting on your way. He's a large genial looking chap, fair-haired, wears a club tie of sorts, cricket I believe, and weighs around thirteen stone. . . .'

'In fact I can't miss him. Bless you, my boy.'

They shook hands formally.

'This is a very tricky one,' the thin man confessed as they parted. 'I'm having to play it with the cards very close to my chest. And between you and me it's a pretty poor hand.'

'Sorry I couldn't deal you an ace.'

'Forget it,' said Mr Campion, 'and I mean that. But you may have passed me a joker all the same.'

The door closed gently behind him and after a cautious escape into St James's he vanished into the merciful anonymity of a taxi.

The Swallow Café was a long dark room with something of the texture of a doughnut about it: pleasant and padded and a thought sticky. There were pictures of Portofino and Italian peasant pottery and a row of little gilt paper gladiators between two of the light fittings which were shaped like sheaves of lily buds with strong brass stems.

Mr Campion glanced around for the jar in which the wallet had been found and discovered it at once on a shelf running beside the tables.

The familiar expresso counter at the far end of the room was deserted and from somewhere behind the wall which backed it a woman's voice was raised in bitter complaint.

'*Ma cammina! Non po' lasciar' un posto nuovo fra dieci minuti, sumara. Che impiastra! Che pazzia! . . .*'

It was the slackest time of the day and very few of the tables were occupied but after a first glance round Mr Campion found himself aware of only one customer, a girl who sat in a corner with her back to the rounded end of the counter. She was unself-conscious and at ease, listening to her companion with smiling tolerant interest.

It was not that she was particularly beautiful. Her quality was grace. It flowed from every bone and curled every line of her into a long casual frond. She was wearing a pale blue suit under a loose white coat and her bag lay on the table with her gloves beside it.

She was hatless and her hair was dark as polished ebony, her wide mouth, laughing and provocative. The extraordinary wave of intrinsic high fashion and contemporary intelligence drew his attention even before the tinkling door bell had concluded the announcement of his arrival.

'I did but see her passing by,' thought Mr Campion and it was several seconds until he realised that her companion was Mortimer Kelsey.

The young man, red faced but shamelessly exuberant, rose to his feet awkwardly as the fixed table pinned his thighs.

'Ah, Mr Campion,' he said, 'I didn't expect to see you. I wonder if you know Dr Dido Jones. She's going down to Saltey this afternoon and I'm giving her a lift. Won't you have a coffee with us? Actually we're waiting for a policeman.'

3

The Swallow Café

IT could well have been an extremely awkward gathering Morty suspected, but he was too entertained and happy to care. The stale room with its treacly flavour was by no means unpleasant after the damp outside and he was sitting next to Dido Jones which made every other circumstance fade into oblivion.

The plainclothed Sergeant Throstle who had appeared almost upon Mr Campion's heels was much as Oates had described him. Like many good policeman of his type his main message seemed to be that he was no fool and, on the whole, kindly meant. He drew up a chair to the narrow end of the table to be sure of conducting the party to his own complete satisfaction.

It was apparent too that Oates had negotiated Campion's entry with discretion, conveying that here was someone to be handled as a V.I.P. from a different but possibly interconnected world. Throstle contemplated the boy friend without surprise. How could such a creature as Dr Jones ever expect to be left without a host of hypnotised companions? He wondered idly if her patients ever took their minds off her to consider their ailments.

On the whole the situation pleased him. He disliked poison pen enquiries but believed that if they had to be handled, the more willing helpers there were on the side of the victim, the easier was his own task. Besides, it was a pleasure to feel that at some time in the future the doctor might be opening wide grateful eyes to express her thanks and to assure him that he was wonderful.

The centre of attraction, who had engendered a certain

amount of unnatural good humour, sat back contentedly in her corner. Each man present was aware of her in a different way and she of him, but as with all natural sirens she did not let the fact worry her.

Mr Campion brought the party to order by turning to Morty.

'How did *you* get here?' he demanded.

The young man grinned sheepishly. 'I was going down to Saltey anyway, as we arranged. Now it so happens that I knew Dr Jones had a house down there so I thought I'd ring her up and ask her if by chance she would like a lift. By chance she did.'

He paused and eyed the older man squarely. 'Perhaps I ought to say that I ask her that nearly every day. This time I was lucky.'

Dido smiled, an embracing glance which took in all three men.

'I'm going down to see the solicitor who's going to show me the house I've inherited. He wants to give me the keys. I went there once before with a friend from the hospital but we couldn't get inside. It was then that I met Morty. This time I thought I'd camp there for a day and find out what it's really like.' She hesitated. 'I'm very glad to see both of you before I go because I'm not at all sure if I ought not to refuse the whole legacy after all those nauseating letters—except that I expect that's just what they hope I'll do. What do you think?'

Sergeant Throstle looked at her sharply but did not speak, for at that moment there was a diversion. The proprietress who had been behind the bar began to serve them. She was a little sallow woman with gold in her ears and at the sides of her mouth and the same shrill voice which Campion had heard as he came in.

'Sorry to keep you waiting but I 'ave no 'elp,' she said. 'I just lost my new girl. I only take 'er on part time and now she runs off. It's a wonderful world when you can pick and choose, come and go, just as you please before you're twenty-one. Kids today they jus' don' wanta work.'

Sergeant Throstle, being the nearest, collected the cups and distributed them and made no offer to pursue the conversation. He shared them round the table and stirred himself enough sugar to make the mixture thick as molasses.

'It's these letters which interest you, Mr Campion?' he said. 'That's right, isn't it?' He smiled at Dido, confiding and confident, conveying that he had the advantage of a longer acquaintanceship. 'It's a little off our normal beat as an enquiry but there are one or two aspects about this particular job which are what you might call intriguing. On the face of it, it looks more like conspiracy than the work of an evil minded vixen who's had her nose put out of joint by a will she didn't do so well out of.'

Mr Campion intervened. It was his turn to smile at the doctor. 'Put me in the picture,' he said diffidently. 'I understand that you've been left this property by an ex-patient? When did this happen?'

'No patient of mine,' she said. 'Old Miss Kytie died about six months ago and I was rather surprised to hear that she even remembered my name. I only saw her about half a dozen times and I certainly never treated her. I'm geriatrics—she was a cardiac.'

'I see. Begin at the beginning, though. When did you first meet her?'

'Early last summer. If it's important I can probably find the date. She shared a side ward here at St Bots with two other old ladies and one of them, a Miss Ridgeway, was my patient. I knew Miss Kytie to nod to. The old things used to chatter away amongst themselves of course, but when a doctor came to see any one of them the other two were usually very discreet—you know how they are—'

'I can guess, I think. But go on.'

'Well, that was all there was to it. "Good morning. Lovely after the rain, isn't it? Did you have a good tea party on

Friday? Mr Tanner, your favourite clergyman, is coming round this afternoon, so save him some cake." Nothing more intimate than that. Then one day when I went in to see Miss Ridgeway unofficially to take her a book she wanted, Miss Kytie had a visitor, a young man who was fairly obviously a solicitor. She was very excited and above herself and insisted on introducing us.'

She hesitated. 'She was one of those old fashioned gushers who talk in alternate italics. "Oh, *doctor*, this *is* a *pleasure. Both* you young people are so *young. Aren't* they, Miss Ridgeway? *So* young and *so* handsome!"' It was an unexpectedly vivid piece of characterisation. She conjured up a brilliant-eyed harridan clutching a lean bosom, by turns embarrassing, envious and pathetic.

'Oho!' said Morty laughing. 'Then she wasn't just a dear old fairy godmother? I'd imagined something rather cosy but...'

'Oh, no. Cosy isn't quite the right word. The trouble is that I really know very little about her as a person. Except, of course, that it was obvious the moment she opened her mouth that she was living for her will and the fun she could get out of it. Some people do, you know. The three old trolls in the ward clearly spent their days chatting it over and over. But it made Miss Kytie the centre of attraction. She was revelling in it.'

'I can see that.' Throstle was professional. 'And she introduced the young man as her solicitor? What was his name? Askew, was it?'

'That's right. How clever of you.' Dido flashed her mind-destroying smile at him. 'She told me all about him to his face. She usually consulted *Percy*, but this was *Hector*, the son, who was just as clever as his father and was just a *tiny* bit more understanding. He *always* found time to help if one was worried which was *so* comforting.'

'Was anything said about you inheriting the house at this meeting—even in joke?'

'Oh, no. Of course not. It was simply a lot of arch nonsense about us two young people getting together. They all saw themselves as matchmakers and they were having a real ball.'

'And did you two become acquainted?'

'We did, as a matter of fact. He's a forceful character—not so young as he looks—and I suppose you could say that he made a pass at me. Anyway, I often seemed to be running into him in the corridor or just outside the hospital. He rather worked at it, you know. At least he got as far as taking me out to dinner.'

She was perfectly frank but somehow it was not a completely satisfactory explanation. All three men sensed it and Morty felt it his duty to intervene.

'I think, if I may say so,' he remarked, 'that Dr Jones is one of those people whom people do fall for on sight.'

They turned to look at him and he smiled.

'Well, I do,' he said.

Throstle opened his mouth to speak and shut it again without making a comment.

'Did you discuss the matter with Miss Kytie at all?' asked Mr Campion.

'No. In fact I never saw her again. My patient was moved into another ward and I'd almost forgotten her. The next thing I knew was some months later when I had a letter from Hector Askew to say that she was dead and had left me her house and most of the contents. She had a serious heart condition when she was in hospital and it was obvious that the poor thing wasn't going to last very long.'

Dido coloured. It was her first sign of embarrassment. 'The notion that she might have been senile when she made her will simply isn't true. I don't think Hector thought so either. I'd say he is a cautious type where business is concerned. It never occurred to me that *anyone* could think so until those letters started arriving.'

Throstle leant forward over the table. 'These letters,' he said. 'I've got photostats of them here, by the way, Mr Campion. They're rather unusual. I'd say they were written by at least three separate hands and possibly seven. Now this suggests conspiracy, especially as they are addressed to various different persons, the hospital authorities and so on. Different postmarks too. Some from Saltey, some from London. Thinking it over, you still have no idea who any of them could be?'

She regarded him with astonishment.

'I still assume that they must be people who had hoped to inherit themselves. Who else?'

'Do you know of any?'

'Not yet. According to Hector she had no living next of kin if you cut out really distant cousins. She was over eighty. His firm were her only advisers and they've been in the business so long that they seem to have the whole district in their pocket. She left quite a lot, one way and another, apart from the house. Several people did far better than I. But I've been trying to find out about your point. I rang Hector as soon as he wrote me and I said that I hoped I wouldn't be depriving someone with a better right. He said certainly not—I was no more likely or unlikely than any of the other heirs. Apparently she was always changing her will and altering the bequests as her old friends died off or she quarrelled with them. Hector assured me—and he was absolutely positive about this—that this was the first occasion since he'd had anything to do with it when everybody concerned was well looked after. What he said was "As her wills went this was a very good specimen—probably the best".'

'You get the house and most of the contents,' said Throstle. 'Now someone must have been in line for that before you—or thought they were. You've no idea who you superseded?'

'No.' Dido hit the table with the flat of her hand and Morty placed his own deliberately over it.

'I think I do,' he said unexpectedly. 'It's the talk of Saltey. Although I'm very much a foreigner down there, I've been told all about it twenty times by the locals who use The Demon, where I'm staying, as their social headquarters. Miss Kytie lived in the Forty Angels hamlet all her life and she'd been the local heiress ever since her brother died in the thirties. I really didn't pay much attention till Dido appeared on the scene. The old girl seems to have been very careful, not to say downright skinflint mean and a bit of a mischief maker into the bargain. She used to play up one person against another and her will has been the one subject of interest in Saltey for years. 'Quack, quack, quack. "She will, you know. She won't, you know. Leave it all to a cats' home, that's what she'll do, mark my words".'

'Now I can't swear to it but my belief is that the person who was disinherited in favour of Dr Jones got a much more valuable piece of property in exchange—half the land he farms, in fact. He's a local character called Jonah Woodrose who seems to be a distant relative of everyone in the place but no more a bona fide heir than Dido. My impression is that they were both used one after the other by the old lady to annoy somebody else. She did it all the time by hints and nods and accepting favours whenever some toady offered them.'

'Who would this somebody else be?' said Throstle.

'I haven't the faintest idea, any more than I can work out who in the village is related to who. There seems to have been a period, not very long ago, when even the bicycle was unknown. That name Woodrose, for example—it's wonderful when you come to work it out.'

Mr Campion sighed audibly. The sound was so unexpected that it surprised everyone and they stared at him. He had the grace to look embarrassed.

'I'm sorry,' he said, laughing. 'I was thinking that "they're all distant relations" are fatal last words. There is absolutely no tangle on earth that is so inextricable and frustrating as the English country family dispute. Time doesn't come into it. Characters live and die and never see the beginning or the end. A rural Jarndice v. Jarndice can take a century. If this turns out to be one of those none of us will ever see the last of it. And meantime, of course, there isn't a moment to spare.'

As soon as the words were out of his mouth it was evident that he regretted them.

46

'I was thinking,' he said lamely, 'that you two have got quite a journey before you.'

As a performance it lacked his usual adroitness and Morty was clearly surprised. He glanced at Dido who gathered up her bag and gloves. Throstle, like a chairman who hopes to conclude a meeting with some semblance of having made progress turned to Campion.

'I'd like you to glance over these photostats and give me your expert opinion. We'd all appreciate that, I think?' He produced a large buff envelope from the folio on the floor by his chair and placed it on the table.

'I'd like to say one thing about them before I go.' Dido spoke with professional dignity and a touch of anger coloured her cheek. 'In the letters which were sent to me and in one of the others I was accused of influencing a senile patient. Miss Kytie certainly wasn't senile when I saw her and I've taken the trouble to investigate her medical history right up to the time she died. Senility is a real condition. Geriatrics is my subject, so I should know. It doesn't just mean having white hair and blue rings round the irises of the eyes. It's a marked state of mental deterioration capable of being accurately observed and recorded. In fact she was a little over-bright. In spite of her heart she actually died of a cerebral thrombosis and you can take it from me that up to that moment she was probably quite as sharp and on the ball as she'd ever been. Certainly Hector thinks so and I'd say he was an expert, with his sort of experience. He won't be very pleased if I keep him waiting. Shall we go, Morty?'

Throstle stood up to let them escape from the confining table.

'How were you going to get down there if Mr Kelsey hadn't popped up with his car?'

'Oh, I have one of my own,' she said. 'I just felt I'd like the company.'

As they went out of the café, Throstle turned to Campion. 'If she's going to meet one young man it's funny to take

another. What would you make of that? Does she just hypno-
tise every man in sight to provide an escort? Or do you smell a
quarrel?'

'It could be.'

'Between her and the young solicitor? It crossed my mind it
might be worth passing on to the County. The whole business
is their pidgin by rights, only the complaint started at this end.
He eyed Campion shrewdly. 'This is the place where Teague's
wallet was found. You knew that, of course? It's him you're
really interested in, or so the Top Brass whisper to me. A lot of
people would like to know where he is just now. I wonder why
he left that little pointer behind?'

'A "Kilroy was here" sign, or would someone like you to
think so?'

'I'm not a member of the Coincidence Club myself,' said the
sergeant. 'The answer is at Saltey—the answer to both enquiries. That's my bet. They'll pick him up down there and
good luck to them. We can do without him in my manor.' He
closed his briefcase. 'Well, it's been nice meeting you, sir. Fancy
you knowing old Oates. It was quite a shock to see him again
this morning. He must be older than God and he's beginning
to look it. Still as bright as a button, though.'

'Aren't we all?' said Mr Campion.

After the rain the pavements were beginning to steam. The
promise of high summer was in the air. He decided to walk, to
sort out the elements of the problem and to restore his own self-
respect by approaching his club without a sense of guilt.

In Soho Square the scent of new cut grass bewitched the air,
whispering of cricket, garden chairs, strawberries and dalliance
in the shade.

He strode briskly, almost jauntily, into the Adam brothers'
masterpiece which is Puffins and was half way across the chess-
board hall before the door porter caught up with him.

'This came for you about half an hour ago, sir. By hand. I
was to give it to you personally.'

Mr Campion opened the stiff white envelope with misgivings. Inside was a single sheet of plain paper inscribed in a precise scholarly hand which was all too familiar. The message was very brief.

'I'm afraid that the position has deteriorated. There is very little time. L.C.'

4

The Road to Saltey

'LADIES and gents,' declaimed Morty in the tones of a professional guide, 'we are now approaching the site of Mob's Hole, notorious haunt of mobsters, dandies, doxies and all the picturesque riff-raff of seventeenth century London. On my left a prospect of Wanstead Flats and on my right a car breaker's yard which seems to have been abandoned owing to pressure of business.'

He was in tremendous form, elated as a schoolboy, and his companion was beginning to feel that it was time to cut him down to size.

'If you drove and talked a little more slowly,' said Dr Jones, 'I could take in more of the lecture. Abandon the Cockney accent which does nothing for your professional image and remember that I want to meet Hector, in one piece, at half past six.'

'Blast his smug go-getting guts.' Morty was subdued but not defeated. 'But I must get this off my chest. Bear with me, share my obsessions. Hear the fruits of my eager researches into this byway of history. If I'm incoherent the fault is yours. Do all your patients adore you, too?'

'Get on with your lecture.'

'If you say so.' Morty reduced the elegant Lotus Elan to a legal limit. 'But right now we are at the start of my discovery. New readers begin here: Mob's Hole, a sort of roadhouse and open air barbecue, really existed, you know. Ned Ward, the London Spy, has a terrific description of it. It was bang in the middle of that heap of decaying ironmongery according to the old maps, and apart from being a picnic haunt of dubious café society, the sort of coxcombs, bullies, whores and pimps Ward

50

wrote about, it was also notorious as a Safe House, if you know what that means.'

'I don't, but no doubt I'll learn.'

'You certainly will if you put up with me for long. Well now, a Safe House was an inn or a lodging with no questions asked. Suitable for thieves, smugglers, political refugees—anyone wanted by the authorities, in fact. You'll find relics of them dotted all round the Thames Estuary. A man on the run was naturally afraid of the main roads with their big coaching inns because they were the obvious places to watch. The road block idea isn't new. The Army, the Preventative Men, the thief catchers and so on have always used it since there was any sort of law. No, a man who wished to move secretly went, generally by night, from one Safe House to the next, making for a quiet part of the coast—some place where smuggling was regarded as being a proper trade and where inhabitants minded their own business.'

'Like Saltey?' suggested Dido.

'You have it in one, my proud beauty. Mob's Hole to Mob's Bowl, in fact. This was the route and it runs through some pretty queer country as you'll find out. London's back door, with a couple of centuries of unemptied garbage pails still awaiting collection by the look of it. It's a dreary run on the face of it but it has its charm for the likes of me.'

'An acquired taste no doubt. Do you include the romance of Gallows Corner and the Great Southend Road in your saga?'

'I can do better than that.' Morty was still enthusiastic. 'I can dodge both of them for you if you don't mind a rough ride. Our eighteenth century friends didn't greatly care for that ominous crossroads. They used a mixture of loops and short cuts. It's not been easy to trace, and if I weren't so brilliant, intuitive and hard-working I would never have found it. But now that this particular piece of research is completed I'll tell you something which really is odd. *Highly remarkable*, as we say in Saltey.'

'Go on,' said Dido. 'Amaze me if you can. And keep both

hands on the wheel when turning sharp corners if you wish to remain just good friends.'

'Sorry.' Morty was not penitent. 'But this is genuinely odd. I was driving down from town last week rather late at night, after midnight in fact, and using my special route which is particularly impressive at night because once you're clear of the streets there are miles where you hardly pass a house at all and you get a tremendous sense of loneliness.

'There I was, idling along—you know my style—when I was aware of someone behind whose headlights were shining in my mirror. I let him pass, making sure he'd turn off, but not on your sweet life. He was right with me all the way, ma'am. Once I stopped and smoked a cigarette just to let him get clear of me in his darned old white jalopy with a bashed-in tail, but in ten minutes I caught him up again, still dodging along, just as I was. He even used my special cut through the ghost town which I always thought was pretty fancy and custom built for me alone. He fetched up in Saltey. How about that?'

'Now that certainly *is* odd.' Dido straightened her back. 'Do you know who it was?'

'Mr Jonah Woodrose,' said Morty, 'whose family name if you trace it back is as ancient as anything in England. Woodrose—Woodwose. The Foliate Man, the Green Man, Robin Goodfellow, the nigger in the original woodpile of Christianity in this country.'

'Play it cool,' advised Dido. 'Fairies and sprites don't drive elderly cars. They go in for nutshell chariots, if I remember. But you've got a point there. What's your theory, master?'

He considered. 'Could be a sort of inherited memory,' he said at last. 'More likely tradition and force of habit. This was the track his forebears always took to Stratford and the other markets, so this is the way he goes. With all that inbred blood in his veins he's likely to be a creature of habit. I wonder what he was doing in London in any case?'

'You sound as if you knew the answer.'

Morty hesitated. 'I don't, and I wish I did,' he confessed.

'But it did occur to me that he might have gone to post a letter, something that he didn't want to arrive with a Saltey post-mark.'

Dido shivered involuntarily and to Morty's delight moved her shoulder a little closer to him.

'It's beastly,' she said at last. 'You know, if there was any sentiment involved in all this I'd give up. I mean, if I was grinding the faces of the widow and orphan by accepting the house, or doing some splendid young farmer out of his rightful home I'd be off like a flash. But I'm not. This is just pure venom and wickedness, and I won't put up with it. I'll ... I'll ...'

'I love a good fight,' said Morty. 'I'm right by your side, lady. When you stick out your chin like that you could have my entire kingdom just for the pleasure of holding your coat. I could start, of course, by holding your hand.'

'You'll keep your hands on the wheel,' said Dr Jones tartly.

Morty, sliding a glance at her, realised not without surprise that she was a grown woman, competent, finely tempered and not quite the beleaguered sylph he had been picturing in his daydreams. The thought depressed him and he drove in silence for a twisting mile.

'I suppose you do know where you're going?' she enquired at last. The road they were following had become little more than an open track through coarse grassland. An occasional broken fence marked a boundary and an empty bungalow standing isolated in an expanse of uneven ground, distemper peeling from its blind stucco face, emphasised the desolation. A narrow board nailed to a post displayed the words 'Victoria Crescent' in fading gothic print.

'This is my Ghost Town,' explained Morty with a certain pride. 'Not unlike the shanty towns of the Gold Rush days— very like them in spirit, now I come to think of it. It's a derelict area and I'd say it always will be. A swamp which used to be called The Trough. In fact it is the site of an old land swindle, the sort of thing which was popular at the turn of the century.

The operator bought a parcel of quite useless country, fairly near to one of the newish rail tracks, marked out a grandiose development scheme on a map—the Royal Esplanade, the shopping centre, Empress Avenue and so on—and divided the whole area into plots of half an acre or so apiece.

'Then he brought down a load of suckers by special train, which you could get in those days, gave them a champagne lunch in a marquee erected for the occasion and held a sale. By then everyone was as high as a kite and the promoter sold off his land at a fantastic profit. One or two of the poor boobs actually built their dream homes here, but the roads and the drains and the Town Hall never appeared. Probably the neatest real estate trick in the calendar and darned nearly legal, too.'

Dido wrinkled her nose. 'And all on the back road to Saltey,' she said. 'It's been a great experience but I think I'll let Hector get me back tomorrow by some orthodox method, like taking me to a railway station.'

'Damn Hector.'

They drove in silence for some time through an area of new open planned villas, writhing television masts, mini cars and mass produced respectability. The uncompromising predictability of street after street was as depressing as the straggling wasteland they had passed through and they intuitively shared the relief of reaching open countryside again. It was flat and uninspiring but now there was a tang of salt in the air and the rain-black road snaked between carefully tended fields, occasional weather-boarded farms with stridently new outbuildings and elm trees which were gnarled and bent by the coastal wind.

'The last of the old forest is just ahead,' said Morty. 'That bit of a rise on our left is probably the highest point for miles. They'd have felled that timber years ago if the land was worth cultivating, but from now on it's sour ground, mostly. That's what protects Saltey from civilisation—it's on the road to nowhere and you have to make a great U-shaped detour to get there anyway. It's virtually an island cut off by the salt-ings.'

The scrawny woodland had retreated from the verge and the road curved gently to the left approaching a sharp T-shaped corner where the signpost read 'Saltey only. No through road.' An ugly red brick farmhouse with a slated roof stood at the corner with its barns and pigsties hard against the tarmac. Tattered posters proclaimed that there had been an auction of livestock and furniture some time since and a notice board announced that the entire freehold property was for sale.

'What the hell!' Morty p lled the car up with a squeal.

Ahead of them two cars were drawn up half blocking the road and immediately beyond, barring the way completely, was a laundryman's van, skewed directly across the turning. A push bicycle leant against the wall.

'Looks like an accident,' said Dido, becoming professional. 'I'll go and see.'

They got out together and as they approached the van they saw that a group of people were confering beyond it. A young policeman, his trousers still in bicycle clips, eased himself gingerly round the obstruction and came towards them smiling sheepishly.

'Been a bit o' trouble,' he said. 'I can't be in two places at once, can I?' He turned and raised his voice to include the three men who stood together in the lane behind him. 'I wonder if one of you gentlemen would mind doing a little traffic duty at the corner or we'll have both roads blocked? Now sir, if you're going to Saltey you'll have to wait, and if you're not will you please move on?'

Dido pushed forward.

'I'm a doctor,' she said. 'Is anyone hurt? Morty, you can keep the road clear for a minute. Is there anything I can do?'

'It's hard to say, miss. I've only just arrived, coming from Firestone.' The constable was flustered. 'If you can get round here you'll see what the trouble is. There's a young girl—or I think it's a girl. She may be hurt but she won't say.'

Beyond the van in the neck of the lane the cause of the confusion was immediately clear. The road was covered with broken bottles which had been systematically smashed and distributed across the surface for several yards. The van which had been approaching Saltey had driven right into the vicious, jagged trap and had skidded to a halt.

Not far from it lay a motor cycle whose owner, dressed in bedraggled black leather and a white crash helmet, stood disconsolately beside it, a muddy back turned to the rest of the company.

Dido, whose shoes were not designed for such treatment, picked her way delicately towards the solitary figure.

'Are you all right?' she said. 'What happened to you?'

The black back turned further away and Dido repeated her question.

'Are you all right?'

There was still no response. Dido took a step forward and swung the leather torso deftly towards her. Its owner had clearly not been expecting such treatment, for the eyes behind the mica visor of the helmet gleamed venom.

'I'm a doctor,' said Dido firmly. 'So don't be silly. If you're hurt at all, you'd better tell me.'

'Oh, get knotted!'

There was no doubt now about the sex of the motor cyclist. She was very female, very angry and twitching with suppressed emotion. A smear of mud and blood down her cheek did not hide the fact that she was white with rage and excitement. Jerking away from Dido she addressed herself to the world at large.

'Can't one of you bastards give me a hand?'

The driver of the van who had been examining the damage to his tyres shuffled towards her, kicking the glass from his way. He and the policeman lifted the machine upright.

'Fork's twisted,' said the van man. 'You were plumb lucky, miss he nearly ran you down.' He considered the massively engined monster with a mechanic's eye. 'Not much wrong with it, I'd say. Nothing that a wrench wouldn't cure. It's a heavy old thing. Sure you're O.K.?'

A shout from over the wall interrupted the discussion and a burly golden head which could only have belonged to a countryman appeared. An elderly birch broom was waved aloft.

'That'll do the trick now, won't it?' he said triumphantly. 'Someone's been having a rare old game here, by the looks of it. That'll give you something for your notebook, eh, Mr Simmonds? Better than hanging round that old Demon come closing time.'

He was a large man, remarkably pleased with himself. Vaulting the wall with the agility of real strength he began to sweep with energy and precision. The two other men followed him, kicking at stray fragments.

'A proper mystery for you, Mr Simmonds,' he continued, 'not but what I could give you a tip where to look. Young tearways. That's what you want to go after if you want my advice. And when you find 'em take the buckle end of your belt to them and ask your questions afterwards. Only sort of talk those young devils understand. . . .'

Dido returned to Morty. Some of the girl's anger seemed to have infected her and she took his arm sharply as a support whilst she pulled off a shoe to remove a fragment of glass.

'Little bitch!' she said. 'One of your friends from the sea wall, I suppose. Damn lucky not to have hurt herself and she curses like a fishwife when I try to help. That machine's far too heavy for her anyhow. This is a foul place, Morty. If it weren't for Hector—and—'

'That's the only good thing I've ever heard about your infernal legal eagle,' said the young man. 'At least it means I'll see more of you. Whilst I've been on point duty I've also been having a snoop around. There's a great pile of bottles behind that wall, all neatly stacked—or they were. Previous owner was quite a connoisseur. Champagne, Haut Brion, Mouton Rothchild, Volnay ... all the best labels. Perhaps that's why he gave up farming.'

'Perhaps,' agreed Dido. 'Don't look now, but isn't one of those cars a white Ford with a badly dented boot?'

'It is, and Mr Jonah Woodrose in person is now sweeping the road and directing the proceedings. None of them can have been here long. Miss Tearaway probably took the corner at speed and came off very lightly considering that she might have cut herself to pieces, smartly followed by the Nine Ash Hygienic Steam Laundry. P.C. Simmonds is the local sheriff and not a very bright specimen. Saltey doesn't take kindly to the law. I don't think he arrived with the speed of light, but merely happened to be cycling this way.'

'I have a feeling,' said Dido, her arm still linked with Morty's as they kept guard over the main road, 'that this was intended as part of the Welcome Home celebration for me. *Beware of our dog, it eats strangers on sight.* I can't see why or how anybody knew when I'd be arriving. It's just a nasty little itch in my bones.'

'Don't forget that I'm going to hold your coat for you, lady.'

Dido's chin came forward. 'Looks like you may have to,' she said. 'But the more I think of it the more I scent organised opposition. You don't know me very well—in fact you don't know me at all—but I just won't be bullied. I come of a large family, all males, and I know something about getting my own way.'

Morty chuckled with delight. 'That's the spirit, my girl. There's a saying in these parts—I picked it up in The Demon —"*I won't be knocked out of my Know*". We'll defy the foul fiend together. And to hell with the Forty Angels and Hector Askew, too, now I come to think of it.'

'Poor man,' said Dido. 'He hates being kept waiting. I ought to have been there nearly an hour ago. At least I've got a good excuse.'

The roar of a motor cycle exhaust announced that its owner was departing for Saltey at speed and in a moment P.C.

Simmonds appeared round the van, notebook in hand.

'I'd best take your name, just in case,' he said. 'Though I think I know you, sir. You're the American gentleman, aren't you, from The Demon, And you're a doctor, miss? You wouldn't be the lady who's come into Miss Kytie's house, by any chance?'

There was a half smile on his face as he spoke which suggested that he was going to add 'and much good will it do you' but he clearly suppressed the thought.

'The van has a tyre that's been cut and he doesn't carry a spare. He will move the vehicle away to the side in a minute which will just give you room to get past.' He cocked a speculative eye at the pair. 'You do want to go to Saltey, I suppose?'

'We're both going to live there,' said Morty firmly, 'so spread the good news around.'

The afternoon was fading as the procession finally moved off. The road swept round in a long erratic curve between low cut butchered hedges separating heavy fields where the saltings, on which nothing but sour grass will grow, had been held at bay by deep drainage. A straggling line of bungalows and villas announced the village itself which was dominated by the squat Norman tower of St Michael's mantled in elms. It was remote, disinterested and apparently deserted, a huddle of mixed dwellings ranging from Tudor to Edwardian, each sited without consideration for its neighbours. Chapel brick and corrugated iron rubbed shoulders with white weatherboard and oak beams which had escaped the restorer's art.

The heart of the hamlet was marked by a patch of grass not large enough to be dignified by the title of Green, flanked on one side by cottages and on the other by The Angel, a sad hostelry which clearly found little favour with its intended public. It stood back from the road and the space in front of it provided a parking area now occupied by a single small station wagon.

'Hector's here,' said Dido sombrely. 'He won't be pleased with us. That's his car. He'll be up at the Hollies, that's the official name of the house. It's a difficult drive to get into.'

The late Miss Kytie's property lay some fifty yards ahead on their left. It was a solid double fronted late Georgian residence faced with stucco, to which two ill-proportioned bow windows had been added. Dark hollies flanked it and at the far side was a brick wall concealing a lady garden with trees beyond. A white five-barred gate stood open at a rakish angle and gave on to a circular drive in the centre of which was a group of un-pruned rose trees guarded by a miniature box hedge. Weeds sprouted from the pebbled pathway and on the ground floor the blinds were drawn.

Morty negotiated the difficult approach with skill and brought the Lotus to a halt directly in front of the pillared porch. He ran up the two steps which led to the door and tried the handle. It did not respond.

'Try ringing,' said Dido. 'He's bound to be here.'

A tug at a wrought iron bell pull which creaked at the un-accustomed insult brought a faint tinkling jangle from some-where far inside, but the echoes died away without producing any other result. The light was now beginning to wane and the air was soft and melancholy after the downpour of the morn-ing.

Morty had raised his hand for a second attempt when Dido caught his arm.

'Listen,' she said. 'There must be someone at home. I can hear music.'

They stood immobile with ears strained. From the depths of the house, faint but unmistakable, came the adenoidal moan of the Mersey beat:

'*I wanna be your rave ...*'

'Damn him,' said Morty. 'He's got a blasted transistor going and he can't hear anything else. One more try here and if that fails we'll take him from the rear.'

He wrenched violently at the handle as he spoke and put his shoulder to the panelling. To his surprise the effort was suc-cessful. The door groaned, hesitated mutinously and finally swung back in surrender. The interior was dim with twilight, a cluttered curtained gloom which offered no welcome.

'Hector!' shouted Dido. 'Hector, where are you?'

Distant and elusive Mersey voices wailed but there was no other response. Morty began to move purposefully through the house, flinging back curtains and shutters, raising protesting dust in his wake. He returned without success and they paused together to listen.

'It's down this way,' said Dido at last. 'It must lead to the greenhouse—a sort of garden room built on the side. I saw it when I walked round without the keys.'

A narrow passage led them to a half glass door and beyond it they found a green overgrown arbour full of ferns and smelling of eucalyptus. The place was furnished with dilapidated cane chairs and a low table filled the centre space. On it stood the tell-tale transistor still bleating out a history of woe. The largest chair in the room was a vast fan-backed affair with wide curling arms containing pockets for magazines and a tumbler, a relic of colonial glory designed for chota-pegs and gracious tropical verandahs. In it sat a man, his head bent forward on his chest and his arms gripping the sides.

Morty, who had snatched up the transistor in some anger, switched it off and they stood looking at the stranger. There was about him a frightening ageless loneliness as if he had been carved out of stone.

Dido took a step forward and caught at her breath, aware that the hairs at the back of her neck were rising. She shook herself involuntarily and became professional with a disciplined effort.

Very gently she took hold of Hector Askew's shoulders and leant his body back against the cushions. His eyes were wide open and his head lolled awkwardly to one side. It did not need expert knowledge to tell either of them that he was dead, but it was some minutes before Dr Jones straightened her back and looked her companion in the face.

'I thought he must have had a seizure of some sort,' she said.

'But he hasn't. I think he's been shot. Very silly of me not to spot it straight away.'

Suddenly her composure broke and Morty held out his arms to her. The fact that she was human enough to weep and be afraid was the one comfort he found in an ugly world.

5

The Company at The Demon

THE investigation of homicide in England is subject to the same considerations which control most other enterprises in contemporary life. This means that laws of economics and the shortage of manpower put a limit on the time and staff which can be devoted to any one problem.

The chain of enquiries into the death of Hector Askew began with P.C. Simmonds, who was just starting an evening meal in his cottage when the news reached him, and ran from him to his superior at Nine Ash, thence to Chelmsford and finally to Scotland Yard. The possible connection between the murder and the poison pen outbreak was remarked with commendable speed and Sergeant Throstle found himself seconded to a murder squad to which he did not properly belong, under the leadership of Superintendent Gravesend, an officer who delighted in being called dynamic when his activities were noticed by the Press. By midnight there were five official cars parked outside the Angel and the inn itself did unexpectedly good business until it closed its doors to the general public with stop watch precision.

Dido spent an uncomfortable night in an attic bedroom at The Demon and slept fitfully. The Superintendent and his team did not sleep at all, nor did they expect to. The modern intensive system of enquiry, which is to work with unremitting pressure until a case is broken, had found a high priest in Gravesend. He guarded his reputation with the care of a gardener watching over a rare plant, for it was his intention to retire early and to move on to better paid appointments.

Throstle disliked him dispassionately but the situation was out of his control.

By Sunday evening The Hollies had been searched from junk room to tool shed and before nightfall every inch of the overgrown garden and the copse beyond it had been trampled, beaten, prodded and given the appearance of an area recently tenanted by a battalion of cantankerous livestock. Nothing of any consequence was discovered.

Hector Askew, it was established, had arrived at Saltey at about four o'clock on the afternoon of Friday, some two and a half hours before his appointment with Dido. He had left his car outside the Angel and gone directly to the house, where he had apparently unlocked all three outer doors and opened two windows at the back. But he had not been seen alive since he had walked up the drive. The transistor was his property and he was in the habit of using it to obtain racing results.

No one had heard an identifiable shot and this was not remarkable since two young men admitted spending their afternoon shooting at rooks and three motor cyclists had rushed through the village headed for Mob's Bowl without benefit of silencer.

By Tuesday evening three hundred and twelve grudging statements had been taken, signed, co-ordinated, corroborated and their makers temporarily eliminated. Askew had died at some time between five and six as a result of a shot from a 3.8 pistol which had not been discovered.

On Thursday in the early evening the Superintendent sat in P.C. Simmonds' office parlour and looked morosely from his official report to his private notes. He had drawn a complete blank and no amount of detail or of word spinning could change the fact. Saltey had treated him and his squad with what amounted, in his opinion, to dumb insolence but he could find no loophole in the facade, nothing to suggest conspiracy or even simple concealment by omission.

The population, in the local Inspector's phrase, was pig ignorant and was enjoying the fact.

The odd incident of the broken glass at the corner of the main road puzzled him but he found no enlightenment. The murderer could conceivably have left the village before it occurred or even have placed the barrier there to delay discovery, but he was tolerably certain that in fact no one had left the village during the vital hour. He put the affair down to the viciousness of modern youth, which was the accepted opinion, but left a query beside it in his notes.

Wider researchers had uncovered a scandalous affair between the dead man and an ex-secretary of the family firm, but the lady had been married and divorced since that period and was now much engaged as a receptionist and managerial friend in a hotel on the Isle of Wight. Apart from an occasional expensive winter cruise to the Mediterranean and the Near East with cultural overtones, Hector's life for the past five years made remarkably dull reading. Nevertheless the Superintendent wrote the word 'womaniser' in his notes and as an afterthought underlined it, adding a query. He stared gloomily at his handiwork for some time, but found no enlightenment. Finally he drew a line across the sheet of paper and inscribed the initials N.U.P.S.H. beneath it in block capitals.

Throstle was sitting on the far side of the table opposite his superior and from long training had the habit of reading upside down. He raised his eyebrows.

'That's a new one on me.'

'It dates from the war, my lad. Same like T.A.B.U. and C.U.M.F.U. A favourite of my old boss in the S.I.B. in the days when preventing Arabs from sneaking motor tyres was the most important job on earth. Damn near impossible too. If you must know, it stands for "No Useful Purpose Served Here" and that's the long and the short of it as far as I'm concerned at the moment. I'm sorry but this was agreed at the morning conference.'

He folded the sheet of notes precisely and tucked them into a wallet.

'You'll stay on here until you can get a lever into some little crevice. Run over the depositions, see who you can shift—you know the form. The answer is either here in the shape of someone who thinks the house is rightly theirs or at Nine Ash, in which case you want an angry husband or a young woman in the pudding club. Quarter the ground every which way, and keep all concerned on the hop. Report in the usual way and if anything breaks ring me at once. Understood?'

He stood up and straightened his back wearily. 'And another thing ...'

'Yes?'

'The mattress of Simmonds' spare bed is made of broken bricks. If you must sleep, stay on at the Angel. I'll give you a week. Liaise with the County. You'll find the man at Nine Ash is the best bet. He's an old timer called Branch who'll tell you all the local dirt, if you can understand what he's saying. If no one cracks, then we're just wasting our time on what ought to be a local job.'

At precisely the same time, which coincided in Fleet Street with the evening conferences, four London news editors were reaching the same conclusion. The adjourned inquest had revealed nothing and the significant phrase 'The investigations are continuing' was on the lips of the official P.R.O. at the Yard. Good reporters are scarce and there was better game afoot. The invasion of Saltey was over and the cash tills at The Angel and The Demon returned overnight to their normal rhythm.

Morty found himself disconsolate and the depth of his feelings surprised and worried him. Dido had returned to London and he was in a mood of bored malaise. He had spent most of the day prodding at the marsh turf covering the site of the pre-Norman fort, a desolate piece of comparatively high ground by the sea wall which offered a commanding view of Mob's Bowl and the huddle of the Forty Angels a quarter of a mile distant on the inland side. Through his glass he surveyed the nearer hamlet which was dominated by the church of St Polycarp, a decaying late Norman shell without a tower, reputed to be dangerous and only used on token occasions. Near it stood a cluster of cottages in brick and weatherboard whose slate roofs uncompromisingly prevented them from being picturesque. Some modern caravans and a small green tent completed the group. The Bowl itself was empty at this hour, an expanse of greasy mud which sucked in sluggish resentment at the ebbing tide. In better days there had been a boatyard, still marked by sheds and a railed slipway running to the water's edge and a group of four sail lofts in lichen grey weatherboard one of which was surmounted by a weathercock above a wooden lantern. Three small rowboats were pulled up on to the hard and several skeleton hulks lay inert in the grey slime.

The Demon itself was an L-shaped building, part weatherboard and part plaster over brick. It had a mansard roof in which there were dormer windows but despite its three floors it appeared squat and sturdy, having the painted and tarred patina which coastal buildings acquire over the years. Only the touches of white and green, the trimmings of geranium tubs and benches, gave it a rakish air, that of a middle-aged man who dons an unlikely hat for a children's party. It stood squarely beside the Bowl separated from the waterside by a broad frontage of pebbled earth which was edged by baulks of timber sunk into the mud. Bollards proclaimed that this had once been a working quay. Seagulls circled perpetually around a white flagstaff and only the incongruous new sign offended the young man's eye.

From where he stood Morty surveyed the back yards and the outhouses, noting the arrival of an elderly Morris Minor from whose interior there emerged a figure of such ponderous bulk that the performance took on something of the quality of a conjuring trick. Magersfontein Lugg, Mr Campion's other emissary in Saltey, had arrived at the inn for vesper refreshment and there was something about the self-importance of his movements which suggested that the old man was bringing news. The idea afforded Morty some pleasure. Dido, with luck, would be banished from his thoughts. After all, he had more important things to worry about.

The saloon bar of The Demon was much as it had been for a

hundred years. It was dark, warm, heavily varnished and smelled pleasantly of beer, baking and scrubbing soap. On the shelves behind the long counter there were concessions to modernity in the shape of miniature bottles, a coyly indecent calendar, bureaucratic edicts concerning drinking hours and a large handwritten card which announced:

DEMON CAKES
Made from the original recipe
1/- each
Box of 6 packed to take away
5/-
'The History of the Saltey Demon'
by H.O. Wishart
On sale here: 2/6d

When Morty entered there were already two customers, an old man sitting in the gloom of the ingle corner at the end of the bar, whose red rimmed eyes were the only living thing in a face which otherwise appeared to be moulded in suet, and the portentous figure of Mr Lugg outlined against the light from a door behind the bar. He was a large man, a thought melancholy, with a bald head and a clipped greying moustache which suggested that it was the relic of a darker and more luxuriant growth. He had discarded his flat cap and overcoat to reveal a white expanse of sweater and now leaned against the bar, a tankard in his hand. His accent was thick as a London fog.

'Wotcher, cock.'

Morty responded conventionally to the greeting.

'Good evening. Good evening, all.'

'Still grubbing around in the 'istoric past, I see from the muck on your boots.' Mr Lugg was disposed to be conversational. 'Not my period, reely, the Roman caper, togas and all that gear. If I 'ad to make a choice it would be Restoration, what you might term the Dawn of Gracious Livin'. I could fancy meself in a wig, leather sports coat and a touch of lace at the wrists but not in a purple cotton mini-skirt and a laurel wreath.'

'I take your point.'

'Exackly. I see my architects today and nice la-di-da shower they are, I might add. Trying to flog me the open plan lark. Asking me to live in a ruddy shop window so that 'alf Saltey can see if I've changed me dickey before I partake of me deep frozen ah lah cart. I give 'em my views on the subject and they looked at me like something that ought to be sent to an 'ome.'

'Was that at Nine Ash? Did you see anyone else there?'

Mr Lugg's foot brushed sharply against his shin and the big man continued, his tone becoming loud with warning. 'Neo Georgian might be the ticket—in a bijou style, of course. Now what about a touch of pig's ear? Think you could keep down a pint?'

Dixie Wishart, hostess of The Demon, who had appeared behind the bar was smiling and matronly, her rather old fashioned good looks sitting oddly beneath hair that had suffered from a blue rinse giving it alarming heliotrope lights in the massed curls above her forehead. A plastic apron decorated with continental bottle labels added another luminous touch and she rustled as she moved.

'Sorry, I missed you when you came in, Mr Kelsey dear. What's it going to be?'

Mr Lugg gave the order. 'My friend will take 'is restorative in your other pewter mug if it 'asn't bin knocked off by the visiting narks. And you'd better give the old 'un his usual.'

'That's sweet of you.' She raised her voice and addressed the immobile figure in the corner. 'Very kind of Mr Lugg, isn't it? Here's a drink for you, Mossy love. Don't forget your manners. Wipe your nose first and say thank you.'

A thin grey hand slipped towards the bar with accustomed if surprising agility. The red rimmed eyes flickered and the glass was raised in salutation.

'Properly kind, I'm sure. I see the Demon once when I was nobbut a boy. I say I seed the Demon. . . .'

Dixie returned to her other guests. 'Don't let him go into the lecture—he still thinks you're tourists and that's what's expected of him. He's my mascot really, poor old gentleman. Over eighty, he is. Very good for trade in the summer. Helps to sell my cakes and H.O.'s little book. I made a new batch today, if either of you fancy one for your dinner?'

'What's in them this time?' enquired Morty. 'I smelt them when I came in.'

'Same as ever, of course, dear.' Dixie was on her dignity. 'Ginger and cinnamon and eggs and cream, all baked like shortbread. It's the original recipe handed down from H.O.'s grandmother. She was there, you know: she saw the Demon too.'

'So you say,' said Morty. 'And very good for trade. I wish I could find something more tangible than your husband's beautiful little essay in whimsy to use in my own researches. A good cook and a poet may create a legend but I'm supposed to be a historian, so where do I go for honey? Don't give me old Mossy in the corner as a reliable witness.'

'There's nothing wrong with his memory of the past,' retorted Dixie with spirit. 'It's only today he's a bit shaky about. And if you're not more civil about my Demon I'll make him go through it again and again. Every session takes twenty minutes and costs a round of doubles, including me.'

She raised her voice again. 'You'll tell 'em, won't you, Mossy? You *did* see him, didn't you.'

The old man lifted his rheumy eyes.

'That I did,' he said, 'I seed that acomin' down the road as clear as yesterday. I see a lot of things in my time and that's the truth, so it is now. I seed the old Prince of Wales when he was a boy. I seed a Zeppelin burn up like a firework show. I seed Jonah Woodrose drink a gallon o' beer come Jubilee night when he wasn't a grown man and never draw a breath.'

He scanned the company cautiously and nodded his head.

'And I seed Matt Parsley alying in his own coffin what he made for my sister, the morning they found him stiff as dried seaweed. If that weren't Demon's work I never seed nothing. And I'll thank you to give me half o' mild, Mrs Wishart.'

He had undoubtedly made an effect. Their hostess cleared her throat noisily and turned on him with a swish of her apron.

'That'll do now, Mossy. Don't you go telling tales out of school or you'll get the place a bad name. One Demon's enough in these parts and we don't want any more fancy work. Don't you listen to him, Mr Kelsey dear. He'll fill your head with rubbish.'

'Oh, but that was great!' Morty was delighted. 'Like old home week in the Catskill Mountains. Let him have his say.'

Dixie bristled. Two spots of angry colour in her cheeks emphasised her wrath.

'Not in my bar, he won't. He's a silly old fool and I won't have my nice little tale mixed up with a lot of dirty village scandal that's got nothing to do with it.'

Mr Lugg nudged his companion and whispered breathily, 'Tell you later, cock. 'Omely little news item it is, now I come to think of it. Go well with a nice plate of liver and bacon.'

The long low room was beginning to fill with its regular evening customers and from the kitchen behind the bar came the appetising crackle of cooking. Dixie Wishart rustled efficiently from barrel to counter and it was some time before Morty could make his peace with her.

'Where's H.O. tonight?' he asked, as she paused beside him to accept a light for a cigarette. She was only partially mollified.

'Doing the chef, poor darling. He's been what he calls overhung all day, which means he had a drop too much last night. I should know. He didn't get to bed until two and snored like a pig until dawn. You'd better skip along and get the good table, the pair of you, if you want any service. The policeman

71

from London will be coming in later and who'll want to talk in front of him?'

The dining room at the inn led out of the saloon bar and also looked directly on to the Bowl. It was furnished in sound Victorian taste, with rounded mahogany chairs upholstered in leather that had once been red and a surprising collection of Rowlandson prints. Rainbow bright tablecloths did their best to reduce the atmosphere to that of a tea shop. Two schools of contrasting taste were also evident in the mixture of pewter and plastic which made up the salt cellars and pepper pots.

Mr Lugg devoted himself to his food with concentration and energy, only pausing for light conversation when Dixie made her appearance to produce the cheese.

'Two loos, ladies and gents, on the ground floor, that's what I'm going after,' he remarked for her benefit. 'Nosh in the kitchbath. Main lounge with fitted bar. Boodwah corner for telly. Wot more could you ask?'

'Got a name for it yet?' enquired Morty.

"S'matter of fact, I 'ave. Considering wot the rest of the place is called, I thought of calling mine "The Villa Lug 'ole".' He sucked a tooth reflectively.

'Right. Now that she's scarpered for a bit, I'll give you the lowdown on Matt Parsley. Undertaker, carpenter and rowboats built, that's what he was and lived very convenient to the church where that big black shed is right now. Now one morning, twenty years ago—and that's a date 'is Lordship 'as been arskin' about though he won't condescend to say why—one morning they found 'im dead as 'orsemeat and twice as ugly by all accounts, lying in one of 'is own coffins.'

'Laid out like a corpse?' Morty was incredulous.

'Well, not exackly. Shame to muck up a beautiful lump of wot you might term imagery, but the poor old worm fancier 'ad 'ad a 'eart attack, or so the doc said. Natural death, classy funeral, wreaths from the Sons of Lebanon, the British Legion, the Ladies' Guild and sorrowing family. All very ah lar. But 'e was found 'alf in and 'alf out of a nice box of 'and finished pine, bung in the middle of the floor.'

He consumed a final morsel of cheese.

'I bin into the facts. Not with old Mossy, who's so far round the bend 'e can see 'imself coming, but with one or two that do remember. Seems like 'e goes trundling up the road to Forty Angels wiv 'is box on a barrer, late at night like wot is customary in the trade, old Mossy's sister being dead and lying there in 'er bed waiting for him. 'E never got there. Hours later 'e comes trundlin' back with 'is box still empty, runs the 'ole issue into the shop and corpses 'isself right across it. Barrer tips up, coffin slips down and there's Matt Parsley lyin' among the shavins wiv 'is 'ead in the coffin where Mossy's sis's feet 'ad orter bin. Simple, reely. 'Cept for one thing.'

'Why did he turn back?'

'Exackly. Might 'ave bin took ill on the way, o' course, but them as 'eard 'im go into the yard where there's paving and cobbles by the stabling, say 'e come 'ome on the trot. And there's another little item.'

'Yes?'

''Appened on a Monday night. Coffin wasn't due till the Tuesday. His regular mate was off duty and wasn't there to 'elp 'im with the corp, like wot 'e orter 'ave bin.'

'That surely is strange, brother. Something must have happened between here and Forty Angels. Don't tell me he saw the Demon, had a long chat with him about what he'd been doing since 1898 and frightened himself into a fit.'

'Might 'ave, of course. Then again 'e might 'ave taken a drop too much, gorn off too soon, fell in a ditch, remembered what day of the week it was and come 'ome in such an 'urry that 'is poor old 'eart give out. That's the Official Voo, according to the doctor's 'andout. I don't go for it meself.'

'Why not?'

''E didn't drink, not to speak of. Particular kind of bloke by all accounts. Everything shipshape and on the dot. You know wot I reckon, mate?'

'I'd certainly like to.'

Mr Lugg swilled the last of his beer around the tankard, lifted it to his mouth and appeared to pour the contents directly from lips to stomach.

'I reckon,' he said at last, 'that if we knew the answer to that one we'd know wot this 'ole perishing shooting match is about.'

Their conversation was interrupted by the arrival of Sergeant Throstle whose broad shoulders were emphasised by the Houndstooth jacket he considered appropriate for country enquiries. With him was a thin sad faced individual whose grey suit, creased and a trifle greasy, was so deliberately non-committal that it could only have belonged to a minor government official. The C.I.D. man waved to Morty and favoured him with a wink but settled himself and his companion in the farthest corner. They were talking in undertones and Mr Lugg, having made an overt effort to catch the murmur, finally turned back to Morty. The sound of a transistor beating out a history of frustrated love drifted from the bar.

'Unless old Dickybird and that other rozzer 'ave got the place bugged, which ain't likely,' he remarked, 'we're as private 'ere as a flea circus wot's gorn out of business. I've bin making researches today, looking up me contacts as you might say, and I've 'appened on a little something wot the official narks 'aven't cottoned to yet.'

'You've been in Nine Ash all day?'

'Exackly.' Mr Lugg was very pleased with himself and was savouring the moment for which he had clearly been waiting. 'I come across an old pal in the Black Bull there. Not a nice class of person, reely. Name of Good, which is wot you might call sick 'umour. 'Orrible face, 'orrible nature and 'orrible record.'

He shook his head reflectively. "Orace Good is not the article, an' that's a fact.'

'What does he do for a living?'

"E's done most things in 'is time from 'ouse breaking to bookies runnin' and informing but 'e's an old man now and

'e's a sweeper. Works at the 'ospital there and does all the truly
filthy jobs wot you, personally, wouldn't demean yerself with.
'E also cleans up the morgue and keeps 'is ear'oles open. 'E was
there when they took a dekko at the late 'Ector Askew de-
ceased.'

Morty leaned closer, for Mr Lugg's voice had sunk to a
whisper.

'What was his big news?'

"E saw the medicos fetch out the slug wot put paid to the
gent on the cold table. Three eight, they said, standard type.
Cupra-nickel.'

He paused for dramatic effect.

'What's so special about cupra-nickel?' said Morty. 'I
thought they were all made of the stuff. I don't get it.'

'Thought you wouldn't,' said Mr Lugg with satisfaction.
'And the corpse fanciers and busies 'aven't got the message
either, from wot I can 'ear. It was made by Seligman's, an old
fashioned lot that went out of business before the war. Their
stuff was very classy. 'Orace spotted it quick as a flash, on
account of its 'aving a point as sharp as 'is own nose and 'im
'aving seen one or two before. They 'ad a special name.'

'Such as?'

'Such as Silver Prince.'

Mr Lugg nodded his head. 'Silver Prince, cock. A silver
bullet, in fac'. And if that means anythink except James
Teague, Esquire, then I'm the 'ead mistress of a Sunday school.'

6

The Poet of the Saltings

MR LUGG concluded his evening meal in the style which he considered becoming to a man of his station in life. He took coffee, smoked a small but virulent black cigar and accepted a brandy from Morty, which he diluted with a great deal of soda. Honour being satisfied he withdrew to the saloon leaving the young man alone, for Throstle and his friend had not lingered.

The dining room at The Demon was an acknowledgment to the world that the inn was also an hotel since it served as a lounge for guests between meals. Morty made a prolonged attempt to read but he was not happy. For the first time since his student days he was in love and he recognised the symptoms ruefully, rather in the mood of a parent who has to face the fact that his offspring is starting chicken pox.

Dido coloured his every thought. Her face came between him and the page and his reactions were slowed because he could no longer concentrate.

When he reviewed the situation in an intense effort to behave dispassionately, he found no comfort. She was elegant and he suspected gloomily that she was probably extremely clever in her profession and undoubtedly surrounded by admirers who spoke her own language. He stood no chance at all. Even if she was not already committed, the competition must be continuous and ardent. She could take her pick from a score of brilliant rivals each with common interests and a start of five years' acquaintance. Except for a brief moment during the alarming adventure they had shared she had remained cool, efficient and aloof. Now that he came to assess the situation he doubted if he had made any real progress with her.

Any man would have behaved protectively and many would have made a better job of it. Dido accepted favours but only because they were strewn perpetually in her path and she was too nicely nurtured to refuse. Damn her, damn her for her style, her elegance, damn her for sweeping him casually into her net, for reducing him to a jelly, for threatening to hurt him irrevocably.

He closed his book with a slam and as the cruets on the table ceased to vibrate he realised that the inn was silent for the first time that evening. The last car, the last motor cycle, the last transistor and the last late drinker had vanished. The lights in the bar were out and through the open window he could hear the lap of the rising tide against the wooden bulwark of the quay. It was a clear, moonless night but not totally dark, for the stars carpeted the whole sky and an occasional window still glowed to emphasise the black silhouette of the hamlet.

Mob's Bowl had closed its doors and had become a secret place, shrouded but still slyly awake.

Morty tiptoed through the stale silence of the bar and strolled out towards the estuary where the air was still warm and tangy. The path over the saltings was irregular but this was familiar ground. Ten minutes' cautious walking brought him to the higher area where the old fort was still marked by stones whose original purpose was so erased that they could have been an outcrop of rock. This was his place, his personal domain, the lookout post from which he could consider the world and the ache in his heart.

From somewhere beyond human sight he could hear the scrape of oars in rowlocks and presently there came the grating of a keel on pebbles and retreating footsteps. A light died in a cottage and a gull mewed forlornly. Now, he thought, now I am utterly alone with my melancholy and I can be as theatrically miserable as I please.

Dido, my sweet, unique, unattainable Dido, where are you now? Do you even give me a second thought?

'To the world's end have I come. To the world's end.'

77

The voice behind him was deep and had an edge of sardonic amusement in the overtones. Morty jerked violently, realising too late that this was the reaction the speaker had intended.

'Wishart!'

'The same. I wonder if anyone reads Macleod today?'

The landlord of The Demon who had been standing directly behind him moved to his side and offered a cigarette. His voice was so low that in a crowd he was difficult to hear but in this silent place each separate granulation of sound lingered like a sustained chord. The young man could just discern the leonine sweep of grey hair above the broad forehead and he sensed rather than saw the twinkle of mockery in the hooded eyes.

'William Sharp—Fiona Macleod, if you prefer his romantic side. You won't have read him. Out of date, out of fashion. Yet he was a poet, you know.'

Morty was still edgy with shock. He retorted brusquely, putting himself at a disadvantage.

'Wrong. You are quoting The Immortal Hour. And if you must know I've read him on Shelley and Sainte Beuve.'

Wishart laughed. 'What a benison a little learning is. Do you know what I miss most of all in this ancient isolation? The mind of man, the single glimmer which goes beyond personal greed. It is a brutal hunger, Mr Kelsey. You are fortunate to be free of it. But perhaps you came out here to escape from company? This should be the quintessence of solitude. You have the time and the place—' he hesitated and blew smoke into the still air, '—but not the loved one?'

'Suppose you mind your own goddam business?' Morty was irritated and off balance. His mood had been broken and the shock of Wishart's appearance still tingled in his bones. His host took a step towards the remaining corner of stone and leaned on it, hunching his shoulders and turning his head away.

'You mistake my motive, my dear sir. In a sense it is my business. I may be an elderly observer but I still have the use of my ears and eyes. Again, I am indigenous. But for the accident of education—and I can assure you that it was an accident—I am the basic man of the estuary.'

This at least is true, Morty admitted to himself. He is a local at heart. Even that unnaturally cultured voice has echoes of the coast. Perhaps that is what saves him from being offensively theatrical here in this unlikely wilderness.

As a gesture of reconciliation he fumbled through his memory of the man's work and found the phrase he was seeking.

'*Let us respect the saltings and the wind.*'

'That is a subtle flattery. Few people recall anything of mine beyond a single line written forty odd years ago. I had supposed Dixie to be the last soul on earth interested in my withered laurels. Yet you say your subject is history and you profess to conduct your researches here?'

'That's certainly true. You are leaning on all that is left of a Saxon fort, if my guess is right. These stones were brought here before the quarry at Nine Ash had been discovered and St Polycarp's, which did come from there, is early Norman. Why did you follow me?'

It was some time before Wishart replied. Finally he threw the end of a cigarette so that it travelled for several yards like a shooting star before it vanished into the water below the bank.

'You do me an injustice. I could argue that it was I who led and you who followed, but that would not be strictly true. I came here because I wanted to talk to you and because it seemed very probable that you would come this way. There is not much that you can do in Mob's Bowl without being remarked. I came to tell you of a letter bearing no signature which I have received and have now destroyed, though some of it is committed to memory. You could also say, perhaps, that I came to offer you a lesson in history.'

A chill caught at Morty's heart and he shivered involuntarily, his resentment shifting reluctantly from his companion.

'Not another of those infernal things?'

'Ah, so there have been others? You don't altogether surprise me for I have heard a whisper of them in the wind. I think I should tell you the burden of the writer's plaint. It was posted, by the way, in Saltey two days ago and was written in block capitals by an elderly person, probably a woman. Not wholly literate but with quite a gift of invective. A woman, almost certainly one who was born in this place.'

'How do you know that?'

'I am building with very trifling straws, but they make a brick or two. I say a woman, since there was a brand of malice in the missive which I believe to be typically female. I say elderly because the hand was not steady as yours would be if you inscribed the same essay. And I say local because it has a peculiar hallmark which no stranger would recognise.'

In the darkness Morty could visualise Wishart's secret smile, the satisfaction of a lonely man who normally finds no audience for private jokes.

'All of us in Saltey who are nearing seventy betray ourselves by it. It was the snobbery of the time, the idiosyncracy taught to us by Miss Jessica Croft our village schoolmistress, the Greek E in handwriting. I use it myself, and it derives from my childhood here and not from my frail knowledge of the classics. Dame Croft went out with the tide when this century was very young and no child has used it since. My correspondent, ergo, is of her vintage.'

'O.K. So you had a letter from some anonymous old harridan. What did she say?'

'You will not care for the contents. I may be an indifferent Boniface but I am equipped to be your mentor in some respects. It said that I should not accept a Jezebel as a guest, a "Whore of Babylon" was the phrase. It stated that the delectable Dr Jones had been conducting a liaison with the late Hector Askew, in order to inherit Miss Kytie's property. This suggestion was colourfully supplemented and in some detail. The writer added that since Askew had been struck, rightly, by the vengeance which Jehovah wreaks upon the sinners of this world, the doctor was now casting libidinous eyes upon the body of Mortimer Kelsey and that he too stood in danger of receiving a retributive thunderbolt from the servants of Nemesis now resident here on earth. Not a particularly Christian document but it struck a religious note.'

Morty snorted. 'There's nothing new in it. Dr Jones tells me she's given hers to the police. You ought to have done the same.'

'A little beyond our local Dogberry, I fear. As for the amiable Throstle, his hands are full elsewhere. The two happenings—the death of Askew and these letters—have only the remotest of basic connections in my arrogant opinion. You don't understand us in Saltey, Mr Kelsey, and there are long odds that you never will.'

'I can see that a group of evil minded jealous and greedy old witches are trying to frighten Dido out of her wits—trying to scare her off by a pack of lies and slanders.'

'Just so. The question is, will they succeed?'

Morty considered. The picture of Dido, angry, cool and determined, came vividly to him.

'I'd say no. She's a hell of a girl. Spooks and mumbo jumbo, wisecracks from old Rip Van Winkle in your bar and all the broken glass in creation wouldn't keep her out if she gave her mind to it. If you want my bet I'd say that the bigger the opposition the more determined she'd be to fight it.'

'I thought you might form that impression.' Wishart pulled a pipe from his pocket and filled it. When it was satisfactorily alight he spoke again.

'You call yourself a historian, Mr Kelsey. Have you come to any conclusion about our Demon? My impression was that you came here originally because you were attracted by that significant piece of mythology.'

'It's largely true—that and my thesis. I've read your book of course. Why do you ask?'

'Because it has a bearing on your problem. If you can read that riddle you can touch the fringe of knowledge. Understand

81

the Demon and you have the clue to our psychology. My pamphlet is a bait for the tripper trade, written at the insistence of my dear wife. Those who can read between the lines will find some amusement at what are called "in-jokes" today. It is an experiment in the forgery of folk lore. Yet the story has an origin, a basis in fact. Have you no idea what it could be?'

'According to your fairy tale,' said Morty, giving his mind to the subject with an effort, 'on June 7th 1895 the village of Saltey, or rather the Mob's Bowl end of it, was visited by a Demon who rushed down the road, smashed gates and windows, broke moorings, took tiles off roofs, destroyed crops and generally had himself such a ball that the place took years to recover. The story has been handed down from those who saw him to their children's children as if they were the warriors of Bunkers Hill or Agincourt. A lot of embroidery has been added on the way, of course—the baby found in the middle of a haystack, the two headed calf, the plague of bats, the cloven hoof marks in the churchyard and the remarkable cakes cooking in the bakehouse oven. I rather go for the bats myself and I should say they were your contribution. But do I believe any of it? No, sir.'

'Yet something undoubtedly happened. What is your suggestion?'

Morty considered. 'Oh, something set the tongues wagging sure enough. Almost certainly a freak storm, purely local. It probably raised a small whirlwind, the sort we call a Dust Devil in the States. They can cause quite a bit of damage and certainly look kind of strange if you haven't seen one before. That would be my reading of it. But you've got nothing to worry about. I'd hate to spoil a good story by supplying a simple corny explanation.'

'You'd be wrong to do so. Doubly wrong, because although there was no whirlwind there *was* a great deal of damage to property.'

Wishart settled his elbows more comfortably on the rock and

Morty was again aware of the man's hunger for more sophisticated conversation than his patrons at the inn could provide.

'The truth about the Saltey Demon,' he said at last, 'is better than fiction—funnier, if you like. It would be a pity to spoil a good legend for the sake of a poor joke but this is a risk I am going to take. It is for your researching mind alone, so you must respect my confidence.

'June 7th 1895 was the day of the Royal review of the troops and militia in the grounds of Sparrows Manor at Nine Ash. It was a sort of a local Field of the Cloth of Gold, with bands, marquees, pageantry, the flags of all nations and of course a royal Prince and Princess. No one in the district had talked about anything else for weeks and nearly every able bodied man, woman and child was determined to be there. Charabancs—horse drawn wagonettes in those days—were hired, dog carts were polished, brakes repainted and those who couldn't afford to ride went on foot. By eight o'clock in the morning, with a few notable exceptions, Mob's Bowl and Forty Angels were as deserted as the central Sahara.

'It was a very hot day, the middle of a heat wave in point of fact, and what is more important it was a Wednesday.'

'I don't get the significance of that.'

'You will, my friend, you will. Wednesday was always a baking day in the village and every housewife made her own cakes, but few had the right ovens for the operation. The mixtures in their pans were brought by the ladies every Wednesday morning to the baker, whose name by the way was Septimus Kytie, a relation of the old lady up the road. His custom was to bake the cakes during the day and have them ready for collection in the evening, thus saving a great deal of valuable fuel. This practice continued here until the advent of the mass produced rubbish which is called bread today. Mr Kytie was therefore excluded from the exodus.

'Now there was a second absentee and he was a predecessor of mine, the landlord of what was then The Foliage, a henpecked and unhappy individual called Waters. I picture an idyllic scene, the sunshine, the deserted village, only the call of the gulls to underline this unique peace. I am improvising a trifle here, but the deduction is inescapable. Mr Waters called on his friend Mr Kytie to comment on the beauty of a world without women and to give an additional quality to the occasion he brought with him a couple of bottles of brandy, probably from a private reserve. We sometimes have such trifles in these parts.

'One thing led to another, most agreeably, and by mid-afternoon they were both fast asleep. The oven and the precious cakes were forgotten. Then the terrible moment arrived when the smell of burning aroused them. They were faced with disaster and inevitable exposure. Fifty potential Furies were about to descend on them and they had perhaps half an hour to save their skins. It was a situation which could well ruin both men for life.

'But one of them, and I suspect that this was Septimus Kytie, had an idea. There was a wretched child hanging about the place, a miscreant who had been denied the treat. The old men seized on him, bribed him and gave him very precise instructions. He was to go and hide in a ditch between here and Forty Angels, get himself covered with mud and reappear when the wagons returned. On his way he was to do as much damage as any small fiend could lay his hands to. His story was to be that he had been knocked off his feet by a Demon. Kytie had spent some time at sea and had probably seen a whirlwind in action. His briefing was colourful and he had a willing pupil.

'At this point a genuine minor miracle came to their aid. The weather broke and there was a sudden sharp storm, the sort of summer drencher which ends a great heat, accompanied by a good deal of thunder. Kytie and Waters added to the confusion by every piece of wanton destruction they could imagine. Mares in season were let out of stables, dogs un-chained from yards, cattle loosed, hens driven into the street, doors were flung open, windows broken and boats turned adrift by the quay. There is no doubt of their success and they

84

probably had the time of their lives. The wagonettes returned to a scene of utter chaos.

'In the face of this major disaster and the convincing evidence of a demoniac visit the blackened ashes of the cakes were a minor detail, though a very useful one from my point of view.'

Wishart paused to tap out his pipe.

'Now mark the frailty of human nature. Within an hour of the return of the populace it appeared that a Mrs Woodrose who was bed-ridden and lived at the back of her cottage had also seen the Demon, and this made her both interesting and important. Next day ten witnesses came forward from Forty Angels who had observed him as he sped over the saltings. The legend was established within a matter of weeks. By midsummer you weren't worth talking to unless you had your own Demon story—something you'd seen, or something strange that had happened to your house. Before the year was out every single man, woman and child firmly believed in their own reminiscences. Except, of course, for the original conspirators. And two of them are dead long since.'

'And the third?'

'The third is old Mossy. He was the delinquent boy. You should have guessed that.'

Morty was delighted. 'It has the ring of truth. As an historian I'd lay odds that half the unexplained phenomena of the ages started in pretty much the same way—the devils of Loudun, for example. Thanks a lot for your confidence. I promise I'll respect it. Your legend is safe with me.'

He straightened himself up, prepared to move. Wishart took hold of his arm and gripped it tightly.

'The story has a moral for you. You should be wise to consider it. If you do not, I have wasted your time and mine and I become an idle gossip who has betrayed a secret to no purpose.'

'The only moral I can see,' said Morty, shifting his elbow uneasily, 'is the one any historian learns very early in his career, if he is going to make the grade. Never take anything

on trust. There's a logical explanation for every accepted
mystery and it's up to the new man to discover whatever has
been suppressed for the sake of a good story. Is that what
you're driving at? I learned that one in Constance, New Jersey
before my old grandma taught me how to make two holes in
an egg.'

Wishart renewed his grip. 'You mistake my meaning, but I
intend to persist. You have referred to the strange happenings
at Loudun, so vividly described by Huxley, and there is of
course a common factor. What do you suppose it to be?'

'Mass hysteria? Undernourishment breeding superstition in
an ignorant, priest-ridden community?'

Wishart wagged his head. 'You are missing the point. The
common factor, my friend, is mischief. The basic human delight in doing evil if the opportunity to do so undetected
occurs. That is why I have taken all this trouble with you this
evening, for I am far too vain to be an ancient mariner by
accident. If you take my advice, you will persuade your young
doctor to keep away from Saltey. Neither you nor she belong
here. I mean it, Mr Kelsey, even if I enjoy hearing educated
voices. *Mischief, mischief, mischief.* Get away, the pair of you.'

The older man was speaking intensely, his voice down to a
whisper and his head close. Morty's reaction was violent. So far
as Saltey was concerned, Dido was his property, his to protect,
his to advise. He shook himself free of the restraining arm.

'Don't shoot me that sort of line, mister. I may be a sucker
for tales of Demons but I can spot a simple piece of phonus
bolonus when I see it. Plenty of people here think they're
entitled to The Hollies—hence all these letters to frighten Dido
off. They'd like to see her pack it all in, to sell the place
cheaply and vanish. Well, my guess is, they're going the wrong
way about it. If you know or suspect who's at the back of it
you'd better tell them so. Spread the word around. Otherwise
you are wasting your time.'

Wishart shrugged his shoulders. Against the stars his head
had a massive dignity which was undeniable. When he spoke

again his voice had returned to its normal depth. He had taken no offence at the young man's outburst but he was measuring his words with care.

'As you wish, Mr Kelsey. I am only an onlooker, too old for active adventures, even if I was attracted by the thought. But I draw your attention to a matter which you appear to have overlooked in your fine dramatic outburst.'

'You do?'

'The matter of Hector Askew. He was killed and killed by intent. This is not a question of superstition or mass hysteria or old wives' tales, but of what I will call mischief. Evil, if you prefer the term. Envy, hatred, malice and all uncharitableness as the prayer book says. It would be a thousand pities if your delectable Dido—or you yourself come to that—were to get yourselves hurt. Good night, Mr Kelsey. Perhaps you would be kind enough to lock and bolt the door as you come in.'

He took a couple of steps and had almost faded from sight when he turned his head.,

'By the way, if you should hear a pebble strike the weather-cock on the sail loft, don't go down to investigate. Just lock your own door as well.'

7
The Mark of Teague

MORTY awoke uneasily on the following morning. His mind struggled to consciousness through mists of sound and scent compounded of the mew of gulls, the grumble of men's voices in the room beneath him, car engines growing louder and suddenly ceasing, a burst of laughter which was not intended kindly and the reassuring hospitable smell of scrambled eggs and bacon.

Dixie Wishart, her blue hair escaping rakishly from the scarf which partially enclosed it, was bustling about the room, pulling curtains, stacking books on the one table the room contained and rattling china on a tray. As he opened his eyes she crossed to the foot of the bed and surveyed him, her hands on her hips. He had the impression that she was not entirely at ease.

'Time to rise and shine, Mr Kelsey dear,' she said. 'My word, but you were late last night. No wonder you overslept. Anyone would think you were courting.'

Morty heaved himself on to an elbow and scratched his tousled head. He was, she thought, a proper man, too clever perhaps but if she were twenty years younger...

The murmur from the room below rose and stopped abruptly as someone banged a hand on a table.

'What on earth's happening? The place sounds as if it were full of people.'

'Plenty,' said Dixie and clicked her tongue. 'We've been taken over by the police. That's why I've brought your breakfast up here. I've been up since I don't know when and it's nearly ten o'clock now. The boiler is sulking, so there's no hot water for you. And Sergeant Throstle said to give you his compliments

88

and he'd care to see you downstairs in the dining-room in half an hour.'

Morty blinked. 'Throstle? What in heck does he want?'

'I really couldn't say.' Dixie conveyed that she disapproved, was deeply suspicious of all policemen and hoped that she was not going to be asked to believe the worst. 'There was some trouble last night. Not here, I'm told, but out beyond Forty Angels. Now they—the police—are all over the place like blowflies and they're using my clean dining room to talk to half the lie-abouts in Christendom—all the caravan and tent lot out by the church. It's bad enough having customers in the bar when you can't tell whether they're boys or girls or raving queers. And they don't spend the money, you know, not that type. Not to say really spend. Shandy for the men and the girls on little drops of vodka and Baby Burpjoys and I don't know what next in the way of gut-rot. Half of them don't wash properly and none of them seem to do a hand's turn of work. They're getting the place a bad name....'

She had run out of breath and turned to pour out a cup of tea.

'Now you drink this up, Mr Kelsey dear. And get yourself dressed. I'll tell the Sergeant you're awake. I hope you've got an excuse for yourself last night even if it's a rude one. He's looking for trouble, that man is. I've never seen him in such a state. A London detective and not even shaved. You'll learn all about it from him, never you worry.'

With a rustle of plastic apron and a final rattle of crockery she departed. From below the voices continued, indistinguishable but punctuated by an occasional phrase spoken in anger.

Morty lathered his chin guiltily from the relics of the tea hot water jug, breakfasted while dressing and within a quarter of an hour descended to the saloon bar which led to the dining room. Beside the far door on a bench sat P.C. Simmonds, his arms folded, his helmet on the table in front of him and an open notebook beside it. The three other occupants of the room lounged in varying attitudes of nonchalance on the window seat. They were dressed in the ritual uniform of their kind which consisted of tight blue faded jeans, decorative boots and leather coats. Each affected hair of the same length and each wore dark glasses which gave the group a calculated anonymity with an underlying note of menace. They were sitting against the light and it was some moments before Morty realised that the slighter figure in the centre who sprawled with hands in pockets and legs stretched was a girl. As she turned her head to survey him he saw that she had an ugly graze on her cheekbone but the masking sun spectacles concealed her thoughts as efficiently as a visor. The mark was identification enough: this was the motor cyclist who had run into the broken glass on the road to Saltey.

P.C. Simmonds nodded formally. 'Morning, sir. It's Mr Kelsey, isn't it? I'll just take a few particulars and then I'll see if the Sergeant can see you.'

'That's a bloody nerve,' said one of the youths. 'What about us? Keep us waiting an hour but a lousy git like him can get served like a dose of salts. I'm packing it in.'

The constable ignored the interruption and began to write.

'You're Mr Mortimer Kelsey, an alien but living here on holiday at The Demon which is your registered address. That's right, isn't it?'

'Sure. You should know that by now. And could you put down Citizen of the United States of America? It sounds better than alien. I'm sorry if I'm jumping the queue, officer. I'll wait my turn. What's it all about, anyway?'

Simmonds eyed him without raising his head. 'Mr Throstle will tell you.' He resumed his script, mouthing the words as he wrote. 'Aged 26. U.S. subject. Tourist.'

The inner door opened and a youth shambled out. Apart from being taller than the waiting group there was little to distinguish him beyond a deep flush on his cheeks which did not match the nonchalance of his expression.

'Next please,' said the newcomer, revealing a mincing London accent and a reedy tenor voice. 'And oh, nursie, my teeth still hurt me something chronic. Could I have a drink to take the taste away?'

Morty hesitated but a jerk from Simmonds' head propelled him into the room.

Sergeant Throstle, his hair ruffled and his chin showing the truth of Dixie's observation, was seated behind the largest of the three tables. Round the corner to his right was the sad grey man with whom he had been dining on the previous evening. He too was unshaven and his face from nose to ear bore a livid mark. One eye was half closed by a swelling that promised a sizeable bruise within the day. The grey suit was no longer respectable, for a sleeve gaped from its shoulder revealing canvas and torn stitching. He looked ill and weary.

'Sit down, Mr Kelsey, if you please.' Throstle's tone was businesslike and his eyes had lost their amiable twinkle.

'Now before we go any further at all, I'm going to ask you one question and I want a complete answer and no argy-bargy. Understood? Just what did you do last night between when we last met here—or say, closing time, which is ten thirty in these parts—and three thirty this morning, when I understand from Mrs. Wishart you returned?'

Morty considered.

'I walked out to the old fort,' he said, 'at about eleven, I suppose. There I met our landlord, the distinguished poet Hubert Oliver Wishart, and we had a long chat about the Demon—the story of it, I mean. Then he came home, or I guess he did. I smoked for a bit, but it was getting kind of nippy, so I went for a walk. That's about all.'

'A longish walk, Mr Kelsey. Where did you go?'

'Right along the sea wall. To Firestone and back by the road, if you must know. It's the longest possible way round, but I wasn't hurrying. Now just what's this all about?'

Throstle ignored the question. 'Meet anyone?'

'Not a soul. I wanted to be alone, as they say, and I certainly was. Even the gulls had packed up.'

His examiner surveyed him levelly for some time and finally grunted.

'Humph. A thin sort of tale. If it's the best you can do I'll have to accept it if only because a child caught stealing apples could have done better.'

He relaxed and appeared to shrink a little in the process. 'Well now, if you haven't heard the story already I'd best tell you before you get the local version. Last night, or rather early this morning, this officer here, who is Detective Constable Sibling of the C.I.D., was on observation duty, at the corner by the Saltey and main road turning to be precise—it's called Ponders End Farm. You walked right past it. He was attacked rather brutally from behind, we believe by more than one person. Somebody slipped a sack or a bag over his head in fact and he was pretty nastily manhandled. Finally he was tied up like a chicken with sticking plaster, which is worse than rope if you want to get out of it, and left like a parcel in the farmyard. Now we don't like that sort of thing, Mr Kelsey, and we mean to nail the customers concerned, good and hearty. You were out the best part of the night, you came within a few yards of where Sibling lay, yet you saw and heard nothing. Not even a motorbike, for example?'

Morty shook his head. 'Sorry, not a thing. Oh, a rowboat came ashore by the Bowl, but that was before I met Wishart. Apart from that nothing but a couple of barn owls and the clock on Firestone church.'

'Well, if you can't, you can't.' His inquisitor was morose. 'We know about the midnight oarsman.' He turned to his companion. 'I suppose you don't recognise this chap, Sibling?'

The bedraggled man shook his head: it was his only contribution to the meeting.

Suddenly Throstle changed his tactics and thrust a photograph across the table. The gesture had the element of surprise about it and was made with professional skill.

'Ever seen this joker before?'

The print was a typical criminal record portrait, which is to say that it was unimaginatively lit and showed the full face of a man in a bad temper. It was some time before Morty recognised the subject.

'No,' he said at last, 'no, I've never seen him in the flesh but his face is kind of familiar—I mean I think I've seen a shot of him before. His name wouldn't be Teague by any chance? It's a lousy photograph to recognise a man by.'

Throstle snorted. 'You're damn right on both counts. A lousy photograph but it is the best the C.R.O. can do, which is to say it is as useless as a passport. Out of date, into the bargain. As you say, that's James Teague. How come you know his name?'

Morty explained. 'I don't know much about him, of course but it looks like a lot of guys are interested to know if he shows up.'

'You can say that again.' Throstle breathed heavily through his nose and retrieved the print, replacing it in a folio. He thumbed through the papers it contained, half extracted a second photograph and changed his mind.

'You know, Mr Kelsey, you're a little bit of a puzzle to me and I don't like little problems when I've got bigger ones on my plate. You're quite sure about all you've said? Anything you'd like to add?'

'Nothing,' said Morty firmly. 'Has there been any sign of Mr Teague? Last night's fun and games for example?'

'It could be. That's what we're here to find out. It's a nasty business all round, so I'll tell you just a trifle more to put you in the picture. Sibling was attacked by two people and he thinks they were both men. They caught him from behind and they could have been locals who don't take kindly to strangers, as you may have noticed. It's possible that they didn't know he was a policeman, for he wasn't in uniform and you could say he was trespassing, in a sense. At any rate, he was behind a wall and keeping an eye on the road junction. They were damn lucky not to kill him for they covered his face with tape and he's a man who mostly breathes through his mouth. After he was hobbled anyone could have come in or out of Saltey for several hours without being identified. In fact several people did apart from yourself—two motor cyclists and a car passed the corner coming this way. Sibling heard them as he lay in the stable yard. He heard you too incidentally. You still can't help us?'

Morty shook his head. 'Sorry. I didn't even see headlights from where I was.' A thought occurred to him and he continued: 'Old Wishart said something last night about being careful if I heard a stone striking the weathercock on the sail lofts. Does that mean anything to you?'

Throstle eyed him sharply. 'It certainly does. The weathercock isn't the easiest thing to hit with a pebble as you may know if you've ever played cricket—or in your case I suppose baseball. But there is a man who came from these parts who could do it. His name is Burrows, Thomas Alfred Burrows, appropriately called "Target", though for a different reason they tell me. A tall tough man with a glass eye or black patch as the fancy takes him. A sailor man with an ugly reputation—no convictions, but a great deal known to his disadvantage. Two evenings ago *his* visiting card turned up.'

'He hit the target?'

'Somebody did. The bird on the roof is made of copper and makes quite a noise if it gets coshed. Rather like a gong, they say. It used to be Master Burrows' way of announcing his arrival when he came ashore in the days when he lived here. He was a very good shot with a stone and proud of it. He hasn't been seen in these parts for twenty odd years but that noise scared the pants off one or two of the ancients, including Wishart and old Mossy, when they heard it again. Here—you may as well take a dekko at this.'

He pulled a second photograph from the folder and skimmed it across the table. The print had evidently been enlarged from part of a group and showed a face dominated by frowning beetle brows under a peaked sailor's cap. The sinister effect was diminished by the lack of focus in the eyes which looked outwards in the reverse of a squint. The impression was of a sly mongrel of uncertain temper, an animal not to be trusted. Morty returned it after careful examination: it was not a face to be forgotten.

'Sorry. No dice at all. But I'd know him again.'

'I hope so. Now listen to me. Mr Kelsey, and get the message loud and clear. There's good reason to think that either or both of these men—and they're what we call villains in our old fashioned way—are somewhere in these parts. One of 'em has killed a man already and for all we know both of them may be booked for it again. If you see or hear or smell the slightest sign that makes you think they're in the neighbourhood get in touch with the police—*at the double.* Understand? No mock heroics, no amateur private eye stuff, no bloody minded curiosity. And that goes for your Dr Jones too—perhaps more so. Whatever they're up to those two are not playing for peanuts. If you want to get yourself and your girl friend killed or maimed for life, let me tell you that the way to set about it is to stick your little noses in where they're not wanted. This place is a mass of dykes and ditches, holes and corners, and at this time of year it would take an army to ferret a man out, especially if he's got friends. I haven't got an army—I've far too few overworked and underpaid policeman who've better things to do than to protect any silly beggar who's trying to play last across.'

Throstle had been leaning over the table, emphasising his points with the flat of his hand. He was angry and irritated at his own display of nerves. He pushed his chair back finally and eyed the young man appraisingly.

'Don't think I don't realise that you feel you've got a stake in this business, somewhere or other. These poison pen letters come pretty close to you. By the way, I know there's been another one. Wishart admitted that to me this morning. But just consider the facts. Teague couldn't conceivably have started this business because he was otherwise engaged at the time they first appeared. As for the man Burrows, by all accounts he is as near as a touch illiterate. One or other of them may—and it's a very long shot—have been connected with Hector Askew's death, but there's no direct evidence as yet. But there are little bits of this and that to suggest that they may be in the neighbourhood and if this is the case then God help you if you try any funny business.'

He paused and smiled wearily, more to himself than to the young man.

'I wouldn't lay it on so thick,' he explained, 'if it weren't for your friend Campion. I've learned quite a bit about him and he's by no means the bland friendly outsider he sets himself out to be. If he's playing some sort of lone hand in a matter that may or may not be his business, well that's his own funeral, and it could well be just that. He's no call to involve you or any other stranger. Take my advice, son. Get out and stay out.'

There was silence for several moments, long enough for the clock on the wall to become audible.

'I get the message,' said Mortimer Kelsey.

'Fine. Now run along, sir, if you don't mind. Perhaps you'll ask the next young tearaway to come in. The girl will do. Her name's Doll Jensen and you can tell her by the scratch on her face. Oh, and before you go, just one thing.'

'Yes?'

'Superintendent Gravesend will be back this afternoon, so cut out the midnight walks. They make rotten reading if he should want a statement in writing at any time.'

8
The String Man

AT the side of The Demon almost at the foot of the flagstaff
stood a red public telephone box and towards this Morty
strode, deliberately ignoring the comments of those who were
still waiting to be questioned. The location was in fact a good
deal more private than that of the instrument at the inn,
which lived on a shelf behind the long bar of the saloon. Any
conversation here was apt to be punctuated by imaginative
advice during business hours.

He made three attempts to convey news of the night's de-
velopments and they were all luckless. Dr Jones was not at her
Bloomsbury flat and could not be reached at St Botolph's
Hospital where she was incommunicado in the wards. Mr
Campion's bell produced no response to a persistent appeal.

Frustrated and not a little angry with himself and the world
in general, he kicked at the pebbles beneath his feet and finally
selected one which suited his purpose. The weathercock on the
lantern above the sail lofts gleamed whitely in the morning
sunlight, an inviting target once the idea had been planted.
Morty possessed a good eye and had been a distinguished
pitcher at Vere University, but the stone sailed high and wide
to disappear beyond the red corrugated iron roof. A flurry of
seagulls announced that it had reached the mud beyond.

Presently his attention was caught by the buzzing rattle of a
motor scooter which was clearly far too light to rank with the
urgent mechanical giants favoured by the London visitors. It
emerged round the corner at a respectable speed, however, and
the rider halted the machine with a crunch of gravel within a
few feet of where he stood. She was a tall thin woman of uncertain age, but well beyond fifty, who wore a yellow sou'wester

97

tied beneath her chin. A leather jerkin which had started its career as army equipment and a tweed skirt completed the outfit. Its owner dismounted as if she were more used to a horse than a scooter and surveyed him with sharp intelligent eyes set above a nose which would have looked normal on an eagle. She kicked the support idly into position propping the machine upright, patted the saddle and took a couple of steps towards him.

'Morning to you,' she said. 'Oh, this is first rate. A left and a right straight off. You're the one man I've been looking for. Never had a chance to nobble you alone.'

'Good morning,' said Morty.

She released her oilskin headgear from its moorings and shook out a mop of untidy white hair.

'You're Mortimer Kelsey, aren't you? I've seen you around. You found that young good-for-nothing's body last week. I didn't get much of a look in at that show, more's the pity. But I hear the game's still afoot and that's all to the good. I'm Monica Weatherby, by the way. I'm the string man in these parts.'

Despite himself Morty was attracted. The woman in front of him, he perceived, had never lost the awkward gaucherie of a schoolgirl and had long since substituted a friendly heartiness for the feminine charm which eluded her. The voice had the unmistakable note of authority which long country breeding brings to women of gentle birth.

'Silly of me,' she continued, twisting her yellow headgear by its strings. 'Ought to explain if you don't know the term. I'm a journalist, don't you know. Write for the *Gazette* at Nine Ash and keep a watching brief for the *Globe* in town. It's called stringing. Quite well paid if you can find a good story. No by-lines of course, but then crime reporting's not really my cuppa tea. Country life, nature in the raw, ancient local history, these are my subjects. You shoot a bit yourself over those converts they tell me. Brought along something to show you, in fact, in case I ran you to earth. But it can wait. First things first. I'll just file my copy and we'll have a nice natter. Did you see anything of last night's little rumpus?'

'Nary a thing, lady.' said Morty. 'I've just been grilled by experts but I've stuck to my story and they're making no charges.'

'Humph! That's a fat lot of help. Can't you do better than that? I got most of the gen up at Forty Angels.'

Morty considered. His new acquaintance was disarming and he found himself anxious to help.

'As far as I know a plain clothes policeman called Sibling was beaten up last night by a couple of men who probably mistook him for somebody else—a trespasser, perhaps. I doubt if it will make headlines.'

'Maybe not, but that's the editor's pidgin and he can work it out as he pleases. Saltey is bursting with policemen and they're all as mum as oysters, so *they* think there's something in the wind. Now just hang on half a jiffy whilst I get this on the wire. Thanks for the name, by the way. Hope it's spelt in the proper way.'

She turned and scuttled into the box, her large sensible shoes making the pebbles leap from her path.

Her methods with the telephone had the same touch of forthright amateurishness which characterised her treatment of transport. She made two short calls and preceded each with a sharp blow to the side of the instrument which appeared to produce instant results. She emerged wiping her hands on a large bandana handkerchief.

'Filthy places. Not enough grooming done to keep them tickety-boo. Still, this one works which is more than can be said of the one up the road. Now, Mr Kelsey—you are Mortimer Kelsey, I suppose?—I think we ought to have a chinwag. Too early for a snifter but do you suppose your landlady could rustle up a coffee?'

Morty supposed that she could and suggested the four ale bar known as The Snug, a small highly varnished nook which was completely private and away from the main saloon. Before she joined him his guest strode back to her charger, opened a container beside the saddle and produced a battered black briefcase, which she tucked under her arm.

'In here, I think, Miss Weatherby.'

'Oh, it's *Mrs* Weatherby. But not to worry. I'm still Monica Sparrow to most people, even if poor old Hugo's been dead these thirty years. Sparrow, you know, of Sparrow's Manor, or used to be. This area is still Sparrow's Hundred though I don't own an acre of it.'

'My respects, ma'am,' said Morty. 'Twenty square miles to the Hundred down here and twenty seven in Yorkshire where they call it a Wapentake. I've done my homework, you see, even if it's not my period.'

'Good man.' Mrs Weatherby slammed her case on to the scrubbed table and planted herself firmly on the bench behind it. 'I know it's not. I've done some research on you myself, which is not difficult for a nosey old woman like me. I always tell 'em "I only ask because I want to know" and that's how I earn my living. And by the way—no jokes about sparrows. I know them all and I know my face is like a dilapidated barn owl. My friends call me Mon and the rest of 'em, behind my back, refer to me as the Sparrowhawk. Very little goes on between here and Nine Ash that I don't know about, and what I don't know I can piece together better than a dozen policemen.'

'I can believe that.' Morty warmed to her. 'That's fine and dandy because a little solid information is just what I'm looking for. You know about Dr Jones and her correspondents, for example?'

'Ha! Your young woman. A fine gal by the look of her. Hook her up whilst the going is good and don't waste your time doing the odd spot of knight errantry just to prove that you're worth your salt. Take her away, raise a family and let that derelict property down the road go to perdition which is where it belongs.'

Morty blushed. The thought that his feelings were so patent

to any outside observer shook him and he reacted defensively.

'I ... I hardly know her, to tell you the truth. But she is the victim of a conspiracy and I'm darn well going to get to the bottom of it.' He outlined the history of the letters.

'Conspiracy, eh?' Mrs Weatherby sipped her coffee meditatively and it seemed to Morty that she was sifting through a forest of family trees, sorting evidence from hearsay and diagnosing by innate instinct.

'Conspiracy,' she repeated. 'Well, I suppose it could be. I haven't seen any of them—the letters, I mean—myself, more's the pity, or I might have put paid to it months ago. You think several different hands are at work? Are they written with a pen, typed or put together out of bits of newspaper?'

Morty explained as best he could. When he came to think of it, his knowledge was very incomplete, but he made a good witness and he recited all that the landlord of The Demon had told him of the latest arrival. Mrs Weatherby listened in silence but she checked the points on the long bony fingers of one hand, tapping each digit sharply down on the table as she did so.

'Four different groups, eh? You could call the first of them Catty and Arch—that would be a woman of course, possibly one of old Mossy Ling's cousins and there are three of those, all as like as turkey cocks. Next, Smug. I'd say that means Jonah Woodrose, for a ducat. Then you say Informed but with Malice and Professional Know-how? There is only one man hereabouts in that category who fits the bill and he's Alan Sullivan, a retired insurance agent who does tax work and knows everybody's business. An acid little runt with duck's disease. Finally, Wicked Religious—a pretty wide field, what? An elderly female on the Kytie side of the fence without a doubt. Choice of three there. Ethel Wishart, a distant cousin of H.O.'s, old Mrs Waters who's practically ga-ga and Bob Felgate's wife Norah, a toothy vixen and a pillar of Nonconformity with a mind like a cesspool. Not a nice collection and just about what I'd guessed all along. Pick 'em by the heels, shake 'em all out, see what drops on to the ground and you'll have the answer.'

'Isn't that a job for the police?'

'Fiddle faddle!' Mrs Weatherby was contemptuous. 'They'll never get near it in a month of Sundays. Only thing to do is to frighten the ringleader if you can locate him or her. I'll have a word with Jonah and see if I can put a pinch of ginger under his tail. He knows more than is good for him and always did. He's not a Woodrose for nothing. You can say I'm an interfering old witch if you like but this place has a bad enough name already without adding poison pens.' She chuckled reminiscently. 'Yes, it would be quite a kick to stop Jonah's earth for once. The Woodroses, don't you know, still talk about "their people", meaning anyone who once worked for them or their descendants. They are not feudal—they're tribal. The Kyties were just the same in their time—playing Montagues and Capulets over less than half a dozen farms and a little bit of coastal business. That's why both factions were so angry when old Kitty Kytie left her house to a stranger.'

'Angry enough to kill Hector Askew, simply because he drew up the will?'

'Bless my soul, no. Use your loaf, boy. Think. *Think.* The thing is done, Kitty is dead and buried, your beautiful filly has inherited. Nothing to be gained by bumping off young Askew. No, not on your Uncle Sam. That young blackguard was killed for his sins, and he committed 'em mostly in London or abroad, I'm told. Jealous husband, girl in the family way, that's the shape of things and you can bet your boots on it. Even the man Gravesend spotted that, which explains why he went scuttling back to town leaving it to a C.I.D. sergeant and the local lot to ferret out the answer. He likes quick results, does Mr Gravesend, and this is a waiting game.'

'The guy is coming back this afternoon according to Throstle,' said Morty. 'I forgot to tell you that.'

'Is he now? That rather looks like business.' Mrs Weatherby switched rapidly from the last lady of the Sparrows to string man for the *Globe*. She made some mental calculations with the aid of an outsize wrist watch. 'I'd better get that on the blower right away.' She stood up and pulled a handful of change from a pocket. 'It's just on opening time. Here, take my case and if the coast's clear in the dining room, we'll finish the natter there. Get me a Harry pinkers—a large one.'

She strode out of the room, her head forward and her shoulders swaying as she moved. Morty had the impression that she was carrying an invisible hockey stick. He gathered the briefcase and did as he had been bidden. Throstle and his aides had departed but it was still too early at the inn for normal business.

On her return the string man seemed pleased with herself. 'Small scoop there, I think. Now let's get down to brass tacks.'

She pulled up a chair, opened her briefcase, drew out a dog-eared photograph which had been folded unkindly in half and spread it out on the table, scooping side plates and cutlery out of her way to clear a space.

'You won't have seen this, even if you've been to the Record Office,' she said, 'because the original doesn't exist any longer. Belonged to our lot and was destroyed in the fire, forty years back. This is all that's left of a survey map of the Saltey area made in 1758 for Sir Thomas Sparrow. It's a Timothy Skynner and must have been quite a peach in its day, what? Take a good dekko at it and I'll show you what I'm getting at. Ten inches to the mile. I remember it as a girl hanging in the old man's library. About two foot by three when it was alive.'

Even in its tattered state the print was a delight to any re-searching mind. It revealed an extremely accurate piece of cartography, made decorative by an ornamental compass and a baroquely framed title. The lower left hand corner had been squared off to list 'The Parcels', the farms and the holdings of the time, given in acres, roods and perches, together with the tenants. Very little had changed it seemed in the course of two hundred and more years, except for the coastline where erosion had redrawn the outlines and a new sea wall had smoothed away the more erratic indentations. To Morty the discovery was a treasure and he pored over it for several minutes in silence.

'This is just great,' he said at last. 'Quite new on me. I'll make a copy print, if you'll allow me. It fits into my thesis like a glove. May I borrow it for a couple of days?'

'Help yourself,' said Mrs Weatherby heartily, 'but don't miss the real point of the whole caboodle.' She pointed a bony finger to emphasise her words. 'All this coastal area is Wood-rose country and always has been, since the dawn of time. Every foot of access to the water in both directions. The Kyties—they were there already you see—owned or rented anything that could be really farmed. Very few of them took to the sea. Jonah Woodrose's grandfather started moving inland in the 90s of the last century, but he kept as much of the saltings as he could. One or two names have changed and families have died out, but the principle's much the same today. Now a modern Ordnance Survey map shows only one way out of Saltey except by water. Correct? Well. look at this, young man, and you'll see that there are half a dozen, or used to be. Wide ditches, little private tracks, footpaths through coppices—most of them have gone, but two or three are left. The police, God bless 'em, think that by watching one corner they can keep tabs on who goes in and out of this place and they always did, or pretended to. They couldn't be more wrong. The area isn't a box, it's a sieve. Get what I'm driving at?'

'Smuggling, I'd say.'

'You're bang on. Everything came through the Bowl and went on to London by the back lanes. Even up to the war you could bet your sweet life that half the families in this place dabbled in it, whatever else they worked at officially. And who do you suppose were the leading lights in the enterprise?'

'I could guess.'

Mrs Weatherby snorted. 'I daresay you could. But I *know*, because I enjoy poking my nose into things. The answer is all your girl friend's correspondents, or their menfolk. Most of them are past it now, but their ringleader still seems to be interested in keeping Saltey to itself. Damitall, I'll beat the truth out of Jonah if I swing for it.'

Morty took a gulp of his second gin: his companion had presented him with a mixture too strong for his taste and he grimaced involuntarily.

'You know,' he said at last, 'there's one thing I don't understand. You're a kind of a local character and in a way I'd say you're being disloyal to your own people. Yet you're taking my side and I couldn't be more of a stranger. Hell, I'm grateful to you and your help is just the greatest but unless you're scouting around for a Sunday tabloid story—and I want no part of that, lady—I don't get your angle.'

Mrs Weatherby rose to her feet, looked towards and beyond the bar to make certain they were alone and returned to the table before she answered. Her voice was lowered.

'Smuggling,' she said. 'has a fine romantic ring about it—once aboard the lugger, yo heave ho and all that kind of malarky. I've had a bottle or two myself I wouldn't care to explain about and my father's taste in brandy and cigars was always ahead of his income. No particular harm in that, so far as I can see. In the old days the gentry were inclined to regard it as a sport and we minded our own business if the others went in for it more professionally. That's why strangers aren't encouraged here, a fact you've already had your nose rubbed in. Bless my soul, boy, I'd no more think of running a story about that than I would of pinching the Crown Jewels. That's why I dislike those letters of yours, because they puzzle me and I hate mysteries.'

'How so? I thought you'd just solved the whole problem, bar the shouting?'

His companion held her head on one side like a cogitating terrier.

'Because they don't fit into the pattern,' she said at last. 'Different as chalk from cheese. The more I think about it the less I like it. I haven't the slightest doubt that these naughty old things have had a hand in it, but just why, I ask myself. Their day has been over for twenty years. They're all as old as God, apart from Jonah Woodrose and he doesn't fit the bill as a modern smuggler. He's an uncouth brute but he's doing very nicely thank you and he was never one to risk his neck. So somebody must be behind it all. Someone is still interested in keeping Saltey to itself.'

She took a sip of gin, breathed heavily through her nose and continued speaking, more to herself than to Morty.

'Apart from the fun of paying a quid or two less for your liquor there was never much to be gained from the old fashioned game—not in terms of big money, anyhow. But today it's a dirty business—nothing sporting about it. Different people, different goods and bigger profits. Watches are worth while, of course, but as far as I know they mostly come by air, in big consignments. In this part of the world I'm afraid it's dope, which is quite a new department for us. *And that I simply will not have.*'

She rapped the table sharply and Morty was vividly reminded of his first schoolmistress.

'I won't have it,' she repeated. 'Morphia, heroin, the reefer cigarette things—what d'you call it, marijuana—and so on, they're all works of the devil. I've seen the effect on kids even in Nine Ash Hospital and they're quite terrifying. It's got to be stopped.'

Morty applauded. 'Quite right, ma'am. Just what do you propose doing about it?'

'Do?' Mrs Weatherby switched two penetrating eyes on her companion. 'Do? Get to the bottom of it, of course. Blow the whole thing sky high. Sink 'em without trace.'

She emptied her glass.

'Now what have we got to go on? First Jonah Woodrose and his gaggle of old women. Unlikely material, I grant you, but the roots of sin are there as Kipling said. Jonah's no master mind, so there must be somebody with brains in the background who's making use of him. Probably not a local, but then Jonah spends quite a bit of time in London. Jonah wouldn't risk running drugs. Jonah is rich. Jonah is a coward. And Jonah is mischievous, like all the Woodroses. I'll start with him. And you—' she tapped sharply on the table again, 'you will take the other end.'

He turned to her in surprise. There was something in her autocratic but slap-happy approach which was both endearing and convincing. If she was determined to be a one woman avenging army it would be as well to become an ally.

'Me, lady? Just what do you think I can do?'

'Keep an eye on the children—the tearaways, of course. Mods or rockers or whatever they call themselves. How do you suppose this racket is conducted? Who else goes roaring over the countryside day in and day out? Apply your mind, my dear man. As far as most people are concerned they're all as alike as peas in a pod—tight trousers. long hair and dirty fingernails— and I don't suppose there are more than two or three of them who are real little crooks. Pump your friend Throstle and see if you can dig up what he knows about them. If he is as obstin- ate as a mule—and he can be—find out which of them he really grilled this morning. They'd be the ones with some- thing known against them, as the policemen say. Find who owns the expensive machines and what they do for a living, if anything. Chat 'em up. Make friends.'

Morty squared his shoulders.

'A large order. They're just as clannish as the rest of the population.'

'Nonsense.' Mrs Weatherby was emphatic. 'You're thirty years nearer their age group than I am. Learn the language, study the customs of the people. History is your subject, what? Well, here's social history of a very uncivilised kind right under your nose. And if you can find anything out just give me a tinkle. Remember, I only ask because I want to know.'

9

Social Evening

BY that especial mixture of perspicacity and effort which is an almost infallible formula for success, Dixie Wishart had built up the reputation of The Demon beyond the confines of Saltey as being worth a visit on Saturday nights. Judicious selection, coupled with flattery and liberality in the matter of drink had produced an excellent team of dart players and she paid handsomely for visiting musicians. The youth who performed on the electric guitar was not only accomplished but personable and the pianist had the true and unmistakable honky-tonk touch, particularly when the majority of the instrument's outer shell had been removed.

The mysterious working of Providence, which often decrees that the occasion produces the man, had also conjured a self-appointed master of ceremonies to complete the circle. Mr H. Hamilton Dashwood was small and dapper from his unnaturally black hair and his boot button eyes to his highly polished shoes. He had suddenly appeared two years before, when the 'Social Evening' was in embryo, taking charge of the proceedings at a moment when apathy was fighting with insularity for the upper hand and had turned impending disaster into triumph.

Dixie, who enjoyed decorative embroidery whether it was plastic or romantic, had decided that he was a widower working in a gentlemanly way as a commercial traveller, a lonely soul who lived for the golden moments when he could command the attention and the ephemeral affection of a crowd. Each Saturday at eight he arrived in a small car, sometimes armed with a cardboard suitcase containing a quantity of false noses or paper hats. To his hostess he was a godsend and even if he never had occasion to buy a drink there were always plenty of others to perform this office for him, so that his glass of practically neat whisky became a miraculous cruse throughout the evening.

Morty, who had dined in solitary by no means austere gloom at Nine Ash, returned to find the saloon of The Demon crowded with seekers after pleasure and the air thick with smoke and noise. His arrival went unmarked, for the 'Social' attracted customers from a distance and apart from Mossy Ling in his alloted corner he recognised only a handful of regulars. Of Mr Lugg there was no sign.

Mindful of Mrs Weatherby's final instruction he had dressed with some care in a pair of slimly cut canvas trousers, a dark blue shirt and a silk scarf of such virulent puce that it glowed as if radioactive. This was the limit his wardrobe permitted but the effect, he considered, was not displeasing.

Mr H. Hamilton Dashwood was displaying a new discovery as he arrived. He spoke in the hearty avuncular style of the old time music hall chairman. 'Direct from the patronage of King George the Fourth, the Duke of York, the Marquis of Granby and the Blue Boar itself, for the first time at The Demon ... I give you a master at the art of spooning—no, not your sort, madame—the manipulation of two spoons as a musical instrument.... A very big hand for the largest dwarf in captivity, Mr Clarence Dodgson.'

There was general appluase at the announcement and Mr Dodgson, who was mild, bald and meagre on first inspection, burst into a rattle of metal with a pair of spoons which he vibrated dexterously over every available section of his person including his head. The pianist picked up his cue and soon the majority of the company were united in song.

'*Knees up, knees up, don't get the breeze up ...*'

Morty worked his way with some difficulty to the bar and finally attracted Dixie's attention. She was hot and dishevelled and her blue hair had lost some of its artificial resilience.

'You want to watch your step tonight, Mr Kelsey dear,' she

whispered. 'I think we may be in for a bit of trouble. I'd send for that Simmonds if I hadn't had enough of him already.'

As she spoke she jerked her head towards a corner of the room where the dart board hung, flanked by a pair of scoreboards made almost illegible from constant use. Five youths surrounded it, flinging darts casually at the target, making no attempt to play but giggling amongst themselves when one of the feathered needles went dangerously wide of its mark. Four of them still affected dark glasses and the group were ostentatiously aloof from the general entertainment. Calculated trouble brooded over their truculent isolation.

The reason for their choice of a strategic position became clear when the artist with the spoons ended his performance and Mr Dashwood stepped forward to take the floor.

'And now, ladies and gentlemen, for the principal item of the evening. I refer, of course, the the semi-final round of the Saltey and District Darts Contest for the Challenge Shield so kindly presented by our gracious hostess, Mrs Dixie Wishart. A big hand, please, for a beautiful lady—I can say that on this occasion since her husband appears to be off duty. Tonight's event is between the challengers from the Blue Boar at Firestone and our own, our very own team at The Demon.'

The applause which greeted the announcement was courageous rather than wholehearted. The eight genuine players began to shuffle forward but the group by the board stood its ground. A silence born of embarrassment and apprehension swept over the room and for a moment or two nobody moved.

It was broken by the thwack of a dart as it struck the edge of the wooden mantelpiece very close to the head of one of the official team. The group by the board tittered and the self-appointed Master of Ceremonies tripped delicately towards them.

'Now I'm sure you gentlemen don't want to spoil the evening's pleasure....'

The tallest of the interlopers placed the flat of a large hand on Mr Dashwood's chest and propelled him violently backwards almost into the lap of the pianist.

'You oughta take it easy, man. We're using the board just now.'

The M.C. recovered his balance and stood brushing an elbow. 'Gentlemen, gentlemen all, please. If you'll just...'

His words were smothered by an angry grumble from the company. The teams of Firestone and Saltey included men with powerful shoulders and despite the restraining twitter of female voices and an imperative but unrecognisable cry from Dixie, several of them moved uncertainly towards the aggressor.

'Wanna make something of it?' He was standing in front of his party, a gangling menacing figure, gripping a dart by the feathered end so that the point faced his audience. He took off his glasses revealing pink lashless eyes which gave his face the unexpected expression of a large and dangerous rat. His companions stood together, each with a similar weapon.

'Come on, big boy. Now's your chance for a punch up.'

Behind the bar a glass splintered on the ground but neither group moved and no single head turned in the direction of the sound.

The frozen silence and the immobility of the crowd gave Morty a chance which he could not resist. The chief destroyer of the evening's peace was standing in the typical position adopted by a would-be attacker in an elementary demonstration of unarmed combat. The moment was too good to miss. Morty edged through the silent crowd and caught the threatening figure completely according to first instructions as given in the Vere University gymnasium course on self-defence.

The effect was spectacular. The youth appeared to twist backwards into the air and then to crumple forward. A judicious and accurately placed knee in the pit of the stomach brought him winded to the floor, the dart still in his hand. Morty stood briefly above the squealing figure and then trod sharply on the clenched fist so that the weapon skidded away amongst the feet of the spectators.

'Out!' shouted Dixie, her voice now clear and authoritative above the uncertain murmur of voices suddenly free of panic. 'Out! Out, the lot of them. Chuck 'em out, boys.'

Tension snapped like a bowstring. The two teams surged forward, propelled by new found courage and the curiosity of those behind. One of the remaining quartet lowered his head and charged through the crowd for the door, leading the retreat.

Within seconds, only the writhing retching creature on the ground remained with Mr Dashwood bending over him.

'He'll be O.K. when he gets a little air, sir. Just help him to the door, gentlemen, and wish him a very goodnight from one and all.'

By inspiration or instinct the guitarist struck a couple of preliminary chords and began to sing:

'Bless 'em all, bless 'em all.
The long and the short and the tall...'

The chorus was widely and uproariously received. Even the insolent gunfire of departing motor cycles failed to punctuate the rhythm and as an acknowledgment of the occasion Mr Dashwood led the company in a verse which would not normally be tolerated in the presence of ladies. It was a concession in celebration of victory which everyone present understood and approved.

Morty alone was uneasy. He had acted on the spur of the moment and achieved a success which was far more spectacular than its actual skill merited. His chance of penetrating the ranks of disorder had been annihilated and he had made enemies where he most needed co-operation. Mrs Weatherby, he decided, might have handled the situation more adroitly but he could not picture her as a patron of a social evening.

The room was now intolerably close and sweaty. Jovial faces

began to bob up before him, loud with congratulations. Hot hands patted his back and he realised that honour could not be satisfied but by the acceptance of drink.

The problem of etiquette in selection was solved by Dixie who announced her decision by the pop of a champagne cork. 'He'll drink with me, ducks, and we'll all toast his health. I've seen it done on the telly but never thought to find it happen in my own bar.'

She filled a tankard with the golden elixir and thrust it into his hand. 'Here's to you, Mr Kelsey dear.'

'Properly smart,' said Mossy Ling from his corner. 'I seen it done on the telly too. Use wires, so they do now. A powerfully good little old trick. Reckon you could teach me, mister? Better if there are two of us when they come back.' He sniffed, managing to put a suggestion of malice into the sound, and gestured down the bar with his glass. 'Some of 'em ain't even gone, I see.'

In the happy back-slapping tumult of the moment the ominous little shaft passed unnoticed or was ignored. Morty accepted his tankard with acclamation and it was several minutes before he glanced in the direction the old man had indicated.

Even before he moved he was subconsciously aware of what he was going to see, as a man often is when his shoulder blades are the subject of concentrated attention from a forceful personality.

The girl leaning with one elbow on the bar was watching him with the deliberation of a cat at a mousehole. Her sombre eyes were over-emphasised in the fashion of the day but she had transformed herself from the leather jacketed virago of the morning into something wholly female. The mark on her cheek had been obliterated by careful make-up and her dark tightly curling hair had been combed over her forehead so that it mellowed the hardness of well defined skullbones and a square determined chin. She was wearing a white sleeveless blouse and black trousers which fitted like a skin.

For a long moment she outstared him and he was grateful to Mr Hamilton Dashwood's mellow claim on the company's attention to witness the official peak of the evening.

When he turned his head again she was standing next to him apparently watching the contest, her shoulder within an inch of his arm.

'I'm Doll Jensen,' she said. 'Remember me?'

Morty took his time before he answered. He was acutely conscious of the animal magnetism which the girl was exerting and he began to suspect that the change in her appearance had been made for his benefit. He looked down at her carefully groomed head and stylish white silk and decided that she had made a very good job of material which was better than he had first supposed.

'Sure. You took a fall in all that broken glass.' He spoke without enthusiasm, but his cautious curiosity was aroused. If the girl wanted to make the running he was quite prepared to let her go ahead.

The attention of the company had now been given entirely to the contest and the hero of the minute before was forgotten. Conversation was conducted in lowered voices to allow the players to concentrate on the game. The girl was looking away from him, but he could feel the warmth of her arm through his sleeve.

'That was Moo Moo,' she said, 'or so the boys reckon. Grotty great bastard. He knew I was coming down that night. He's the one you put on the floor. That was a laugh. Lucky you didn't knock his wig off or he'd have done you up rotten. He's as bald as an egg and doesn't like jokes about it.'

'Moo Moo?'

'They call him Moo Moo the Dog Faced Boy, up at the Flats. Comes from Wanstead. I hate his guts.'

'Not a boy friend of yours?',

She continued to stare directly in front of her, talking out of the corner of her mouth.

'Never fancied him ... he's just a layabout. They let him

string along because he's a fixer. You know—gets spares and all that jazz. Works in a garage and knocks the stuff off I shouldn't wonder. Likes boys mostly. I don't go for his type.'

It was on the tip of Morty's tongue to ask what her type was, but he thought better of it and enquired mildly, 'Why do you come here? What's the attraction in a dead end like this?'

An obstinate frown crossed her face. 'Because I bloody like it,' she said. 'It suits me. I've got a pad here in a caravan and the rest of them can mostly find a shed or a hut to doss in if they don't want to go home. Nothing to pay. No questions asked. If the boys want a lay or a giggle or a kick-up they can please themselves—that's their business—and there's no one to tell them to get the hell out.'

'If it suits them, why make trouble?'

She shrugged her shoulders. 'Search me. If you find life a bind don't you bang around and get yourself a rave? It's something to do. Better than a caff or a godawful youth club.'

Morty began to feel old. There was a gap here which he could not bridge. The philosophy of life, if it could be defined by such a phrase, was beyond his grasp. The girl continued her deliberate touch against his arm with just enough pressure to make conversation intimate.

Derisive groans and faint applause announced that the men of Saltey had lost the first leg of the match. He turned away from her to the bar but she moved with him so that they remained in contact. She accepted a vodka and tonic water much to Dixie's disapproval and as she raised her glass to him he realised that she had established a degree of possessive intimacy which he could not defy. In Mrs Weatherby's phrase book, he was being chatted up.

Doll Jensen, he felt, was not a girl who did anything without a reason and yet he did not altogether credit the superficial purpose she conveyed. He found himself mildly excited and very curious.

'What do you do for money?' he asked. 'You can't go burning up the road on a Honda just with a handful of dimes.'

She shook her head. 'That's for sure. I do a lot of things. You'd be surprised. I've been a waitress. I've worked the knocker if you know what that means—the door-to-door selling racket. I tried the yachting crew-girl lark in the Med one summer but came unstuck in the winter. I get along.' She talked easily, as between equals of two different worlds, giving him a glimpse of lives and backgrounds outside his experience or imagination.

After a long reflective drink she looked up at him. She was a year or two older than he had first supposed, about twenty-one perhaps.

'What about you? You're a prof of some sort. And a Yank. What's in it for you at Saltey? Digging up fossils or old bones?'

'Hardly.' Morty felt an urge to be entertaining but did not rate his chances as a lecturer very highly. 'I'm researching. Manners and customs—history round about two hundred years back. Maybe I'll write a book about it.'

He struggled to explain without condescension but knew he was failing.

She shook her head. 'Beyond me, that's for certain. I just wouldn't know. History's strictly for the birds if you ask me.'

Suddenly she brightened. 'Old stuff—you're keen on old bits of nonsense. Did you ever see the Sex Pot? It's ever so antique and groovy as all hell. Ever see that?'

Morty was baffled. 'You have me beaten. No one's told me anything about a sex pot in these parts.'

She laughed, showing very white even teeth. Her head was perhaps a shade too large for her body but in this oncoming mood she was undeniably desirable. Different clothes and change of warpaint, he decided, would make her a real eye-catcher.

'Not what you mean, lover boy. We just call her that. She's carved and painted—must be hundreds of years old. You ought to put her in your book. Want me to show you?'

The guitar and piano were now pumping out pop rhythm

and despite the open windows the smoke thick atmosphere was tepid as a London tube. She took his arm. . . .

'Let's get the hell out. I'll show you.'

The prospect of fresh air and adventure was too great to be resisted. Morty followed her as she twisted through the sweating revellers.

The forecourt of The Demon was still lit by a single arc lamp focused on the hanging sign and as they emerged he saw that she had slung a black leather coat over her shoulders and was carrying a long business-like torch. She slipped a hand into his, not confidingly, but by right of being the leader. They crossed into the shadows and walked slowly towards the dim grey bulk of the weather-boarded sail lofts which stood on brick piles as a protection against the highest tides. Wooden steps from the road led to the main doors which were padlocked but she picked her way carefully by the side of the buildings through a confusion of small unpainted hulks, wire hawsers, ropes, planks and rusting marine engines on the muddy slope which led to the Bowl. At the back, within a few yards of high water, a ladder was propped steeply against a door, a small entrance which was part of a larger frame.

She climbed lightly as a cat, pushed open the rotting timber and flashed the torch back on the rungs.

'Up here.'

He followed her nimbly enough and they stood together in the engulfing blackness of the great barnlike structure which smelt of the sea, tar, varnish and decay. With the door closed she took his hand again and led him cautiously, the beam directed to the wooden floor.

The buildings were made up of four long sheds, each with an open communicating door. The torch threw brief scudding shadows from a dusty medley of masts, spars, coiled ropes, empty cases and sacks. From high above them an imprisoned bird, scared by the light, beat blindly against the corrugated iron of the roof.

The girl did not pause until they had reached the far angle

of the final section. She was still keeping the illumination on the floor, for much of the planking was unsound and treacherous. Abruptly she halt d her companion and for a moment they waited in utter darkness.

'Now,' she said. 'Now. There she is.'

The sudden shaft of light which flashed upwards into the corner was almost blinding. Morty, who had no sort of theory about what he was going to see, was quite unprepared for the shock of discovery. Above him towered the blind eyed figure of a woman with jutting voluptuous breasts who appeared to be soaring between earth and sky, a wooden giantess whose cold unreality was emphasised by crude faded colours, pink, blue and grey. Snakes writhed about her forehead and the carving was cruel and incisive.

He drew a long breath and whistled. 'She surely is a shocker. What a beauty, though. Do you know what she is?'

Doll Jensen played the torch over the massive body and the shadows on the wall appeared to dance.

'Not a clue. I think she's just the coolest thing ever. Glad you came?'

Morty moved closer and ran an exploring finger over the formalised folds of drapery which concealed nothing of the gross curves of belly and thigh.

'She's a ship's figurehead. About eighteen ten, I'd say at a guess. A real peach. She ought to be in a museum. H.M.S. *Medusa*, if you want to bet on her name. Doll, I'm certainly grateful to you.'

Her grip on his hand tightened.

'You'll put her in your book?'

'Surely.'

The girl was facing him now, her upturned head level with his chin.

'Glad you're pleased. I wanted to please you, see?'

The kiss was slow, deep and quite inevitable. The girl gave her lips and her whole body to him with an intensity which quivered between them without any restraining instinct. The torch clicked into oblivion and for a time they swayed together, mindless and hungry.

Presently she relaxed and took a couple of steps backward dragging him with her. Morty, putting out a protective arm, found himself collapsing easily on to musty sacks whose presence he had scarcely noticed.

The girl nestled and twisted beneath him and he found her mouth, wide and soft as velvet.

For a long minute neither of them moved and he could feel her heart beating hard and regular against his chest.

Quite suddenly her body became tense. She was still gripping the torch in one hand and it now burst into light over his shoulder. Her high pitched scream of pure terror was directed at something immediately behind his head.

'No!' she shouted. 'No, you ...'

Morty had a split second vision of being plunged into the interior of a meteorite. Agony seized him like a flame which devoured and paralysed and he collapsed into a pit whose depth was not to be guessed.

He did not wake to full consciousness for many hours. Lights, faces and voices drifted about him like strange fish seen through a distorting glass. With focus and perspective came pain which dragged him mercilessly back to reality.

Dr Dido Jones was bending over him and standing diffidently beside her was Mr Campion.

10

Doctor and Patient

YOU'LL probably have a splitting headache for a couple of days, so relax and take it easy. There's no great harm done.'

Dr Jones' voice was cool and her hands straightened the coverlet brusquely. Until that moment Morty had considered that she was the ideal ministering angel to smooth the fevered brow and in his wilder daydreams had envied anyone fortunate enough to be her patient, but now there was an inflection in her tone which he found too impersonal for his peace of mind.

'Don't bother about explanations. We know most of them, anyway. Drink this.'

He raised himself painfully as the world swayed giddily about him and did as he was told. He was lying, he realised, in a large Victorian four-poster bed in a room which bore all the fussy ultra-respectable hallmarks of the period. Faded photographs mounted in crimson velvet and the more ponderous works of Burne Jones and Watts looked down placidly from walls decorated with ribbons and roses. The back of his head still opened and closed with searing irregularity.

He made a supreme effort.

'It would be a help if you told me where the heck I am.'

Dido's voice came to him from a long way off. 'You're at The Hollies. We brought you here last night. This is Sunday morning ... Sunday morning ... Sunday...'

The pain slowly dissolved into clouds of cotton wool and he slept.

When he next awoke he was dimly aware of a large lugubrious face looking down on him. Mr Lugg was standing at the foot of the bed, a massive arm supporting one of the posts.

For some time he eyed the patient without moving and Morty returned the stare. To prove that he was awake he winked.

'You dropped a clanger last night, cock.'

Morty sighed. 'You're telling me. It fell right on top of my head. What happened?'

'Gawd knows.' Mr Lugg shrugged his shoulders. ''Er ladyship 'as decided to open up the 'ouse for the summer season. I'm on tempor'y loan to make the party respectable and do the washing up—what the Frogs call a Conscience. They came down together last night lookin' for yer.' He sucked a tooth reflectively. 'Well, it was me wot found yer.'

'And brought me here?'

'Exackly. If you'd been took back to the pub in the mess you was in 'alf the rozzers in the place would be asking questions and 'is nibs is in no mood to give 'em answers. I never seen 'im in such a state. As for Doctor D, it'll take more than a bunch of forget-me-nots to put 'er feathers straight. You was a bit public, mate, with your amoors last night. You can't go playing Errol Flynn in front of a full 'ouse without getting your name in the gossip columns. *You was noticed.* Mrs. Dixie blew the gaff on your bit of nooky in black tights so I didn't 'urry meself to find you. Then when you didn't come 'ome and I see yer bit of nonsense messing around in 'er van all on 'er tod I knew it was safe to look for yer. You was out like a light in that shed which I might add is one of the best known local boodwah love nests. That's the full strength of the 'ow d'ye do.'

Morty groaned. His head still ached intolerably and for the first time he became aware that a bandage was closely swathed over a lump the size of a tablespoon. He put a tentative hand to the spot.

'You 'ad an argument with a blunt instrument. Know 'oo 'it yer?'

Beyond his line of vision a door opened and he recognised a familiar voice.

'A very good question. Have you any idea?'

Mr Campion joined Lugg at the foot of the bed. He was as bland as ever but the lines on his face were more defined than Morty remembered. The patient started to shake his head but abandoned the attempt.

'Not a clue. It came from behind me. I don't think I walked into a trap. I—I think that damned girl was as surprised as I was.'

'So I gather.' Mr Campion's tone was diffident. 'I ran the lady to earth this morning—not without difficulty. She seems to have been thoroughly frightened and to have left you to it. Not a loyal type I'm afraid. She simply fled. She claims she dropped her torch in the rough and tumble which is probably true since I found it this morning. I returned it to her. It made a convenient introduction.'

'But she saw who it was. She shouted out.'

Mr Campion's frown deepened. 'That's just the trouble. I don't care for her information at all. It complicates the whole picture. This is a private war and the fewer people who join in the better.' He sat down on the edge of the bed and eyed the young man seriously.

'You wouldn't consider dropping out of it? I asked you down here to do a little innocent on-the-spot observation for me, not to get your skull cracked. No? I was afraid of that.'

'If I run away now I'm a lost soul, so include me in. I'm free, white and I feel as old as the hills, but I'm staying on the tail of this bandwagon until I find exactly where it is going. Now come clean. Who coshed me last night?'

Mr Campion sighed.

'The lady says she'd never seen him before in her life. She's quite emphatic about it and swears it wasn't one of the tear-away boys. A big man, she thinks, but she's only really certain of one thing. He had a black patch over one eye.'

'Burrows, the man who can hit the weathercock.'

'As you say—Mr Target Burrows—a very unpleasant personality. Manners none and customs beastly. From my point of view he has another unfortunate characteristic—he is liable to attract official attention.'

For the first time that day Morty smiled.

'You're being goddam mysterious. Don't you want all the help you can get?'

Mr Campion took off his glasses and polished them with a handkerchief before replying.

'My lips ought to be sealed,' he said at last. 'Like the third oriental monkey—I see and hear evil but I shouldn't speak it. For the sake of your health—and possibly Dido's—the less you know the better. You could say that I am trying to find some Government property. If I succeed I shall misappropriate it, because I have an excellent reason for doing so. That is why I am not overjoyed when little items like poison pen letters, unsolved murders or simple unexplained bangs on the head crop up and attract official attention. I hope I make myself clear?'

'You know damn well you don't. These two guys, Teague and Burrows, have the same idea, I suppose?'

'That's roughly the picture.' Mr Campion was choosing his words carefully. 'This—er—property was probably concealed somewhere in Saltey about twenty years ago, and if that is the case then Teague should know where to look for it. Unfortunately he has vanished extremely efficiently but there's evidence to suggest he's not far off. Burrows on the other hand probably doesn't know where to look or he'd have done so long ago. He may be waiting for his partner to show up and discouraging other enquiries in the meantime. If they are working together again they make a nasty pair and if Teague, in particular, gets caught...' He hunched his shoulders and hesitated. 'If he's caught, we're finished.'

'How come?'

Campion stood up. 'Teague has kept his mouth shut all these years when he knew that a few words could earn him remission—possibly immediate release, if he played his cards right. He's a cold blooded adventurer and it looks as if he's made his long term plans very carefully, as a man often does when he's got plenty of time to think. If he's caught before he gets what he's after, nothing on earth will make him speak. He'll die with his secret.'

Outside the church bells had begun their evening peal and a shaft of light was making the room appear as if it were filled with golden dust. A motor cycle roared past the house headed for Mob's Bowl and Mr Campion waited until the fusillade was over before continuing.

'If that happens,' he said, 'the consequences could be tragic. It would almost certainly cause the death of a perfectly innocent woman whose survival is extremely important and it might set up a chain reaction which would involve a great many more lives. My dear chap, I do know that this sounds melodramatic and mysterious but the trouble is that it happens to be unpleasantly true. It's also a trifle urgent, because I have very few days left. So you see, Teague simply mustn't be caught.'

The efficiency of Dido Jones as a doctor, never a matter of doubt to her patients or her admirers, was demonstrated with clinical clarity all through the evening. She had looked in several times, using a thermometer which she wielded so as to make conversation strictly limited, but despite his misgivings Morty found his headache evaporating more quickly than he had dared to hope. Now she returned bearing tea and toast. She was wearing a linen suit of pale cream which emphasised the gleaming ebony of her hair.

'You're doing very well,' she announced. 'Temperature normal, pulse normal, bruise coming up nicely. If your head is clear tomorrow you can go back to The Demon—or whatever else you please. Take it easy for a couple of days and don't try to drive a car.'

'Thank you, doctor.' Morty put as much penitence into his voice as he dared. 'I—I guess. it's no use saying . . .'

'Forget it,' she said. 'I'm going back to town now. I've got work to do in the morning. Lugg will look after you for tonight. He's staying on as caretaker. Goodbye.'

He caught her arm as she turned. 'Goodbye?'

'Yes.'

'Dido, you couldn't get around to seeing me as a wounded warrior—a casualty in some goddam heroic cause that I'm not even allowed to understand?'

Her laugh was cool and almost conventional but there was a trace of real amusement in it.

'No, Morty. I simply couldn't. It wasn't blood on your face and your shirt, you know. Just a rather off beat brand of lipstick. Very unflattering.'

He did not relax his grip.

'I guess there's no future in this conversation. Could you give me a consultation about my health, say next Thursday at Quaglino's? It would give me something to live for.'

Dido freed herself. 'No. Mortimer Kelsey, I could not. The plain truth about you at the moment is that you are in the doghouse, which is a very appropriate place for you, now I come to think of it. Goodnight.'

'Goodnight is better than goodbye.'

'If you think so.'

'Just one thing, lady.'

'Yes?'

'Oh, Dido, Dido, Dido . . .'

The door closed behind her so quietly that he did not hear it. Suddenly he felt old and drowsy. The tea on the table beside him grew cold and through his dreams the ticking of a clock marked the passing of long empty hours.

Mossy Ling left The Demon at five minutes after closing time on Sunday evening, a custom by which many inhabitants of Mob's Bowl set their watches. He was not in a good mood since despite all his efforts to turn attention his way he had not been entirely successful, with the result that he had been compelled to pay for rather more beer than his carefully calculated economy permitted. Strangers had been sparse for the time of year and he depended upon their support for his refreshment. To add to his difficulties the main topic of conversation had been Morty's exploit in humiliating the tearaways and there had been too many other witnesses to make his account of this affair of particular interest. He had tried a new gambit in the morning but with little success, for the company had been rather too sophisticated for his line of approach. Had it not been for his skill in removing unfinished drinks during the temporary absence of their owners the evening would have been a total failure.

Now he teetered across the pebbled frontage of The Demon, his footsteps making a distinctive clip-clip-crunch as he moved, for he was stiff in one leg and supported himself nimbly enough with a blackthorn. He passed the silent mass of the sail lofts and shuffled purposefully past the row of brick and tile houses known as Salt Street. At the far end he turned into a narrow alley which emerged on to an area of twitchy grass beyond which lay a huddle of darkened shacks which had once been fishermen's cottages. His own habitation, originally a tarred wood stable, had been converted into a two-roomed bungalow but it still kept its half door. The latch clicked sharply as he entered and he left the upper section ajar to give himself sufficient light. Like many old countrymen he kept the place hermetically sealed in summer and winter alike but the stale reek of tobacco, cooking, undisturbed dust and blankets innocent of soap for fifty years did not distress him.

The room was cluttered with a magpie's hoard gathered from the carcases of ships and the discarded junk of attics and rubbish dumps. He lit a small oil lamp, shut himself in for the night and began a long systematic scratch which he found infinitely pleasurable.

Having satisfied the first demand of comfort he unlocked a heavy brass-bound sea chest and took out a bottle, calculating the contents against the wavering flame in the blackened glass casing. For some time he sat sipping at the nightcap from a tin mug.

A brass ship's clock hung on the peeling wall, but it no longer indicated time, so that the sound when it came could not be mistaken. A floorboard creaked, making the old man jerk his head to one side so that his better ear was towards the inner wall. There was someone in the next room, someone who was waiting just on the other side of the door. He listened for a full minute whilst his hand moved cautiously forward to grip the stick which had been propped against the table.

'If that's you, Jim Teague, you can come on out. I ain't afraid on yer.'

There was no answer to his call and he moved stealthily towards the door. With one hand on the latch he spoke again, whispering now.

'Target? Is it Target Burrows come 'ome?'

He pulled the latch so violently that he almost fell into the stale darkness beyond. Hands, strong as iron, gripped him by his shoulders and began to shake him as a dog might deal with a rat.

127

11

At Cheffin's Farm

'THERE is a female party by the name of Weatherby askin' for Mr Mortimer Kelsey, and she was kind enough to add would see her pronto.'

Mr Lugg stood in the door of the dining room at The Hollies, a sombre apartment whose sage green walls were adorned by maple framed engravings from the works of Sir John Gilbert illustrating the plays of Shakespeare. Titania languished over her ass's head and Falstaff caroused with thespian vigour.

Morty was making a late breakfast whilst Mr Campion did his best to encourage the younger man's indifferent appetite. He had removed the bandage but his head was still uncomfortably sore.

'You know the lady?'

'I certainly do,' Morty admitted. 'She only asks because she wants to know. I warn you, she's a—'

He got no further. Mrs Weatherby strode into the room swinging a shoulder bag as if it were a set of golf clubs. She had discarded her sou'wester and her wild white hair was partialy concealed by a batik scarf. She took in Mr Campion, recognised his type, approved and overcame her surprise in a single breath.

'Sorry to barge in on you like this but I've dug up a piece of gen which may be rather hot. Didn't realise you weren't alone.'

Morty made the introductions, adding, 'Mr Campion's man Lugg is going to keep an eye on The Hollies for a day or two. Dr Jones has gone back to town.'

'A jolly good wheeze,' said Mrs Weatherby. 'Keep the

snoopers and nosey parkers out. Everyone in Saltey wants to know their neighbour's business.' She glanced round the room. 'Not that Kitty Kytie had much that was worth pinching. A little Waterford and one Chinese red lacquer cabinet, that's about the lot as I recall. Still, you never know today. Things turn out to be valuable antiques that I wouldn't give house room. No thanks, no coffee for me. I looked for you at The Demon this morning and they told me you were here. Dixie Wishart made quite a song and dance about it but I think a parlourman—if that's what he is—makes everything perfectly respectable. You had a house warming party last night?'

'You could put it that way,' murmured Mr Campion. 'I assure you that the proceedings were strictly formal. Morty, for example, had nothing stronger than tea.'

Mrs Weatherby surveyed the younger man critically. 'If you ask me he's either been in a fight or has a severe hangover—probably both if my information is accurate. However, that's his affair. I came to bring news.' She turned to Campion. 'Are you in the picture about our local troubles?'

'I have a watching brief.'

'Good-oh. Then I don't have to explain about this wretched man Woodrose. I promised that I'd look him up and put things to him straight from the shoulder. I went over to Cheffin's Farm last night—that's his place, you know—intending to have a bit of an up and a downer with him. And what do you think? In my opinion he's done a bunk.'

Morty put down his cup and both men turned on their guest. Mrs Weatherby continued, clearly enjoying the sensation she had caused.

'I dropped over on my phut-phut about half past eight last night. It's a good safe hour because country people always eat extraordinarily early, in fact on Sunday evenings they generally have a sort of high tea after evensong. Not that Jonah ever goes to church, but his housekeeper Mrs Carp does. Apart from her he lives alone. She's a Felgate you know and all that family manage to look remarkably like fish, so it's just as well she married that poor clodhopper before he died. She teaches at the Sunday school and spends her free time in the village, but I thought I'd be certain to catch Jonah. I found Nellie Carp all right, but there wasn't a sign of the man. He apparently went off by car for his usual Saturday night spree in London and never returned. Nellie sleeps with her sister on Saturdays and doesn't come in until the morning. What do you think about that?'

'Forgive me,' Mr Campion was diffident, 'but the man appears to be quite a lively character. Is there anything remarkable in his having a night on the tiles?'

'Oh, bless you, no,' said Mrs Weatherby. 'He's a one for his roll in the hay. But always back by two in the morning, regular as clockwork. Whatever else you can say about him, he's a worker. I wouldn't give a thought to it if it weren't for what I happened to notice whilst I was walking round to the back door. The front is kept permanently locked, except for funerals of course, and it took me a minute or two to rout out Nellie Carp. She certainly expected him back on Saturday night or early Sunday morning and was very cagey about telling me anything. You know how suspicious these country people are— they won't let you in the house if they can help it. It was just as well I took a peek inside before the light went. Jonah uses one of the front rooms with big french windows as his office. I wouldn't call him a tidy man at the best of times, but the place was a shambles—cupboards wide open and papers all over the floor. In my opinion Jonah did a moonlight flit on Saturday afternoon and did his packing in about four seconds flat. He drives a terrible old Ford that I'm sure isn't road worthy. He's still not back because I rang up half an hour ago. What do you make of that? I only ask because I want to know.'

Mr Campion considered. 'I think you can take it that *something* has happened,' he said at last. 'The housekeeper isn't thinking of going to the police?'

The suggestion drew a snort from Mrs Weatherby.

'You can bet your boots that she won't. Jonah hates any sort of official and he'll take a shotgun to a man in uniform at the drop of a hat. He's done it before and landed himself in hot water. Nellie Carp is scared stiff if I'm any judge and she won't make any move in case she does wrong. He's a hard man and inclined to blow his top if he's put out.'

Mr Campion stood up. 'I think,' he said judicially, 'that we might pay Cheffin's Farm a visit. I'd like to have a look at the room which Mr Woodrose has left so untidy before anyone else does. Do you think you could arrange suitable introductions?'

It was some moments before Mrs Weatherby answered. Finally she shook her head.

'Difficult,' she said. 'Damn difficult. That woman will behave like a frightened oyster if I know her. We could have a bash at it, of course, but I doubt if you'll get over the doorstep.'

'Not even if Morty who is handsome and persuasive found some pressing reason to ask permission to investigate, say, the hammer beams in the old barn? With your help he might be able to spin out the conversation for quite a time. Ten minutes ought to be sufficient.'

Mrs Weatherby's expression became conspiratorial.

'Synchronise watches, what? We create a diversion at the rear whilst the main attack goes in from the front?'

'Something of the sort,' admitted Mr Campion. 'Perhaps you could show us the way?'

Cheffin's Farm was at the mouth of the road leading into Saltey and the land opposite the ill fated corner on the seaward side. The approach lane, long twisting and narrow, was ill kept and pock-marked with dangerous holes which Mrs Weatherby skirted on her motor scooter with impressive flair. Her skill was constantly demonstrated for at each bend she turned in the saddle and waved to them over her shoulder as they followed in Mr Campion's comfortable Hawk. The solid Georgian house of grey brick and slate had a cold unwelcoming air even in sunlight, emphasised by untrimmed laurels and a large weeping willow which sprawled like a yellow octopus beside the pillared portico. Several of the upper windows were shuttered and the whole establishment proclaimed that it served a bachelor whose interests were not domestic. Only the outbuildings behind the house showed signs of prosperity and Mrs Weatherby led Morty towards them with the slogging tread of a route marcher. Mr Campion could hear her authoritative tones long after the pair were out of sight.

'Old? My dear man, old as the hills. Why, in my grandfather's time we thought there was a prehistoric barrow in the long field. It turned out to be a mound built for a windmill, of course, but that didn't prove ... Ah, there you are, Mrs Carp....'

Mr Campion gave them plenty of time before he moved. Then he slipped quietly out of his car and disappeared like a shadow into the enveloping branches of the willow. No professional burglar could have asked for better cover.

He was back in the driver's seat long before his fellow conspirators returned. Morty, putting his head in at the opposite door, found him apparently asleep at the wheel.

'That was real hard work,' said Morty, breathing heavily. 'I had to talk my head off before the old woman would even admit that she could see me standing in front of her. She's more like a terrified codfish than a human being. But Mon was just great—gave me the biggest build up of all time. Still no dice at all as far as any news about Jonah is concerned. How about your end?'

The thin man smiled. 'Have no fear, young sir. I will reveal all when we get back to The Hollies,' he said as Mrs Weatherby sped off down the lane. 'This is no place for a conference. I hope Lugg has provided us with sherry.'

'If I know the lady, she'll take what she calls a Harry pinkers,' said Morty. 'She likes it dryer than the driest Martini in the business. I didn't know you bred them like that any longer. What odds will you give me that she says "Bung-ho"?'

Mr Campion appeared to give the matter earnest considera-tion. 'Evens on "Down the hatch",' he decided and continued the journey in silence.

Mrs Weatherby disappointed both of them. Despite a re-markable assortment of drinks ranging from stout to white port laid out by Mr Lugg on the table in the conservatory, she refused refreshment.

'Can't stay more than half a jiffy,' she explained. 'Got to catch the dreariest Institute lunch for my local rag. But I simply must know about Jonah. Has he really skedaddled, and if so, why?'

Mr Campion eyed her thoughtfully over his glasses.

'Off the record?'

'Never a word, may I die. Has he bunked?'

The room was heavy with the aroma of eucalyptus from the thrusting rubbery tree which was rapidly outgrowing the glaz-ing of the roof. Mr Campion opened the long glass doors and looked round the lush wilderness beyond before he answered.

'Mr Jonah Woodrose,' he said at last, 'has had visitors. I don't know the chap's personal habits, of course, but no one in his senses makes a mess like that in his own house if he has a clue where to look for what he wants. He's been broken into and entered, as we say in court. Somebody has made a pretty thorough search of the place and this includes a couple of large secret recesses built into the back of fitted cupboards. Jonah would have known how to get at them. His visitor didn't. He evidently had a rough idea where they were but he didn't know the trick of opening false backs. He just smashed them, probably with a poker. Only Jonah could tell if anything was taken but the visitor certainly wasn't looking for spirits. Both hidey-holes are full of brandy and most of it appears to have been there for quite a time. Whether the raider took anything or not is anybody's guess. But one thing is clear. All this must have happened after Jonah left.'

'And he's not back yet,' said Morty. 'I'd say he'd been hijacked—kidnapped to keep him out of the way.'

Mrs Weatherby was delighted. 'It'd do the old ruffian a power of good. What a lark, eh? So glad I dropped in on you two this morning. Now a promise is a promise but you won't be able to keep the news quiet for long. Give me a buzz if anything breaks. Now I really must fly like a bat out of hell but you do give me your word—'

Mr Campion nodded solemnly. 'You have my personal guarantee,' he said, 'and none genuine without the signature on the wrapper. Unless, of course...'

'Unless what?'

'Unless he turns up. I doubt if he is a very truthful character. His explanation, if he's forced to give one, might be simple but unprintable.'

The birdlike speculation died in Mrs Weatherby's eyes. 'That would be disappointing,' she said. 'We must all hope for the worst, mustn't we? A disaster to Jonah would make tophole copy. Now I really must say Toodle-oo. I'll let myself out. Keep in touch, chaps.'

The pleasant green arbour seemed curiously empty after her departure. Mr Campion stretched his legs from the verandah chair to the low table in the centre of the room and sipped his drink absently. Outside late chestnut candles mingled with the profusion of may trees and the scented air was warmly lazy.

Morty broke the silence. 'Where do we go for honey?' he enquired.

It was some time before the older man answered and when he spoke he was clearly thinking aloud.

'Jonah Woodrose is a predictable creature,' he said. 'Dozens of people know his routine over a weekend and probably one or two know precisely where he goes. The cause of his disappearance is more likely to lie here, rather than in London. Anyone who wanted him out of the way could set a trap for him quite easily, especially as he always takes your back road home. The back road passes through The Trough—your old ghost town. We might be doing ourselves and him a service by restoring him to the agitated bosom of Mrs Carp before there are any official enquiries.'

He stood up. 'This is a time for long shots. I think we should explore Victoria Crescent and the Royal Esplanade.'

12

Beware of Ghosts

THE difficulties and hazards of exploration are usually formidable in any part of the world and the area marked on the Ordnance Survey of 1900 as Eastonville, a title which has long since vanished, could be classed as inhospitable terrain. Mr Campion, driving cautiously down a track labelled Runnymede Road, regretted that he had not equipped himself with a Land Rover or a Bren carrier, for the landscape suggested that it could well have been a battlefield abandoned for a century after a brobdinagian barrage.

'These mounds,' explained Morty, 'are ancient rubbish dumps and the swamps between them are just goddam swamps.'

'Probably malarial.' Mr Campion spoke with feeling. 'I think we should turn off here at Albion Terrace. There are tyre marks going that way.'

For some time they followed the trail which led through a group of caravans, multiplied and split tantalisingly in three directions. The area was not entirely uninhabited and since it was unapproachable without some form of transport, each decaying villa or shack appeared to possess its own means of communication with the outside world. Passing the completed half of what should have been a semi-detached villa marked by an inscription 'Glastonbury. *No Hawkers, no Circulars. Beware of the Dog*', Mr Campion halted the car at the intersection of four rutted roads. The afternoon had been exhausting. No one, it seemed, had remarked Jonah Woodrose or his white Ford and the search of a dozen empty ruins had revealed nothing more exciting than broken tin baths, discarded corsets and the rusting carcases of dead vehicles.

He got out. 'If we walk to the top of the next mountain we should command a reasonable view of the landscape. It will give us a peak to stand on, even if my wild surmise turns out to be a busted flush as empty as a shark's egg.'

The ascent over the uneven slope was not easy but at the top it was possible to see that the derelict wilderness had once been planned to develop logically outwards from a circular track far behind them. It was late in the afternoon and from the chimney stack of a distant factory to the north a single plume of white smoke hung in the pale sky. Nothing moved and even a dog who had resented their approach and continued his complaint long after, was satisfied that it was safe to be silent.

As they turned to go Campion, who had been ranging the squalid countryside through binoculars, caught his companion's arm.

'Don't look now,' he said. 'Or rather—do. There seems to be an ancient Briton standing by the car.'

He passed the glasses to Morty. In front of the Hawk, looking up at them with one hand shading his eyes stood a wild figure, bulky, red faced and dishevelled. He was draped in a ragged army blanket which he clutched to his stomach and apart from that appeared to be completely naked. Seeing that he had their attention he waved.

'And that, if I mistake not, Watson, is our client,' murmured Campion. 'He seems to havs spent a discouraging weekend.'

Jonah Woodrose greeted them with a sheepish smile which did not entirely conceal a hint of truculence.

'Had a bit o' trouble.' he said. 'I wonder if you two gentlemen ... why, you're the American chap from The Demon, ain't yer? Properly glad to see you, so I am. Could you give me a lift, now?'

At close quarters his appearance was startling. His fair hair which had once been carefully combed over a bald dome of forehead hung in a lank wisp behind one ear and a heavy stubble sprouted from his chin. His cheeks were grazed and scarred and there was a blue lump beneath one eye. Morty was reminded sharply of the last time he had seen those signs.

'What in heck have you been up to?' he demanded. 'Kidnapped by gipsies?'

Jonah scowled at him. 'Never you mind. Just give me a lift back to Saltey, that's all I ask. I'd be properly grateful and that's the truth, but I'll mind my business and I'll thank you to mind yours. If it's the price of a gallon of petrol you're afraid of—'

Mr Campion cut him short.

'Didn't you come here in a car?' he enquired mildly. 'Any idea where it is now?'

The man in the blanket jerked his head. 'Over yonder. In a little bit of a barn with half a roof. And a powerful lot of good it is, with the leads gone and the keys lost. No, no, you get me home, mister. I'll take care of that, come the time.' He shivered involuntarily. 'Uncommon cold it is, standing here in a rug full of fleas.'

Mr Campion opened the door of the car and returned with a flask. He unscrewed the cap and poured a tot.

'You'd better drink this,' he said. 'Then perhaps you might tell us what's happened to you. Unless, of course, you would prefer us to talk to the police. They should be interested. You look like a good example of common assault.'

The big man seized the cup and drank without drawing breath. He took an unsteady pace backwards and supported himself against the car.

'It's my business what happened to me. You can talk your head off to any blasted busybody you like and good luck to you. But get this straight, mister—I'm telling you nothing. Now do I get a lift or do I walk until I find someone who'll do a Christian act without any bloody questions?'

Mr Campion refilled the cup but kept it in his hand.

'I think you'd better listen to me, Mr Woodrose. On Saturday night or Sunday morning you were waylaid by some little trick hereabouts, probably by someone you recognised. You were made a fool of. Your head was put in a bag and you were tied up with sticky tape. It must have been intensely painful struggling out of it—very exhausting, too. Don't deny it, my dear chap—the marks of it are all over your wrists and your legs. You were bundled off in your own car to this barn where you were stripped in order to make escape more difficult for you. Your house has been ransacked whilst you've been away and your secret cupboards smashed open. Do you still want to keep your mouth shut?'

An expression half fury and half bewilderment crossed the man's face. He opened his lips, framing words. but no sound emerged. Finally he held out his hand for the cup.

'It's nothing to you,' he muttered at last. 'You've no call to have any business with me. You can get the hell out and leave me here for all I care. I'll not be catechised by any man alive.'

'Oh, but surely you have been already,' said Mr Campion mildly. 'You should look at your face in a mirror when you get home. Somebody has been scratching it around your eyes— somebody with a sharp knife. Somebody who threatened to blind you, unless you answered questions. Somebody who has killed one man already. Did you talk, Mr Woodrose? Just who did you talk to?'

The big man lowered his head like a cornered bull, moving it from side to side as if he were deciding to charge. Suddenly he shook himself and stood to his full height, so that on the uneven ground he dominated his rescuers.

'Hold your wind. you wilting blasting knowall,' he shouted. 'You'll get nothing from me. I'll settle my own scores in my own way. Go on, go to the police if you're playing their game. But I warn you that if one of them puts so much as a foot on my land he'll get a backside full of lead. That's God's truth and it goes for you, too.'

Campion turned to Morty. 'He's still afraid,' he said. 'And maybe has good reason to be, so we mustn't blame him. Next time it might mean a silver bullet.'

Jonah rounded on him, but it was clear that the thrust had been felt. 'You won't get me with that sort of birdlime, mister.

Keep your nose out of this or you'll be sorry for it. Now get to hell, the pair of you. I don't care for your company. I'll walk.'

He turned his back and took several paces not without dignity, for he was limping and the rutted clay was unyielding. Campion caught up with him and barred his way.

'Better take a lift,' he said. 'As it happens we shall be passing your gate. You know, you'll have to get used to the idea of new neighbours. Some of them have come to stay.'

In the conservatory of The Hollies which, by common consent, was the pleasantest room in the house, Mr Lugg greeted the returning warriors without any show of enthusiasm. His considerable midriff was covered by a sacking apron which had once graced an Edwardian charwoman but a towel draped over one shoulder suggested that he might recently have stepped out of a boxing-ring.

'You've 'ad visitors,' he announced. 'The vicar called to leave 'is compliments and a parish mag. Sergeant Throstle 'appened to drop in as 'e was passing by. 'E left 'is compliments. Mrs Weatherby 'appened to nip in round the back 'arf an hour ago, she left 'er compliments and a little news item. I've bin sweeping up perishin' compliments all the afternoon. And a couple of blokes come to instal the telephone. That's the lot, except a load of coke, someone trying to flog tea on the cheap and a boy scout who'd like to do the front drive for a bob.'

'Telephone already?' said Morty. 'That was quick. Dido only applied for it a week ago.'

Campion smiled. 'We have our uses. That happens to be a wire I *can* pull. I hope they put in two instruments?'

'Exackly. One is for common persons and the other's an 'ot line to the Archangel Gabriel as far as I can make out. That's in the room you're dossing in. It has a very classy ring, like a ding-dong in an 'orrible ideal 'ome. It's Mrs W's news you ought to be interested in by rights. She gets about, does that mechanised scarecrow, I'll give 'er that.'

He waited to make certain of their attention.

'Old Mossy Ling's dead. Dropped off the 'ook, very sudden, some time late last night. The milkman found 'im in 'is shack this morning lying on 'is bed and says he thinks it was natural causes such as old age, never washing, telling lies and drinking too much. Mrs W said to say "Were you interested? She was arskin' because she wanted to know".'

'The ancient mariner in the corner of The Demon?' enquired Campion. 'The professional oldest inhabitant?'

'That poor old guy,' said Morty. 'How come you know him? I thought you were a stranger in these parts.'

'Ours was not an intimate acquaintance,' Mr Campion admitted. 'In fact, I only saw him once and that was yesterday morning. I dropped in after returning some lost property. He struck me as being too good to be true but healthy enough. Our conversation was strictly limited because he wished to give me a full account of your exploit and I didn't greatly care for the topic. I put him off with a pint, so the custom of the country was observed. Foolish of me. I should have paid more attention.'

He hesitated, casting his mind back to the incident. 'I hope this isn't one of those mistakes which cannot afterwards be rectified.'

'If I know Mossy,' said Morty, 'he'd spot you for a foreigner from a mile off and therefore a natural sucker. Did he try you out with the Demon story?'

Campion brushed him aside. 'It wasn't that,' he said. 'I had the preliminaries, of course, but he saw he was unlikely to succeed there, so he switched to your demonstration of judo. At this point he collected the expected reward, which he'd worked pretty hard for. I'm afraid we both lost interest in each other after that and he began to look around for some new source of supply. He found one too—an elderly couple who certainly weren't local. Oh, my dear Morty, what a curse hindsight is.'

He sat back in the big verandah chair and closed his eyes. It was some time before Lugg broke the silence.

'You might let us 'ave a basinful of your beautiful thoughts,' he remarked at last. 'What was the next item on the song sheet?'

Campion sighed. 'A swan song as it turns out. He tackled these people with what I took to be a normal opening gambit. They didn't respond with any great enthusiasm and he began to raise his voice so as to include a larger audience. He was trying to attract attention, to make himself interesting, and he could have been getting at anybody within earshot. I detected a note of simple naughtiness as if he was hinting, or trying to make a joke with a double meaning. Dixie Wishart—the lady with the blue rinse—shut him up as if he'd been using a string of four letter words.'

'That's all fine and dandy,' said Morty, 'she often does when she doesn't approve. But just what was the poor old buzzard using for bait?'

Mr Campion paused before answering.

'His exact words were: "I seen a ghost last week, so I did now. I reckon I weren't the only one neither. A powerfully strange thing that no one ain't thought fit to mention it." End quote. Dear me. I hope he wasn't signing his own death warrant.'

142

13

The Moving Finger

THE letter came by the afternoon post on Tuesday. Morty, returning after an exploration of the odd windings of the little Rattey River inland from the Bowl, found it on his bedroom table in The Demon when he went up to change a shirt, for he had invited Campion to dinner at the excellent hostelry at Nine Ash. It lay prim and unremarkable amongst several others. There was an air mail from the States, full of his mother's limpid charm which flowed from the page as easily as her especial brand of small talk, a publisher's circular announcing, inaccurately, the impending appearance of his book and a couple of bills. He left it until the last, since the italic minion type reminded him uncomfortably of a pedantic mentor on his own subject who never corresponded except to demolish theories and to point irrefutably to gaps in scholarship.

The West Central London postmark reassured him however and he opened it with mild curiosity. It was very brief and bore no address or introduction. The typing was competent but not professional.

'Tell Doctor Jones that she must not come down to Saltey again. Not if she values her sight. Try squirting acid in a dog's eyes if you want to know what will happen to her.'

He read the message twice before his flash of belligerent fury passed and a chill, which had something of animal panic in its hinterland, took a grip at his heartstrings. Dido walking, swift and graceful from the hospital through the maze of staid streets to her Bloomsbury flat. Dido seized from behind whilst a plastic spray was pressed before her face. Dido blind, scream-ing, helpless. He began to feel sick.

London was at most two hours distant, far less if he drove with all his wits. He could surely find her before midnight, warn her, tell her that she was the girl he was determined to marry, tell her that she must never return to this God forsaken countryside with its sly venom and its abominable secrets. Plans, pleas, imploring phrases, surging sentences of desperate urgency chased through his mind. Her expression of quiet mockery, the look that he had last seen in her eyes, came clearly to him and he knew that the battle was lost before the opening shot could be fired. She would never give in to threats and entreaties would only show him up as a craven ass. The voice of the man he had assumed to be his correspondent whispered in his ear: 'Remember that in England the snob-bery of Cool is the offspring of the cult of Sangfroid.'

It was not a time for philosophy. He rang every number in London where Dido might conceivably be contacted, but found nothing beyond sympathetic offers to record any message he would like to leave.

'*Go home under escort and await my instructions. I love you.*' What else was there to say? He abandoned the idea.

Mr Campion received his companion in the garden room. He made no attempt to smooth Morty's brittle nerves beyond supplying a long iced drink of his own devising. He examined the letter carefully but without comment and presently pro-duced the folder which contained the photostats of some of its predecessors. The younger man watched him for some time as he compared one with another, matching or rejecting. Finally he closed the folder and placed the new arrival on top of it.

'I suppose we ought to be grateful,' he said at last. 'At least it keeps matters on the boil and that is rather vital at the moment. Time is our enemy, amongst others, you know. It could be the greatest of them. That thought doesn't make much appeal to you, I suppose?'

Morty was not pacified. 'But this is a threat, not a wisecrack.

What the hell can I do about it? If I can't make Dido listen and she goes—'

Mr Campion cut him short.

'I know it's a threat, my dear chap, but it has its merits from our point of view. I don't think the gallant doctor is in any greater danger now than she has been for some time but this is a new departure. It has a little something that the others haven't got, and that makes it very interesting.'

'The minion type face?'

'It's not important. The letter is very short and anyone could knock it out in a few moments in a shop, whilst pretending to try out a machine. It's very sharp and clean, so I imagine that was how it was done.'

'What then?'

'It introduces an entirely new note. Technically it's quite different, a new school of thought. Compare it with all the others and you'll see what I mean. I'm not an expert armed with a computer which is the way to deal with this sort of problem but I can tell a hawk from a handsaw.'

The evening was still golden and the sloping shafts of sunlight made dappled patterns over the ferns, the long low table with its collection of drinks and glasses and the threadbare turkey carpet on which it stood. Midges and tiny black heat flies were dancing in the warm air and outside the swallows were swooping in shallow arcs over the grass. A storm was moving lazily southward from beyond the estuary. When Campion spoke again his tone was mild and almost conversational. 'You know, I think the time has arrived when we should consult the oracle.'

'Mrs Weatherby?'

The older man shook his head. 'No. She's more inclined to ask than to answer. I mean an expert in the craft of letters. I've only seen him out of the corner of my eye but he's the odd card in the pack. Our resident poet, Hubert Oliver Wishart.'

' "Beware of me: I cast no shadow when I pass," ' said Morty. 'Don't quote that line to him—he's rather touchy about it.

Some of his later verse has a better right to be remembered, or so he thinks. Dixie is the only one who is allowed to refer to it.'

Mr Campion stretched his legs. 'The poet and peasant,' he said. 'They make an unlikely couple. I've been doing some research into H.O. and it's a curious story. Early success, which after all isn't unusual, but there's no sequel of failure—just silence. Silence and a gap. Then one book of verse—a *succes intime* but no great sale. He was born here in Saltey, got himself a series of brilliant scholarships—school, university, travel, everything a man could wish. He shot up like a rocket and vanished. The spent shaft seems to have fallen back where it started but where did it go in the meantime? From just before the war until about five years ago there is no trace of him. That could mean that he became a literary hack and he's not proud of it. Then he reappears with a nice wife who could well be a landlady or a landlady's daughter. He fits into the jigsaw somewhere—the question is: is he a shape which could key the whole thing together, or is he just a piece of the background which is decorative but unimportant?'

'I doubt if he'll tell you that,' said Morty. 'But he's open to flattery and he likes the sound of an educated voice. You might try demonology as an opening gambit.'

The poet was not at the inn when they enquired. He had gone out shortly before sunset and Dixie was unhelpful.

'He took what he calls his staff with him.' she explained. 'It's a tall walking stick. That means he's going to walk for miles and it could be two in the morning before he's home. I don't know what he gets up to but sometimes he has a little drink on the way, so he may go as far as Firestone or Nine Ash. I hope he doesn't get caught—it's going to pour in a minute or two.'

She was right. The storm arrived in a flurry of wind with a swift opening tattoo of rain which gave way to a solid downpour. Custom at the inn dwindled rapidly at the first sign of a pause and before the official closing hour the two men had the bar to themselves. Somewhere above them a door banged and Dixie put her head on one side.

'He's home,' she said. 'He may have been back some time. If you must see him, Mr Kelsey dear, go up to his attic. But knock. It's his private den and he considers himself off duty when he's there.'

The long low room under the roof was only unexpected because of its location. The sloping ceiling ran almost to the floor and the space was reduced by bookcases between the dormer windows which made the chamber alternately narrow and wide. Wishart sat at a table heavy with books and papers at the far end, a single green shaded reading lamp emphasising the craggy lines which scarred his face from nose to chin and formed an intricate tracery about his eyes and forehead. A scholar in a scholar's setting: only the upward glow of light gave his dignity a touch of theatre. A bottle of brandy faced him and there was a glass in his hand. He did not rise as they came in but gestured vaguely towards the shadows. His voice, deep as the G string of a cello, was glutinous and slurred.

'There are chairs,' he said and swayed dangerously as if he might slip sideways. 'Anything on them can be treated as d-detritus—sweep it away. You are late visitors for the country. Do you bring news or shall we sit and tell sad stories of the death of kings? Or speak of cabbages? Ling was no king—nearer a cabbage if the truth were told. But he is dead. Abominably, stupidly dead. Told his last lie, cadged his last drink. Will we consider him for an overture and so work to a conch ... to an Emperor.'

Morty glanced significantly at his companion.

'Tomorrow, perhaps?'

'No,' said Campion. 'Tonight.'

He took out the letter, unfolded it and placed it in the pool of light.

'Intelligence from London, Mr Wishart. I think you should pull yourself together and read it very carefully. We want your opinion.'

The poet's head with its impressive mane of grey hair weaved uncertainly over the paper. Then he shook himself and groped in a pocket for a metal case from which he produced a pair of steel rimmed glasses. He read the letter slowly, holding it at varying distances to keep the words in focus. Finally he replaced it on the table and peered from Campion to Morty over the top of the lenses.

'This came to you today?'

Morty nodded. 'You had one, you told me, last week. Now this. Mr Campion thought you could help.'

The old man gave a long shuddering sigh. He had clearly received a shock which was totally unexpected and the effect was sobering. Drained of colour, his face could have been carved in ivory.

'What can you tell us. Mr Wishart? Have you no opinion to offer?' Mr Campion spoke gently but there was no kindness in his tone.

The man at the table rounded on him. 'Tell you? I can tell you that it is cruel, that it is ugly, that it is the work of a sadist or a lunatic. What more do you wish? It is meant to frighten. I find it frightening. Is that what I am to say?'

'But different. You have seen one at least of its predecessors. Does nothing strike you?'

It was some time before Wishart answered. He had begun to drum on the table with long dark ribboned fingers. Finally he picked up the tumbler which had been perched on a pile of books, took it half way to his lips and replaced it without drinking.

'Mr Campion,' he said at last. 'You are trying to make a point, or so I suppose. You are proceeding with nods and becks but there is no wreathed smile. You ask for enlightenment. Now I ask you a question: who am I to ease your burden of ignorance? I have already given my advice to this young man and he has chosen to ignore it. I wish no part of his troubles. They are nothing to me.'

'But I'm afraid they are.' Mr Campion was persistent. 'I

148

think you know just where the difference lies and that is why you are a frightened man. This letter breaks a pattern—doesn't it?—a pattern which you understand. This letter is not a malicious piece of libel but a direct threat. I do hope you follow me.'

Wishart pushed back his chair and straightened his shoulders.

'You are talking in riddles. I don't know you, sir, or I might suspect that you hoped to spring a trap. You have the bland air of eminent counsel dissecting some wretched incompetent in a witness box. Given a chance you would become hectoring. At this hour my senses may be impaired but I am not totally blind. I may see through a glass ... but not darkly. I see with tolerable clarity, in fact. Tolerable clarity ... tolerable.... I also behave with as much tolerance as I can muster. What the devil are you getting at?'

Mr Campion accepted the challange.

'I'll tell you,' he said. 'Dr Jones and her friends have received a round dozen of letters, all of them originating from somewhere in this district even if some were posted in London. They fall into groups. Each group suggests a type of writer—a disappointed venomous old woman—a man with some knowledge of what could damage a medical reputation—a canting religious hypocrite and so on. The police are interested because they are thinking in terms of conspiracy. I am interested because these letters suggest forgery. I think they are exercises in caricature—the work of a single dilettante.' He waited to let the words sink in.

'You enjoy little essays in forgery, don't you, Mr Wishart? Think of your Cambridge friends, Colquhoun, Middlemass and Swinstead. Three dull men and all of them rich. Yet each of them produced an unlikely volume with remarkable literary qualities—very flattering to their vanity. I wonder who really wrote *Mosaic to Machine* or *Mandragora Days* or *Oh, Mr Cromek*? Odd books to keep on your shelves, Mr Wishart, yet there they are right behind your head sitting next to the fifth volume of Georgian Poetry in which you figure.'

For a long minute the old man stared towards Campion looking through and beyond his visitor. He was still gripping the table with both hands and the muscles around his right eye had begun to twitch. Shocked and ill at ease, Morty watched from the shadows. Wishart broke the tension by picking up his tumbler and emptying it at a gulp.

'I do not understand you,' he said flatly. 'And I do not propose to try. You force your company upon me and you make sly references to my friends. You accuse me by inference. Very well. I deny any part of the slander. Now go. Get out whilst I still have a hold of my temper. Go! Go! Go!'

Campion shook his head.

'Not just yet. We have a point to settle between us. I'm not concerned with the original letters because I rather think there won't be any more of them. But if I'm wrong and there *is* a recurrence then I shall dig deeper, I shall ask questions about years in your life which ought to be forgotten. It—er—it could be extremely embarrassing, don't you think? Jonah Woodrose wouldn't care for it either.'

Wishart frowned in an effort to focus his eyes. 'Jonah?'

'Yes, Jonah Woodrose. These letters were his idea, I fancy, at the start. His pressure at your elbow. Your execution, your inventive skill. There was even a touch of his style in some of them, but I don't suppose he appreciated that subtlety.'

Campion's tone was quiet, almost conversational. Wishart did not respond for some time but sat immobile with bowed head until the silence in the room was oppressive. Suddenly he seized the paper on the table before him and crushed it fiercely.

'This is not my handiwork. I deny your right to say so. I deny every part of your accusation. I could never have written this in a thousand years. You cannot hold me responsible.'

Mr Campion sighed. 'Oh, but I don't,' he murmured. 'This is by a new hand, someone who has decided to take over from you. Someone who is not your partner or your master. Have you any idea who it is? Jonah knows. I think Mossy Ling knew. It is possible that Hector Askew stumbled on the truth. Have you heard from James Teague lately, or Target Burrows, Mr Wishart?'

The poet shook his head. His voice had become a whisper and the fire had left him. He looked old and exhausted.

'Teague ... Burrows. They are dirty words hereabouts. It's twenty—no, nearer thirty years since I saw either of them. Now they or their ghosts are walking again. Mossy Ling said he saw a ghost and suddenly he is dead. Whatever Jonah saw was real enough to frighten the living daylights out of him. I saw him tonight but he told me nothing. Nothing at all, except that he'd had enough. He knows when he's beaten. But you'll get no answers from him if you cross-question from here to eternity. As for myself I know nothing of any value so I can neither help nor hinder in whatever mischief is afoot. In any case I am too full of years—perhaps that is why I have been left alone.'

Morty at least was convinced. The nerves around the poet's eye continued to twitch, emphasising his age and underlining the unease he was not attempting to hide. His face was still ruggedly handsome but it was the mould of an actor accustomed to playing strong roles caught in a revealing moment of weakness. It invited pity but not sympathy.

Yet he had fenced very neatly, making no sort of admission, giving no fact or hint which could be held against him. He sat very still for some time and then as if jerking himself back to reality took up the bottle and poured out three fingers of brandy. The voice was steady now.

'I shall not court a rebuff by asking you to join me. We each of us have our own touchstones against ... calamity. This is mine.'

Campion stood up. 'Just one other question before you apply your remedy, Mr Wishart. You know this area down to the last puddle. Give me an expert opinion. Could a man hide here for a fortnight and not be seen? A man must eat, drink, sleep soundly. Could it be done without friends?'

The old man took a long, reflective drink. Finally he shook his head.

'I've given some thought to that. The answer must be no. The police have been very active, poking their noses into cellars, which are very rare hereabouts since the land is only just above sea level, and exploring every shed and barn in the place. There are no priest holes that I know of and even an undiscovered hay loft presupposes an accomplice. Teague had a few real friends, rascals and mountebanks like himself, but most of them are dead and the remainder are gone long since. Jonah Woodrose is certainly no longer among them. As to his women—and there were several of those—the survivors are middle-aged by now and more likely to betray than to hide. Burrows was a shifty, foul mouthed bully who made nothing but enemies whilst he lived amongst us. Every man would play Judas to him given the chance.'

'Yet their ghosts are walking, as Mossy Ling remarked.'

Wishart drank again. 'You're such a clever theorist. Mr Campion, that I marvel you don't answer your own question. Where would a sailor man hide—a man who knew the coast better than any chart?'

'At sea, presumably.'

'Just so. At sea. There are three out of work tramps lying up in the main channel, each with a couple of men aboard to watch the riding lights. A paying guest would never be found if you searched all day. Not that I commend the idea to you. Burrows has a very odd sense of humour as I recall. It would amuse him to watch a man drown.'

14

Conference

SERGEANT THROSTLE had a number of questions on his mind but the one which lay uppermost was a question of demarcation. During his patient and astutely professional enquiries he had unearthed a number of family secrets but at every point he found himself tempted to follow leads which beckoned far beyond the orbit of his official instructions. Somewhere in the untidy ragbag of facts, rumours and personalities lay a thread which must bring him to the truth about Hector Askew, but each likely strand, if judiciously pulled, led to an area in which he had no authority. Superintendent Gravesend, reappearing briefly after Sibling's misadventure, had decided that it was not related to the main enquiry but was the work of tearaways from London and, in Saltey at any rate, a matter for the County police.

He had returned to London leaving the field uncomfortably clear. Throstle, who found his disapproval of his chief's methods deepening into a cordial dislike, was suspicious of any facile diagnosis. Every event of the past ten days had convinced him that the motive for Askew's murder could not be simplified into a single sentence. As he said himself, he was not a member of the Coincidence Club and there were too many apparently unrelated happenings in the village for his peace of mind. But the common factor, if there was one, eluded him.

He now sat in the neo-Georgian police station at Nine Ash in a pleasant green and white office which still smelt of paint, a pile of folders on the table in front of him, awaiting the arrival of Inspector Branch of the local C.I.D. with whom he had made an appointment. The idea of the conference had considerable merits from Throstle's standpoint for the old man who was due for retirement at Michaelmas was less touchy in matters of protocol than the rest of his colleagues and indeed was the only one to whom his heart warmed.

Branch had not earned the nickname 'Jumbo' for his figure alone; his long and incorruptible memory was considered to be more reliable than most filing systems. He came into the room so quietly that Throstle who was organising his notes did not hear him and the big full blooded man was sitting at the opposite side of the table before he raised his head.

'Shopping list, eh?' Branch had a strong East Anglian accent and the appearance of a substantial farmer. A cherubic fringe of golden curls still decorated the dome of his forehead and a healthy growth of hair sprouted from the upper part of his cheekbones.

'That's the way, boy. Sort it out, then we'll know where we stand. A powerful lot of thrashing around there's been but not a single rat has put his nose out of the stack. Mustn't let 'em stay in their holes.'

Throstle snorted. 'I've had a sniff at everyone I can find,' he said. 'And I'm no forrader. I know enough about Hector Askew's private life to fill a book and very dull, dirty reading it makes. I know every scandal in Saltey for the past ten or twenty years and I think I could put a name to nearly every one of my letter writers. But there's nothing that would stand up in a court of law and nothing to connect them with Askew. You're right about my shopping list. Here's item one—Askew's past. Is there a point I've missed in this lot?'

Throstle's extensive file with its prim wording seemed to delight the Inspector. He thumbed through it, mouthing an occasional name and chuckling reminiscently. 'Mavis Prentis ... no ... Prunella Wisdom, there's a proper joke for you .... Helen Price-Cattermole ... wouldn't waste powder and shot on her ... you've done a thorough job. You could have ten for a penny if you ask me without any man in the country giving anything more than a hearty vote of thanks. Now, what about the property angle? That's a subject people get wholly riled about if they're crossed. Askews have always dealt in property and pretended they didn't. Crompton Badger and Keene in Silver Street, which means old Sid Badger in fact, handle the business officially but he and the Askews are thicker than thieves. They have a regular method. Old Percy or the boy Hector run a place down to the sorrowing widow who is their client—say a house that's too big for her now her husband's dead. She takes their advice and sells out quick and cheap—Cromptons buy for an alleged client who's just a nominee and they split the proceeds. It's a dirty game and a man could make enemies by playing it. Thought of that?'

'Yes,' said Throstle. It pleased him to be a little ahead of his mentor. 'In the next folio. But it's The Hollies I'm interested in. Askew was killed there and all the letters are aimed at scaring Dr Jones into selling. That suggests the Askews, but Hector's death wouldn't help or hinder the sale by a day if she decided to pull out. Then who could want the place and why? See page seven for my list of possibles.' He paused while Branch turned the leaf and added ruefully, 'They're nearly all over seventy and all female, except for Jonah Woodrose and he has the most watertight alibi I've ever come across and I've broken a few in my time. I accept it, in fact. He's out. Bringing me to a dead end so far.'

Branch's eyes twinkled. 'Item two, to my way of thinking, is what you might call "A funny thing happened on my way to Mob's Bowl". Am I right?'

'I have it down under "Unexplained Incidents",' said Throstle stiffly. 'The broken glass. My man beaten up. Dr Jones' young American friend walking round the place with the kind of black eyes you get from having been hit on the head. Jonah Woodrose showing signs of having been in a fight, probably in London if my information is accurate. And an old man called Mossy Ling has died suddenly of thrombosis apparently. There may be no connection but I'd like your opinion.'

Throstle detailed his information. The careful accurate

summary took some time and Inspector Branch opened his eyes very wide and pursed his lips as he listened. The London man. he decided, was rather brighter than he had first supposed.

'All of this brings us to Teague and Burrows,' he said at last. 'That's about the size of it. You're wondering if they could be back in circulation?'

'It's just about on the cards.'

Branch considered the proposition. 'The last of the Pirates,' he said at last, 'Dashing Jim Teague and One-Eyed Target. Very romantic. That could be, I reckon, but somehow it makes a wonderful untidy fit. If there was loot on the barge *Blossom* and she did lay off the Bowl that time, then both of them should know where it is, for one wouldn't trust the other and that's for certain. I'd bet my pension on it. At most it was about six hundred quid, as I recall, and in pound notes which you couldn't hope to pass today without a powerful lot of explaining. If anything else was hidden up near the Bowl, and I'm thinking of The Hollies in particular, Target who was never caught, never even charged, would have sneaked back and pinched it long since. If they're both around they must have met up by now and what their game might be is anybody's guess. I doubt they're lying low in Saltey but there's a lot of old tubs anchored out in the creek so we'll lay on a search there, just to be certain. Teague has failed to report after coming out and Burrows is still wanted for questioning for his share in the raid twenty years ago.'

'Someone has been throwing stones at the weathercock lately,' remarked Throstle. 'And that was Thomas Alfred Burrows' trademark according to the locals. I don't see why he should advertise himself.'

'Nor don't I.' Branch laughed reminiscently. 'You know why he used to do that? That old lantern on the sail lofts was used as a lookout post by Harry Morgan who used to be the Customs chap in these parts. He'd hide up there all day with his glasses to watch what came into the Bowl and where it came from. Target knew that, of course, and he used to fling him up one for luck whenever he came ashore. It was his way of cocking a snook and he was a wonderfully good shot with a stone. He could hit a man on the back of the head at twenty paces and half brain him but we could never catch him at it. He and Teague were the biggest villains for miles when it came to the smuggling business, but for all we could prove we might just as well have sat and twiddled our thumbs. Old Waters, who had The Foliage as it was called then, Septimus Kytie, Matt Parsley and Jonah Woodrose himself—they were all in the racket one way or another and the only man we ever caught was a yacht steward who came ashore there with a packet of heroin in '37 and he was a poor silly foreigner from Kent.'

'Smuggling.' Throstle seized on the word. 'Could it still be going on? Those tearaways who seem to make the Bowl their headquarters—could they be mixed up in the racket?'

'They're a nasty bunch of young hoodlums and one or two certainly use Purple Hearts if nothing worse.'

He turned to a third file. 'Three have records: Norman Catchpole, 20, mechanic, theft from employer. Ronald Lewis, 18, grievous bodily harm, and Desmond Riddler, 17, breach of the peace and offensive weapons, meaning razor blades. They mean anything to you?'

'Trouble-makers,' said Branch promptly. 'They come from outside my baileywick, North London, Islington way, and organise punch-ups at the coastal resorts mostly just for the heck of it. But drugs in a big way? I doubt it. They wouldn't be reliable enough, for to my way of thinking they haven't a brain between them. Maybe someone's using them as carriers. It's possible, but...'

He paused and eyed Throstle over his glasses.

'You're a little off course, mister, aren't you? Drugs—narcotics—that's a job for the boys in the next department. Vice squad they call 'em now. Pass it on, man, pass it on. I doubt Hector Askew ever saw anything stronger than aspirin or cough lozenges in his life.'

Throstle's expression became obstinate. 'I know where my manor ends,' he said. 'Officially, at any rate. But those young no-goods fit into the picture somewhere. They're violent and there's been violence.'

As a concession to the conventions he added, 'I'll watch my step, though. Narcotics can have anything I turn up and welcome.' He glanced down at his own notes and asked, almost as an afterthought, 'Does the name Hamilton Dashwood mean anything to you?'

It was a long shot and to his surprise the older man responded more respectfully than he had anticipated. Inspector Branch sat back, brushed a cloud of cigarette ash from the furrows on his stomach, closed his eyes and began to recite from his celebrated filing system.

'That could be a wonderfully smart question, Mr Throstle. H. Hamilton Dashwood, eh? Real name Henry Harvey Done—same initials—they often do that. Changed it quite legally by deed poll in 1947. Small time crook who used to hang round the halls in the days of variety shows. Occasional job as the chap they threw custard pie at. Robbed or swindled old ladies on the strength of being an actor. Did a bit of time for it, six months if I recall aright. Nothing known in the past five years, but he gets around—all along the coast from Southend to Yarmouth. Travels for a small firm in Ipswich who make carnival novelties, streamers, funny hats and so on. Short wave radio ham but registered and apparently all above board. We keep tabs on him every so often, when we can spare the time.' He patted his waistcoat absently. 'Yes, you might get someone from your end to look him over.'

He pulled out a gunmetal watch at the end of a leather strap. 'Ten to twelve. I think we'd be the better for a pint. By the way—one other thing about your tearaways. Nearly forgot it because it's one of my headaches and no concern of yours. Next Saturday to Monday—Whitsun weekend and Bank Holiday.'

'What about it?'

'Trouble expected with the ton-up lads, the mods or rockers or whatever. Apparently there was a fight last Saturday at The Demon. The word is that they're coming back in strength for a real old fashioned punch-up. I'm sending down all the chaps I can spare, which will be about four—say six with the local man and a sergeant. It should be enough but we're liable to be thin on the ground if Clacton or Southend ask for additional chaps —as they have.'

He stood up and stretched himself.

'It might give you a lead if you're still minded that way.'

15

The Night of the Demon

SATURDAY, the first day of the Whitsun holiday, began so gently that the sun did not disperse the veil of mist until it was no longer dawn but full morning. In the main estuary the three anchored merchantmen remained silhouettes without detail, sleeping on water as featureless as frosted glass. The promise of heat hung in the air and only the gulls failed to recognise that this was an hour for laziness and whispering. They swerved and screeched about the Bowl as the tide ebbed, quarrelling petulantly over mysterious treasures in the mud.

From his bedroom window Morty observed the plain clothed figure of Sibling emerge from a door in the sail lofts on his extreme left, retrieve a lady's bicycle from behind one of the brick piles on which they stood and vanish silently towards Forty Angels and presumably breakfast. A solitary bather crunched across the pebbled yard, still rubbing his back with a multicoloured towel and presently two men in yellow oilskins loaded a boat with baskets and tackle and rowed away towards the shipping, their path making a wide swathe of light on the pearly water.

Morty descended to the reassuring atmosphere of bacon and eggs and put his head into the kitchen to announce his arrival. The poet of the saltings had avoided his guest since their encounter but Dixie appeared to be at some pains to ignore the affair, if indeed she was aware of it. She greeted him cheerfully as she looked up from a large pan of Demon cakes which she was cutting into squares.

'A lovely day, Mr Kelsey dear. Makes you want to sing "Oh what a beautiful morning!" I hope it stays that way.'

'Any reason why it shouldn't?'

Her forehead puckered as she concentrated on the equal divisions of cake. 'Well, there is, you know. We had that silly man Simmonds here last night, full of warnings about mods and rockers and I don't know what else, telling me I needn't open the pub if I didn't want to—as if I didn't know my rights —advising me to watch my step. I told him it was up to him to keep things in order outside and that indoors I'd look after myself, thank you. *I have*, too.'

'Hired a few chuckers-out?'

She laughed. 'That's about the size of it. A couple of lads from Firestone are coming in as extra barmen and the whole of the darts team are spending the evening here. You'll be away all day, I expect? I hear the doctor is coming down ... ?'

Morty accepted the enquiry with a grin.

'I guess I'll look in at The Hollies. You can count me out if you're worried about tables for lunch.'

Dixie patted his hand. 'Just as well,' she agreed. 'You've made your peace with her, then? You should never have let that wicked little tart pick you up, Mr Kelsey dear—it's no way to do your courting with a real girl. I'd give Saltey a miss over the holiday as far as you can. It'll be overrun with trippers and tourists which is fine for me, since I've a business to run, but no good for people like yourself. I doubt if we'll see half a dozen regulars all day. They don't like strangers. Run along now and I'll get your breakfast.'

The invasion began whilst he was still eating. Three motor cycles roared and skidded over the forecourt, disappearing towards the sea wall and reappearing from the opposite direction, having established a rough-riding circuit of the inn regardless of property. Presently a vehicle which had once been a London taxi but was now painted shocking pink and decorated with slogans arrived by the edge of the Bowl and disgorged a group which might have come from a quatrocento harlequinade.

'Don't blow your cool,' proclaimed their transport. 'This is a Freak Out. Watch it, Fuzz!'

A sexless face framed with dark unkempt hair appeared at the open window and a hand holding an enamel can was thrust towards his table.

'Hey, you. Get us some water will ya? We wanna brew up, see?'

It was a demand made with conscious truculence. Morty surrendered to it with as much grace as he could muster. Prudence, however, suggested that he should remove his precious Lotus Elan from the doubtful security of the stables of The Demon and he drove slowly out of the hamlet towards the comparative security of The Hollies.

Overnight, several more tents had appeared on the open land between The Demon and the derelict churchyard and the occupants in various stages of undress were taking the sun. A new caravan and three or four cars rested on the twitchy grass. An ice cream tricycle was already doing good business and a diversity of transistors sprayed the air with a confetti of competing rhythms, but the true inhabitants of Mob's Bowl had locked their doors and barred their windows as for a siege, offering no welcome to visitors.

Morty was relieved to see Dido's trim little car drawn up by the portico of The Hollies but as he approached the garden room his spirits began to wilt and he found his heart beating uncomfortably. Mr Lugg greeted him with a conspiratorial grin.

''Er ladyship will receive you shortly,' he announced. 'And I might add that I think you're going to be lucky. My Mr C is comin' down this afternoon and 'e seems to 'ave told 'er that you're not the 'orrible Carsonoma that you make out. You're to stay for luncheon which will be served out of a lot of very classy tins.'

Dido, emerging unexpectedly from the garden with a sheaf of early delphiniums, found them deep in a discussion on bachelor cooking. She was wearing a white blouse with trousers of saxe blue linen and her hair shone like a blackbird's wing.

162

'The patient has recovered, I see,' she said formally. 'One of my swifter cures. No headaches, I hope?'

'None, lady, none. The marks under my eyes are simply visible signs of my anxiety for your safety. I get bad dreams but that's my private terror complex. Campion says not to worry but I can't play it so cool....'

'Forget it,' she said and put out a hand. 'This is a holiday. My official week off from the rota.'

He held her at arm's length, surveying her from head to toe.

'Anything you say. Just stand there just as you are and let me get my breath. If your week turns out to be a century that will be too short for me.'

It was an idyllic morning. A cuckoo shouted from the copse beyond and was answered by an echo from inland. From the road behind the high brick wall came the occasional rattle of a motor cycle, but the garden remained a remote sunlit arbour unconcerned with the passing parade.

Mr Campion arriving late in the afternoon found them asleep on cushions and Edwardian travelling rugs on a lawn which was beginning to show respectful signs of Lugg's handiwork.

He left them silently and applied himself to the telephone in his bedroom, comforting himself with the thought that no young woman could retain such limpid perfection even in her dreams without a certain amount of forethought. Morty, it was clear had made a deeper impression than he supposed.

His six calls brought him no comfort and he descended to the tinkle of teacups punctuated by the ripple of Dido's laughter. Mr Lugg, another of her willing slaves, had decided that an Edwardian tea party was fitting, and had produced a three tier 'curate's friend' cake stand which supported small triangular sandwiches of cress and paté.

'No silver teapot,' he announced regretfully. 'It's been 'ocked or nicked or given away, I suppose. Below stairs spoons, too, but the china's O.K. Came out of one of the knick-knack cases. . . .'

He paused disapprovingly as a passing motor cycle drowned his words. 'And that's another item which is not the article, if you take me. Very mackaber. Ton-up kids wearing voodoo masks. They're 'orrible enough themselves, without that.'

'Masks?' enquired Mr Campion mildly. 'Did you say voodoo masks?'

'That's exackly what I said.' Mr Lugg was forthright. 'Like those shrunken heads which are just the job for making the parlour look 'omely when you come back from a luxury cruise to central Africa. You can get 'em at any shop when you 'appen to be laying in yer stock of itchin' powder, green deformed 'ands, vampire's teeth and what not. Only these 'appen to be more Chinese tiger type.'

'Or Demon style?'

'Young demons 'ell bent on 'aving a kick-up at The Demon, I shouldn't wonder. If I was you, Mr Kelsey, I'd give your 'otel a miss until they've gone.'

'The trouble with a mask,' said Mr Campion, 'is that the face behind it can be any age you like. Who's to tell? I think Lugg has a point there, you know.'

Mob's Bowl was having one of those days which Ned Ward, the London spy, would have recognised as belonging to his own age. Londoners flooding out to the coast to catch the holiday sun were seeping like a tide into every byway and The Demon, as the last hostelry on a road which ended at its doorstep, caught a large share of the trade. Sandwiches and the celebrated cakes disappeared by battalions, washed down with beer more easily measured by the barrel than the pint. By midday the narrow road from Forty Angels was blocked with cars unable to turn and only cyclists infiltrating by footpaths could reach the inn or the sea wall, except by abandoning transport and proceeding afoot.

Dixie, working with concentrated skill and apparently inexhaustible energy, was not happy. Money was pouring in but the total occupation of the house by apparently militant youths dressed in what looked like uniforms cast off by S.S. troopers or Austrian Hussars made her nervous and at moments actively frightened. The rockers, who by definition ride more powerful machines than mods and who make a display of living dangerously, had established themselves in the main bar shortly after noon and occupied it exclusively by strong arm tactics, so that less forceful customers crammed the Snug and passed refreshments by hand to those outside.

The masks, evidently agreed upon in advance as the smart wear of the day, produced their quota of sensation, for the designer had avoided the accepted pantomime convention of wickedness and created a face with narrow oblong eyes, wisps a horsehair for a Capricorn beard and a mouth of the same cruel shape outlined in scarlet. Stripes of yellow and black like tribal markings scored the cheeks. The intentionally shocking quality was increased by the modernity of the presentation of mindless wickedness which yet had echoes of the ancient pit.

There was no doubt of their success in creating an atmosphere of dangerous uncertainty, but the heat of the day cut the triumph short. The penalty for wearing such an emblem of terror for more than a few minutes in a close atmosphere is a suffocating bath of perspiration and the denial of refreshment. Having achieved their purpose the owners either pushed them to the tops of their heads or discarded them altogether.

A police van, a uniformed motor cyclist and an official car had arrived before noon and the vehicles were prominently parked in front of the inn. Embarrassed and impotent, the occupants sat with apparent indifference whilst the revellers danced invitingly around them, resuming their masks for the purpose. It was a display of defiance, half comic and half menacing. Discomfited Authority is always a delight to holidaymakers and the free entertainment was received with relish.

Sergeant Throstle having taken stock of the situation

muscled his way into the main bar and drank a pint of warm beer with rather less opposition than he had secretly hoped. He took mental notes of those he recognised, but since he himself was known to several of the customers, his eavesdropping was limited to well chosen insults aimed at him from a safe distance. Presently he retired discreetly to the sail lofts and ensconced himself in the comfortable but unpleasantly warm eyrie of the lantern. The lookout point of Harry Morgan had been wisely chosen. With his glasses he could pick out every detail of the anchored shipping, admire the figures of the water skiers from across the estuary who careened around them and count the crews of small yachts with billowing multicoloured spinnakers far out to sea. Bathers along the sea wall defied the mud and struggled out into the flat water. Inland, the narrow neck of road to Forty Angels was clearing and picnickers dozed amongst their papers and bottles on the verge. A concentrated roar of engines from the ground closer to him caught his attention and he leaned forward counting heads as the invading army departed as noisly as it had arrived.

He followed its progress across the saltings and finally lost it as it vanished like a swarm of angry bees heading towards Nine Ash. A dancing curtain of heat hung over the further hamlet and for a long time there was no human movement. Presently Throstle eased his body on the straw padded sacking which covered his perch, stretched himself and fell deeply asleep.

He was awakened by a clang above his head which startled him into a cold sweat and made his ear drums dither. The second sound, that of a stone rattling and sliding down the corrugated iron roof just below him, explained the cause and he jerked himself forward in an effort to discover the origin of the missile. From the forecourt of The Demon a group of picnickers and a solitary policeman were looking curiously in his direction and he watched grimly as the man in his blue official shirt set out to discover the disturber of the peace. The search was careful enough but plainly fruitless for it was impossible to guess the direction from which the stone had come and each caravan, tent, shack or abandoned boat offered cover for a marksman.

Throstle descended from his perch and made his way towards the uniformed man. He was not the local P.C. Simmonds but the young mobile officer who had remained after the main party had left.

'Any luck?' he enquired.

The youth shook his head. 'A skylarking kid, I reckon. Makes a din, that old weathercock. You want a good eye to hit it.'

Throstle nodded towards the police cycle with its shining aerial parked by the inn. 'Are you in touch with Nine Ash on that thing?'

'Just about—it's only short range. If you're interested in the tearaways they headed off towards Maldon and Mersea. Inspector Branch said to tell you if I saw you. He thinks they may come back.'

The long twilight of late May did not bring peace to The Hollies for after sundown the roaring rattle of motor cycles began again and the trees beyond the walled garden flickered into spasms of unnatural detail as the turning headlights took the corner on their way to the Bowl. With nightfall came a small, chill wind which shivered the last of the may blossom to the grass and brought wisps of shouting and laughter across the saltings. An occasional rocket swept into the air to burst in a plume of stars and the erratic banging of squibs and small fireworks added their quota to the atmosphere of discomfort and unease. The Bowl, whether it had been invited or not, was having a party on its doorstep. Nearer at hand even the Angel was having a share of custom but the barrackroom quality of its welcome did not encourage visitors to a second drink.

Dido and her guests ate a cold meal almost without conversation in the formidable mahogany-laden dining room. The drop in temperature had wiped out the day's magic and Mr

Campion after his afternoon with the telephone sat with one ear directed towards a bell which refused to ring in reply. His face was drawn as if the lines about his mouth and forehead had decided to become permanent. They drank coffee in the garden room where with twilight the scent of eucalyptus had become heavier. The table had been spread with a map of the eastern suburbs on which he had traced in blue pencil the western end of the ancient route linking Saltey with the original Mob's Hole at Wanstead.

Beyond this, towards Stratford, Hackney and Ilford as far as Islington, the area was spattered with small crosses whose meaning he did not explain beyond saying vaguely. 'All drinking pools, you know. Every wild animal drinks somewhere, sooner or later. The trouble is, there is such a hell of a lot of them.'

The wail of a siren like the melancholy warning of wartime air raids came distantly to the group and instinctively they turned their heads in the direction.

'The fire station at Firestone,' said Morty. 'They make that noise to alert part time members. I wonder what's cooking?'

Mr Lugg's voice from inside the house but above their heads brought news. 'A tidy little blaze out at the Bowl. I'd say. Come up 'ere and take a dekko. Might be the sail lofts by the look of it.'

Morty caught Dido by the shoulder. 'Nothing to do with us,' he said. 'You'll stay right here. If you want a view go and watch from a bedroom, but no joining the fun tonight. What do you say, Campion?'

'I? Oh, I agree. Probably too many spectators already. All the same, I think I shall add to their number. You never know who may be helping on an occasion like this.'

He slipped quietly into the garden and disappeared among the shrubs and trees beyond, evidently making for a door in the wall which was normally kept locked.

Towards the Bowl the sky was ominously red and flames were lighting the low clouds which had gathered unnoticed since sundown. Morty and Dido stood by the landing window at the head of the staircase.

'Not the sail lofts,' he said at last. 'Not the church either. I can pick them out. It must be this side of The Demon—the cottages, perhaps.'

Mr Lugg descended breathily from the attic, an enormous pair of binoculars slung round his neck.

'Matt Parsley's coffin shop, what used to be. Gorn up a fair treat. Tide's out too. They'll have a job putting the dampers on that old box of shavings.' He turned his head. ''Ere comes the engine. Reminds me of my old days in the 'eavy rescue squad. Lovely work when you could get it.'

The clamour of the bell swept to a crescendo as the engine roared past the house and swayed gallantly on its way to the Bowl. The exciting sound continued for a few moments and then ceased in a final desultory clang. A screech of brakes was borne on the wind.

A more discreet ringing within the house, drowned by the urgent warning on the road, suddenly became dominant and Morty made a move to the hall.

'Telephone. I'll take it. It may be for Campion.'

Lugg had forestalled him, standing by the receiver in his best upper servant manner and speaking with an unctuous refinement which was ephemeral.

'The 'Ollies 'ere. Dr Jones' residence. Can I 'elp you? Oh ... I get you. ... Well, 'ang on, cock, and I'll see what I can do for yer.'

He placed a hand on the mouthpiece and turned to Dido who was half way down the stairs.

'It's the police, miss. Simmonds the local nark by the sound of 'im. Shall I tell 'im to bung off?'

Dido took the instrument and waved them away. When she returned her manner was determined and professional.

'A man has been hurt down at the Bowl,' she said. 'They think he may have broken something. I'm on my way.'

*

The fire in the ugly black shed which had served so many generations of carpenters, wheelwrights, boat builders and coffin makers marked the peak of a riotous evening, in which temper and hysteria had fought mindlessly for the upper hand. With the return of the Demons in their masks the demarcation line between friend and enemy had been clearly drawn. In the saloon of the inn the invaders, arriving in a body, attempted to repeat their tactics of the morning, but on this occasion the reception committee was organised and formidable. A dozen youths waiting for trouble faced as many as were looking for it.

After a few minutes' uneasy silence the storm broke. A fire cracker tossed between the two sides leaped and spluttered like an animated gauntlet, an insult which called for satisfaction.

For a moment or two a tense almost stilted formality hung over the room. When the squib had made its final kick the captain of the Saltey darts team, a bullnecked giant with red hair and a virile display of side whiskers, walked from his corner towards the masked figure whom he suspected of issuing the challenge.

'I don't think much to that,' he observed and swung a hammer fist to the offender's jaw.

A police whistle blown piercingly just outside the room added its oddly appropriate note, as if the film director of a thirty year old western had taken charge and a generation reared on the tradition of such bar room battles rushed to share in the pandemonium. Behind the shouting and the breaking of glass the curious high pitched scream of youth enjoying its lack of inhibition made a background of light headed frenzy.

The resentment of the local men against the possessive arrogance of invading strangers had reached the point of no return. Each man sought out his opposite number, happily determined to repay months of calculated insult.

The fight in the bar itself was brief but destructive. Dixie's first shout had brought the professional henchmen into action.

They moved into the melée with the vigour of rugby forwards, seizing the brawlers without favour, and a group of four policemen who were forcing their way in found themselves presented with struggling partisans gripped from behind but still hitting and kicking at any target offered. One by one the contestants were flung into the forecourt where the fighting continued as if it had never been interrupted.

With the doors of The Demon locked and bolted the larger arena presented greater problems to the uniformed men and the illusion of total war was increased by the clattering of football rattles and banging of squibs which were flung towards them at each attempt to break up a scuffle.

Lesser spirits straddled their motor cycles, roaring the engines, darting venomously in and out of the groups, flashing their headlights into the eyes of all who stood or struggled in their path. Stones rattled against the wooden walls of the inn and windows splintered.

The fire in Parsley's coffin shop passed unremarked until it was well under way. A tongue of flame streaked out from beneath the pantiled roof and a long barn door fell outwards with a crash followed by a gust of smoke and sparks. The effect was as dramatic as a gong which ends the deciding round in a prize fight for the sudden draught gave the blaze all the force it needed to become a furnace.

The shed stood on the landward side of the road and directly faced the sail lofts. Beyond it lay the straggling range of brick and weatherboard cottages which made up most of the Bowl. Here was the communal danger which overrode minor enmities. Police and local supporters took in the fact without hesitation and the invaders found themselves abandoned. They stood together in groups watching the new entertainment, shouting, jeering, waiting for the next mischief that offered. Excited girls twittering like early morning starlings flocked round those of their heroes who had been visibly injured, but the focus of attention was on the fire which leaped and crackled into the night sky.

The body of a youth from Firestone named Alfie Binns had lain beside a car in the forecourt for some time before it was remarked. He lay very still, his quick shallow breath hardly moving the strands of hair which covered his mouth, and one leg was twisted unnaturally beneath him. It was Dixie, who had been organising a chain of buckets from the back of the inn where there was a working pump who found him and for a terrifying moment she wondered if he were dead. She knelt beside him feeling for a pulse and leaned back to call to the hovering figure of her husband some paces away.

'He's hurt pretty bad. Get a blanket. Get a policeman. Get a doctor. Look sharp about it—we mustn't move him.'

She was still beside him twenty minutes later when Dido appeared escorted by Morty.

In the meantime the fire had reached its zenith and the brigade, arriving to discover that a single pond was their main source of water, were working desperately to keep the blaze to the doomed shed. In and out and round about the Demons danced and jeered, flinging more water on themselves than on the flames.

The night's mischief was suited to their mood and the excitement was more intoxicating than the little grey blue pills which purchased only evanescent thrills.

The group around the prostrate figure watched Dr Jones warily as she made her examination. Finally she stood up, brushing her hands together.

'Fractured tibia, I'm afraid. Probably caused by a kick. And he's concussed, meaning that he's had a nasty crack on the skull as well. We must get him away. Ambulance?'

P.C. Simmonds smirked. 'All arranged, miss. Should be here any minute. I phoned for it when I found I couldn't get a doctor—I mean when Dr Thornton couldn't . . .' His voice trailed away and in the flickering light his face showed a brick red. 'I mean before you came along to give a hand.'

It was towards midnight before any member of the party

could relax. The ambulance had come and gone. Parsley's shed had subsided into smoking ruins: the revellers had lost interest and vanished into the chilly darkness.

Dido, Dixie and Morty sat exhausted in the kitchen of The Demon which faced on to the stable yard.

'It's better here, ducks,' their hostess explained. 'No one to watch us for one thing and the windows are still all there.' She dispensed whisky in generous tots. 'What a night! Makes poor old H.O.'s book look like a kid's fairy tale. Perhaps I could get him to add a chapter about it.'

Morty kept a protective arm round Dido's chair. 'Where is he, by the way?'

He was answered by the appearance of the poet who opened the passage door and stood beside it, his face very white beneath black smudges of soot. He was out of breath and shaking violently. He leaned for a moment against the lintel and then collapsed on to a bench by the table. Dixie moved over to him like an anxious hen but he waved her away.

'I'm not drunk,' he said. 'But in a state of shock. The act of burglary brings with it a sense of insult—a personal affront. I find it very disturbing.' He looked up and spoke directly to Dido. 'Would you agree to that, Dr Jones? It is the impact on the mind, not the deed itself which destroys the balance.'

She nodded. 'Certainly. The unexpected is always shocking. But you said burglary? Where?'

'Right beneath your feet, madame.'

'In the cellar?' said Dixie. 'But there's nothing to steal. Have those wretched tearaways been ... Oh, come on, H.O. dear. Don't keep us waiting.'

The poet knotted his forehead. He was very near nervous exhaustion and he ran the fingers of both hands through his coarse grey mop of hair before he answered.

'The cellar. Quite senseless and wanton.' He turned to Morty. 'You've never been down to it, of course. It is damp, uncomfortable and too low to stand up in. We use it only for the draft barrels and for storing idiotic possessions which we are too idle to destroy. It has been broken into, two barrels have been emptied and a hole has been smashed in one of the walls. A silly ignorant thing to do, even for children crazed with drugs or drink.'

Morty interrupted him. 'I don't get it. You said a wall had been smashed. What's on the other side of it? A secret passage or something?'

The old man sighed wearily. 'It's nothing of any significance today. It was a secret of sorts in the time of my predecessors. Beyond the wall, which is only the thickness of a brick, is another cellar which is perhaps a foot deeper. It is useless because it is inclined to flood at high tides. It may have been valuable once for hiding smuggled goods and it has a separate entrance, under this very floor, a trap door which is never used. But not even a rat could make a home there. Yet someone— someone who knew it was there—broke his way into it this very evening. A mad world, my masters.'

Dixie, who had armed herself with a torch, bustled away to inspect the damage. When she returned her face was pink with fury.

'The young brutes,' she exploded. 'Two whole barrels of best bitter gone to waste and a mess like you never did see. I'll give 'em Demons. Not another single one of them sets foot in this place again. If Simmonds weren't such a hopeless ape I'd...' She paused as a new idea occurred to her. 'It must have been done whilst we were away at the fire. That's the first time the place has been empty for years. I left the scullery door so that the men could get to the pump.'

Mr Campion was waiting for Dido and Morty when they returned to The Hollies. They had driven back in her tiny car past the damp skeleton of the shed, past darkened caravans and through the silent street of the Bowl where not even a cat moved.

He came to the door at the precise moment when Morty was speculating on his chances of attempting a farewell embrace and deciding that the situation was too hackneyed to risk disaster.

'Lugg is brewing cocoa,' he remarked. 'But perhaps some thing a little stronger is in order. I prescribe tea, myself. Very soothing after the return of the Demon to these parts. Quite a day for the memoirs.'

They poured out their news to him in the garden room and he listened gravely.

'Very interesting. Significant too, as the man said when he heard the last trump. As it happens I can add a couple of items. You didn't, I suppose, drop into the church during the course of the evening? I know it's supposed to be kept locked— a very wise precaution considering the state of the roof—but the vestry door at the back is remarkably insecure and no match for a man of my determination.'

He surveyed them over his glasses before continuing. 'No? The place has had a visitor, the same intruder, perhaps, who smashed down H. O. Wishart's cellar wall. Almost certainly the same crowbar would be needed. Two tombs in the lady chapel have been opened very unskilfully and an engraved flagstone has been prised away from the centre aisle just below the altar steps.'

'Goddam vandals,' said Morty. 'Not that they could do real damage there. There's not much of interest. The Lady Margaret tomb—fourteenth century—and Jonathan Woodrose, gentlemen, seventeen hundred and two?'

'As you say. And in the aisle Jeptha Kytie, vicar and benefactor, Jessica his wife, James and Enoch his sons with Jennifer Honiton, his beloved daughter, laid to rest between 1784 and 1810. By the way, there was nothing unexpected in any of the tombs, if you exclude a mummified cat, and I don't think there has been for many years—if ever.'

'An organised search, though,' said Dido. 'What were they looking for? Treasure?'

Mr Campion considered. 'You could call it that, I suppose,' he said at last. 'But it's a little word I don't care to use at the moment. Whatever it was they didn't find it, for the simple reason that it wasn't there. The searcher wouldn't have gone on to the Demon if he'd found what he was looking for. We know pretty well when the cellar was raided—the fire gives the time within the hour. The church could have been desecrated any time in the last week or two as far as I can see because nobody has been there officially since Easter. The fire may have been arranged to create a diversion for the raid on the inn. Again whoever it was didn't find what he wanted.'

'Why so?'

'Because,' said Mr Campion with authority, 'of the wanton damage to the barrels. It's a commonplace reaction on the part of a thief if he's disappointed. Ask any policeman. A man who gets what he wants generally removes his traces and skips away like the wind. What a pity I didn't keep an eye on The Demon tonight. I spent far too much time observing who was helping and who was hindering the valiant men of the fire brigade.'

He sighed and sipped his tea. 'Oh, well; a nice long day tomorrow, *mes enfants.*'

'Just a minute,' said Morty. 'You're holding out on us. You said "a couple of items". What's the second?'

The thin man eyed them owlishly.

'The second item is a matter for me alone. It's no real concern of yours and you will please put it in the top-secret-burn-before-reading class. An old friend of mine called Stanislaus Oates who has been helping me in my enquiries, as he would say, telephoned half an hour ago. He has located the elusive Mr James Teague.'

16

Twenty Years After

THE retired Assistant Commissioner was remarkably pleased with himself. He sat beside Mr Campion whom he had just joined as they drove sedately through the secondary streets which lie between Islington and Walston and gave directions on the route with appropriate pride.

'Turn left at the next launderette opposite the Bingo Hall, then right at the Home Bonus Self Service and take the left hand fork at Honest Bob Eachways betting shop. Not your sort of area, my lad, but you'd be surprised at what goes on if you lift the lid. This is Ramsden Lane where an old woman called Mother Carey kept a snake farm. The whole house was full of 'em, cobras, pythons, boa constructors, everything you've ever seen in a zoo. She walked off one fine summer morning and never came back. The sanitary people got on to it in the end and they had the devil's own job to clear the place because the creatures had got under the floor boards, into the roof and into every cupboard and wainscote. The last thing she did before she vanished was to set them free and it was six weeks before the matter was even reported.

'Ron the Rajah lived two doors up, just above the Chinese Expresso. A very good forger, specialising in foreign currency and doing his business with coloured people. He did five years for his trouble and died a rich man.

'The hole in the ground is where the old Imperial used to be. Almost the last of the Halls apart from Collins. They found out too late that it ought to have been preserved as a national memorial to the good old days but they kept the pub next door. That's where we're going.'

'The Cap and Bells?'

'That's it. A Victorian masterpiece, so they say Four different bars—and a couple of cubby holes where you poke your face through little glass windows to ask for your drink, though why that should make it respectable I don't know. Pull up further along beside the radio shop.'

The Private Saloon of the big red brick hostelry was a small, eminently correct cubicle, upholstered in red leather and decorated with cut glass advertisements for long forgotten brands of spirits: McNab's Dew of Kirkcudbright and Auld Laird Malt Special.

At this early hour on Sunday evening it was a quiet family place where elderly couples sat together gossiping placidly. Time appeared to be standing still and the newcomers were observed without comment. The sound of children drifted in from the street for the doors were open to the warm city air.

'Better settle for a long one,' muttered Oates. 'We may have quite a wait ahead of us. This is going to cost you a packet. Time and a half and all expenses, you said.'

'I feared as much,' said his companion. 'How many men did you have on it?'

Oates smiled reminiscently. 'After it occurred to you that I might still be useful,' he said, 'I had six—all ex-officers from Foxy Foster's bureau. You wouldn't know him but he used to be a Super in S Branch. Then I added two old pals from Records and a couple of women who retired years ago to get married. Quite a team if you include me as the brains of the act. You know, Albert, I've enjoyed this enquiry—it was quite a challenge. We old 'uns can still teach the boys a thing or two—especially when it's a money-no-object job. You can't ask men to comb every pub on a list of two or three hundred and not take a drink. If you do they'll be rumbled straight away. That's the advantage a private firm like Fosters has over the regulars.'

'That, and of course brilliant direction from a real expert.'

The old man snorted. 'It was just putting all the available evidence together and it was precious thin on the ground let me tell you. Man of sixty odd, woman forty fivish, possibly a pro in her time, a woman who could have been dressing "old fashioned". Apparently because of modern styles women of that class sometimes do—it puts older men at their ease, gives them confidence that they are not going to be snubbed or made to look like silly old goats. Then again, this disappearance was prearranged, very carefully planned indeed by someone who had taken a lot of trouble to think it out. I think you'll find that our man has a well established identity—probably in the name of someone who's dead or gone overseas, so that he has all his health cards stamped and in order. That gave us a woman with a genuine background, probably quite a respectable one, a woman who very likely owns a small car—Teague must have gone by car when he disappeared—someone who prepared the way by announcing that her brother or uncle or cousin was going to join her from up North or wherever you please, so there's no surprise locally and very little gossip when the new lodger appears. It narrows the field quite a bit.'

He eyed Campion respectfully over his half finished pint. 'Your idea helped, of course, but it was still the leg work that produced the result.'

'Skipper?'

'That was a long shot of yours, but it paid off. Yes, he's called the Skipper, because he talks about boats, just as you said. I haven't seen him myself, mark you, but the identification is pretty positive. Sergeant Openshaw, one of Foxy's men, found him. The woman's name is Medway, by the way, Mrs Rita Medway, and her new brother in-law calls himself Connor which suggests that he bought his papers from an Irishman. It's pretty nearly exactly what we expected.'

He sighed. 'That's the end of the trail as far as I'm concerned. A pity. I enjoyed what there was of it. I'll just stay to see you make your contact. You wouldn't care to take me...'

Mr Campion shook his head regretfully. 'If he spotted you he'd recognise an old enemy and he'd get me confused with the police, which is the last thing I want. My chat with him has got to be friendly or it defeats its own purpose. You did say your man thought he was a regular here?'

'Most evenings, he said. They have a couple of doubles, a bit of a chat with the governor and a few old cronies and go off early. It doesn't sound like Teague, I admit, but our chap is quite certain. He smokes like a gaolbird, too—keeps the fag end turned into the palm of his hand, which is a habit you find difficult to break after twenty years.'

The main saloon with its ornate Victorian carving, formal plastered ceiling and gleaming cut glass panels was beginning to fill. The little bar in which they stood was protected from prying eyes by a grille of square decorative glass windows moving on swivels so that an order could be given in complete privacy from the general public and the drink pushed discreetly beneath the barrier. It provided a perfect screen for an observer and presently Oates who had been keeping one eye on an opening caught his companion's arm.

'They've just come in,' he said. 'The woman in the green scarf. That's Teague with her all right.' He stood aside to let Campion move closer. 'I think you're in for a shock.'

The first impression of the man in the blue reefer suit which no longer fitted him was that he was nearer seventy than sixty. He was standing beside the bar and as the landlord produced two glasses he carried them very slowly to one of the small tables against the upholstered wall benches where a woman was waiting. A black beret hid most of his forehead but the stiff hair beneath it was white and there was a trimmed stubble around his mouth which was nearly a beard.

Steel-rimmed government spectacles with a strong magnification gave his eyes the appearance of staring blankly and he blinked continually as if he found the light too strong. Only the genuine flash of very white teeth gave an indication that there had once been strength and ruthlessness where only their ghosts remained.

The woman in the scarf beside him, a bravely unfading

blonde with unfashionably red lips, sat erect, emphasising her companion's stoop, defiantly protective, her eyes flickering cautiously over the customers.

Mr Campion shook himself.

'Not a good advertisement for our prison system,' he murmured. 'But it goes deeper than that, I think. He looks to me like a chap who's given up, retired, lost interest in life. He could also be afraid. The fact that he's torn up his ticket and changed his name could explain that, of course, but he certainly looks like a non-starter to me. What do you think?'

The ex-A.C. shrugged his shoulders.

'A long term does that to men sometimes. No one's proud of it, but it happens. Go round and have your word with him. You know, I think I'll wait and keep an eye on you, just in case.'

Mr Campion left his companion and made an unobtrusive approach to the table in the further bar. He drew up a chair apparently by chance with the merest inference of an apology at the intrusion and sat for some time sipping whisky without interest in the two who were facing him. Finally he leaned across and spoke directly.

'Skipper Connor?'

Suspicion chased by anger flashed across the woman's face and she placed a thin hand with blood red fingernails over the man's wrist.

'We don't know you. What's your game?'

Mr Campion turned to her. 'It's Mrs Medway, isn't it? I'm not a policeman, not even a friend from the past. I think you could describe me as a negotiator—a man with a proposition. I'm prepared to pay for the information I need. The sum I had in mind is very large.'

A sudden impish smile flickered across the man's mouth and for an instant it was possible to glimpse the charm and the force which had withered. The spark faded as swiftly as it had appeared, leaving the face cold and expressionless.

'You're wrong, you know. You're dead wrong. I've nothing to sell.'

'Leave him alone, you bastard,' said the woman. 'We don't like your sort. If you won't go then we will.' She stood up. 'We'll go now.'

'Not for a minute.' Mr Campion's tone was unemotional. 'Skipper, I'm talking about the barge *Blossom*. One question. One answer. A small fortune in any form you like and no strings attached.'

The man in the beret sighed. He was looking at Campion as if he saw him from a distance.

'The barge *Blossom*,' he repeated slowly. 'Do you know, mister, that for twenty years people have been asking me about that God-forsaken hulk? Men in nice suits, men in suits they'd only just changed into because they wanted to pretend they weren't officials, screws, con men, big timers, water rats, the whole crew. I've seen the inside of every interview room from the Moor to Parkhurst, from the Governor's cabin to a cell that looked and stank like the heads in a Greek tramp. Always the same question.'

'And always the same answer?'

'Too bloody true, mister. Always the same answer. I never saw the *Blossom* in my life so far as I know and I certainly never sailed her. Why do you think I'm hiding like a rat with a pack of yard dogs sniffing after me? Because I never want to hear the blasted name again.'

'You could name a price. No string attached.'

'Not for a Chinese harem or the Crown Jewels. I don't know a goddam thing, and that's for free. Ask Rita and she'll tell you.'

Mr Campion turned towards her. 'For ten thousand pounds?' he murmured. 'It's a lot of money, I would have thought.'

The woman drew a deep breath, closing her eyes and leaning hard against the shining leather.

'He doesn't know a thing,' she muttered. 'He's just a

damned old fool without the price of a light to his name.'

Gradually her tension slackened and she put up a hand to primp her hair. A smile which was sly and confiding crept across her mouth showing teeth which were smeared with lipstick.

'You've lost your bet, dear. They all have. Now sing for your supper and get us a couple of drinks. Sid knows what we want.'

Mr Campion returned to the smaller bar feeling old and melancholy. The elderly couples had disappeared and Oates was sitting in a corner by himself, his deplorable grey felt hat on the table beside a glass of overbright port. He looked up as the thin man came in and the wrinkles in his forehead were quizzical.

'You did yourself no good? I was afraid of that. Teague's got old and tired like the rest of us. He'll go no more aroving as the song says. Did he tell you that?'

'Just about. In almost as many words. Were you watching the proceedings?'

'I kept half an eye on you.'

'And the other? Something is amusing you. Never laugh at a comrade's downfall. It's a punishable offence in the Navy and considered very bad taste even in the police force.'

Oates raised his glass and sipped it thoughtfully as if he was considering whether to share a private joke.

'I couldn't resist it.' he said at length. 'It's sheer habit I suppose—idle curiosity now. But I recognised the landlord of this joint. He's Sid Lowenstein, a man who's had a bit of wife trouble in his time. You can hear him quarrelling with the present one now—she's the fifth—without straining your ears. Just as a matter of private interest I eliminated a suspect in the case of the death of Hector Askew down at Saltey.'

'Teague?'

The older man nodded. 'Teague of the silver bullet. Sid's a very reliable witness, especially in a matter which doesn't concern him. Askew was killed on a Saturday just over a fortnight ago. On that day Teague, or the Skipper as he calls him, and his girl friend were here just after half past five. He remembers it because he does a little bookmaking on the side and they'd won quite a packet on the Kempton meeting—twelve quid to be exact. It puts him out of the running. If you want to know my opinion and I admit you haven't asked for it. I'll tell you.'

'Go ahead, by all means.'

'It's straightforward logic when you consider the facts. Someone who knows Master Teague's handwriting is forging his signature, copying his style, just to lead you on a wild goose chase. It explains why that mysterious wallet of his turned up so conveniently, for one thing. Has that occurred to you?'

Mr Campion sighed. 'It has now,' he said. 'In fact it's been occurring to me for some time. So don't demobilise your forces just yet. There's some unfinished business to be handled if you're still in the old war horse mood. Teague may be a busted flush—he was pretty convincing—but the woman knows something, or she thinks she does. Can you find out *all* about her, how she's living, who pays the rent and who her visitors are? She isn't the fairy godmother type so someone has invested money in keeping that poor old pirate out of the limelight.'

Ex-Assistant Commissioner Stanislaus Oates rose to his feet.

'Just what I was thinking myself,' he said. He looked about him. 'You know, Albert, I don't like this place. It's all very fine in its way, but somehow it's what I call sordid and the port is terrible. Come along, my lad. Drive me to St James's and I'll give you a drink at my Club.'

17

The Picture on the Wall

MR CAMPION found his ex-chief L. C. Corkran in the office in Killowen Square on the afternoon of Whit Monday. 'The Department', as he invariably called it, does not recognise Bank Holidays, for its connections are largely with countries who honour different feast days.

It was not a pleasant occasion for either man. When Morty had described 'Elsie' Corkran as commonplace close to but distinctive from a distance he had been remarkably shrewd, for across a desk the face suggested an officer who had served his country without achieving either seniority or character, whereas at twenty paces his precise white moustache and curling hair conveyed that he might be a doyen of diplomats or a Major General of cavalry. His voice was scholarly, clipped and completely colourless.

'It comes to this,' he said after hearing the recital of Campion's adventures. 'We are back to square one. Teague is not in the running as a lead and is quite prepared to die with his secret. One cannot, I suppose, blame him for his attitude. The rest of the riff-raff, as you depict them, seem to me to be small villains, stirring up trouble to see if they can force or frighten someone else into making an informative move. We appear to be in much the same position ourselves. Would it be fair to say that?'

Mr Campion who was always acutely reminded of long impersonal sessions in his tutor's rooms at Cambridge on occasions when he visited Killowen Square, took his time before replying.

'Not quite,' he said at last. 'The opposition is still unpleasantly active, but there are one or two untidy threads which may lead me out of the labyrinth. It's a question of time. How long have I got?'

'Days, rather than weeks, if I may misquote an ill-advised politican. Until dawn on Thursday to be precise. The transport problem can be overcome by using diplomatic cover but that is the last—the final limit when I can be sure of getting an aircraft and the right man as a courier. Provisionally it will be at Southend Airport from Tuesday night, awaiting instructions.' He hesitated with the flicker of a self-deprecatory smile. 'I took that chance. I hope it is justified.'

'You have news of Monique, then?'

The use of code names in the Department was designed for many reasons, but partly to reduce the personal element to a minimum. But the woman behind the old-fashioned pseudonym with its wartime echoes was nearer to being a personal friend than either man was prepared to admit. Acute danger was always conventionally discussed as a 'temporary difficulty' but the phrase did not conceal the terrifying anxiety it carried so lightly. Corkran made a pretence of looking at a folder on his desk, as if to refresh his memory.

'Only indirectly. Our man thinks she will be moved from her present captors at the end of the week. They are instructed to hand her over to central authority and they've held out as long as they dare because they're not sure of themselves. They also want the prestige of arresting her in case she talks. But a transfer to the big boys means new interrogations, different methods. Knowing her, I doubt if they would be successful, but we all have our breaking point. Unhappily, she has one of those damnable capsule things and she might—just might— use it. The difficulty, of course, is that a suicide like that always argues a professional. If one link is exposed and broken then the rest are too easy to identify. That could be rather unfortunate.'

He sighed. 'You know all this. Have you any suggestions at my end?'

Mr Campion was shocked. The man across the desk rarely

showed more emotion than a don correcting a mathematical exercise, but now he was pretending an indifference which was not convincing.

'There is something you can do—a long shot, I admit, but we can't afford to neglect it. Can you send me a mine detector and a man who knows how to work it?'

'Of course.' He had raised his eyebrows by the fraction of an inch at the suggestion. 'A mine detector? You have some particular area in mind, I hope. That house you're lodging in—The Hollies, isn't it?—has been gone over rather thoroughly by the police within the last fortnight because of the man who was killed there. They used an apparatus of that sort since there was some question of finding the offensive weapon. They covered the grounds, too. I took particular note of it at the time and sent for all the reports because the suggestion frightened me. It would have cut across our plans awkwardly had anything been found. The connection between the killing and the anonymous letters and the inferred "keep off" warning was rather too obvious for my taste, but if anything had been there it would have been found at that time. You have a fresh zone to explore?'

'I have an idea. The letters, by the way, were inspired by two other seekers after truth, but the lesser snake is scotched. I'm afraid the viper remains but he is probably more in the dark than we are. I can have my mine detector? When?'

Corkran glanced at the wall clock behind his visitor's head. 'Tomorrow morning will be the earliest, I'm afraid. You'll be down at that end-of-the-world hole to meet him?'

'I'm going there now,' said Mr Campion. 'Goodbye, Elsie.'

A conventional smile of farewell crossed the face which was so nearly handsome.

'*Quod petis hic est*, I hope,' he said. 'Good God, Albert, how out of date I sound. But it would be pleasant to retire knowing that one had slipped a final fast one past the New Establishment. I do not love its silly face.'

'Ora pro nobis,' said Mr Campion.

The traffic of a Bank Holiday which was dizzy with sunshine had turned the suburban streets into solid queues of frustration. Mr Campion sighed with relief when he reached the horrific area of Victorian-Arabian architecture which marked the start of the old road to Saltey. It was not easy to remember, but once mastered, the route for all its twists and deviations was uncannily free from obstruction. He drove slowly, a sense of guilt sitting uneasily between his shoulder blades. To offer false hope to a man in Corkran's state of mind was unforgivable but the gesture had to be made, because of the remote chance, the last stone which had to be turned.

He quartered the problem from every direction, putting himself in the place of each of the protagonists in turn. Finally he returned to himself. There was something which he had missed, an idle thought which had sneaked up on him when he was half awake and now refused to be recalled.

An ancient joke suggested by the cluttered furniture of his bedroom at The Hollies? The childhood memory of a great uncle booming dull anecdotes over a dining table to which he was admitted on sufferance in uncomfortable clothes? A faded picture framed in red velvet? An overblown Duchess opening a Bazaar, conjured by flowered wallpaper?

There were two vehicles standing in the awkward circular drive when he arrived at Saltey. Morty's Lotus and the dilapidated scooter which announced the presence of Mrs Weatherby.

She had discarded her working clothes for tailored tweeds which suggested that she might have arrived to pay a conventional call and she now sat upright in the big verandah chair facing the remains of another of Mr Lugg's delicate teas. Morty and Dido, a trifle exhausted by the energy which vibrated from her, were patently relieved to see him.

'Too bad you've missed the excitement,' she proclaimed. 'All hell's been popping whilst you've been away. You'll simply blow a gasket, my dear man, when you hear. These two good samaritans saved my life, or I don't know what I'd have done. The last phone box in the place has been smashed by vandals, or that's what the notice says, The Demon is impossible and if it weren't for the doctor I should never have got my story off. I was going to drop in for a chin-wag in any case, but when I saw the wires were connected to the house again, it was providential.'

'Times are hard for us poor pigeons,' said Mr Campion. 'There hasn't been another fire, I hope?'

'Nothing so ordinary. The trouble with a fire is that one can never get a scoop—too many people see it from a distance and cash in simply by ringing up the office from their bedrooms. They get a cut price and do honest journalists out of a job. No, this was a hot tip from an old pal. Mob's Bowl has been raided by the police and all the tearaways and rockers in the place have been rounded up and searched. The place has been literally buzzing with blue-bottles and black marias. What about that for a story?'

'Any arrests?'

'Several, I hope. It's so difficult to distinguish between an arrest and a detained-for-questioning, so we must all keep our fingers crossed. But I do know that they've found a lot of purple hearts and what d'you call 'ems—black bombers?—all over the shop. I picked up a paper bag full of them myself; found it lying on the grass by the churchyard. They're just like the pink cachous one used to eat as a child to take the smell of gin away. The police simply swarmed all over the Bowl so I suppose the smarter boys promptly threw them overboard when they scented trouble. Damned unsporting, but what can one expect?'

Mr Campion sipped lukewarm tea reflectively. 'You didn't recognise any familiar faces amongst the malefactors, I suppose?'

'Not a hope. The trouble is, all these children look exactly the same to me—like Chinese coolies, you know. Even their trousers seem to be patched in the same places. They chant and scream about freedom and then they wear a uniform which is as rigid as a subaltern's at a Trooping.' She stooped and brushed a shower of crumbs from her lap. 'I must trickle along now. If I drop in at the Cop-shop at Nine Ash they'll give me the gen about who's really been kept in the cooler. I'll see myself out. Goodbye, doctor, it was tophole of you to lend me the blower. Cheero, Morty.'

At the open glass door into the garden, she turned. 'Better luck next time, Mr Campion. Whenever you want a purple heart give me a buzz. What a jolly good room for summer weather this is, doctor. I don't blame you for living in it. Kitty Kytie always did. She had no taste, poor creature, but then none of that family ever had. Still, they made themselves comfortable and that's better than kicking yourself in the pants.'

Her departure did not slacken the tension since Morty and Dido were eager for news. Mr Campion was soothing but evasive. He sketched the scene at the Cap and Bells but omitted any account of the morning's interview.

'So James Teague is out of the picture,' he finished. 'His colleague, Mr Target Burrows, is still advertising his presence rather curiously, so for the moment any moonlight walks are out of the question. Tomorrow looks like being a long and possibly tedious day, so I shall retire early. Just at the moment I have some research to do in my bedroom.'

He left them abruptly.

The end of a Bank Holiday in the country is closely connected with the local closing time of the inns. For the Londoners nothing remains but the dull necessity to get home, to rest, to recuperate for the demands of the working week. By half past eleven Saltey was as silent and remote as if the city existed on a different continent. Morty had been dismissed with a friendly coolness which forboded a sleepless night and only the light in Dido's window indicated that she too was still awake.

Campion descended the stairs silently to discover his aide

brewing cocoa in the kitchen. Mr Lugg, in trousers topped by a string vest, lifted a steaming mug.

'Care for a drop?' he enquired. 'It does wonders for your slumber graph and stops you 'aving 'orrible dreams, whilst you're snorin' yerself stupid.'

'Not at the moment, if you'll forgive me. You and I have a little exploring to do. It may take some time so don't drink too much of that anaesthetic. If we have any luck what we'll both need is a nice stiff brandy.'

It was after two in the morning before Lugg made his final tour of the house, locking the outer doors, slipping bolts and checking window catches as he moved cautiously in the darkness.

In his bedroom Mr Campion undressed and sat for some time looking at the telephone which had a direct line to Killowen Square.

Finally he picked it up and was answered by the melancholy voice of the Duty Officer. He identified himself and was acknowledged.

'Gadsden here. The dog watchman.'

'What of the night? Elsie is no longer on the bridge, I take it?'

'Not since six bells. Can I take a message? I have one of these taping devices which I can play back so you needn't go over every point twice. I'll stop you if I don't understand.'

'Very commendable. Will you please say to him that I would now like to add to my mine detector a lot of surveying equipment, a theodolite and surveyor's level, tripods, poles and so forth and link measuring tapes. I want to make an impressive show. Two good operators and two drivers—four in all. I want tough boys who could look like council employees. And two vans or trucks, decently anonymous. Today is Tuesday, just. They'll be away for a couple of nights or until dawn on Thursday morning. Dawn on Thursday is a deadline which will be understood.'

'It's more than I do. Anything else?'

'Yes. Half a dozen cases of champagne. That is not a joke, though it has a certain irony. Krug '59 would do very nicely. Got that?'

'Every word of it. Having a party?'

'You could put it that way. Tell Elsie that among other things—say *"inter alia"* for his benefit—I am hoping to exorcise a ghost. Refer him to the gospel according to St Matthew, Chapter 24 verse 28.'

The voice at the other end of the line sounded depressed.

'The Bible is in the Code Room which is locked at this hour. Do I need to look it up?'

'Don't bother,' said Mr Campion. 'Let him do his own research.'

CARGO OF EAGLES

18

The Tethered Goat

T HERE is an especial quality about the first working day
of a new week in any village which suffers from urban
visitors, a communal sigh which whispers 'Now we are ourselves again'. On Tuesday morning in Mob's Bowl this spirit of
relief from siege was abroad. Greetings at chance encounters
were warm, the baker did excellent business in cakes and gossip and the Salt Street Stores which sold everything from lobster
pots to synthetic cheese and backache pills was comfortably
crowded.

Even the sprinkling of early holidaymakers taking the sun
outside their bright tents and caravans seemed to relish the
sensation of superiority over the ephemeral London starlings
whose paper and carton refuse still scampered aimlessly up and
down the gutters.

Morty alone found no satisfaction in the occasion. Dido had
agreed to dine with him in Nine Ash but had made it clear
that she intended putting The Hollies in order by purchasing
new household equipment and that this task was not to be
shared. The idea that she intended to keep the house filled
him with misgivings. He was in no mood for his own work and
by eleven he wandered unconsoled and purposeless towards
the blackened ruins of the burnt out shed.

The arrival of two grey green 15 cwt. vans, whose anonymity
suggested officialdom in some workaday form, in front of
The Demon offered an excuse and he watched with rising
curiosity. Three young men emerged, large cheerful youths
in denims, in charge of a tow-haired leader whose jacket
was so patched and trimmed with leather that it could well
have been home made. Having conferred casually with his staff

he left them to unload a variety of equipment and made his way towards the single stump which marked where a lych gate had stood at the entrance to the churchyard. He was carrying a small board to which papers were clipped and he referred to them from time to time, taking measured paces, halting and retracing his steps.

Finally he called to his assistants.

'O.K. Wonderboy. Starting from here. Bring us the poles and the number four quad.'

Morty knew very little of the mysteries of surveying but the opportunity to waste time by watching men at work was not to be resisted. He strolled across, accompanied now by various idlers equally intent on enjoying the prospect. The young men drove black and white metal poles into the ground, measured distances and calculated angles with a theodolite. They were in high spirits, shouting incomprehensible slang phrases as they worked but their purpose remained obscure. After a conference they concentrated their attention on the furthest corner of the enclosure where coarse grass and cowparsley concealed everything but the tallest headstones. A mine detector looking remarkably like a vacuum cleaner was carried from one of the vans and an area marked out by pegs and tape was covered inch by inch. It provided a mystery in which none but the initiated could share.

The deep familiar voice of the landlord of The Demon made Morty turn sharply to find the old man leaning on an oblong stone tomb immediately behind him.

'That is the Wishart section of God's acre which is being marked and explored. My grandfather rested his bones there in 1870 at his own request next to Victoria Ann, his first wife who was childless. He was the last of us to find peace in this ground before it was closed. My grandmother, a Woodrose, who bore him two sons and three daughters lies solitary in the earth of St Michael's at Forty Angels. I often wondered if she resented it. What do you suppose those young men are up to?'

Morty shrugged his shoulders. 'You could always ask them, of course.'

'I took that step. They are making an official survey which, it was pointed out, was none of my business. They appear to be using a quantity of expensive government equipment so they must have some *locus standi*. What is your opinion?'

'I'd guess they were looking for the same thing as your visitor of Saturday night. Your buddy Jonah had callers not long ago, or so I'm told. You should get together on the quiz programme.'

The poet was discomforted. He had aged in the past week, and the sudden years had exposed the weakness of his face without bringing dignity.

'The days of collaboration are over,' he said. 'You have never been blackmailed, I suppose, Mr Kelsey? If you had, you might be more compassionate, even if you have been affronted at second hand. But when the shadow lifts it is like the sun coming up on a soft day. One believes in everlasting mercy.'

He turned abruptly and strode off towards the inn. Morty, watching him as he picked his way between tents and caravans, found the retreating back infinitely depressing. As he disappeared into the yard of The Demon he became aware of a newcomer to the collection of idlers by the broken gate. It was Mr Campion.

For a reason which he could not analyse an intense irritation seized the younger man and for some minutes he made no move to join the slim spectacled figure behind the main group. Finally curiosity overcame him and he strolled across.

'What the hell goes on here?'

The thin man continued to survey the workers in the churchyard. They were standing with their heads together, poring over calculations on the tow headed youth's board. There was obviously some technical disagreement between them which could only be settled by a slight change in the area they were quartering.

'Ducdame. Ducdame,' said Mr Campion at last.

'I don't get it.'

'A Greek invocation to call fools into a circle, according to the melancholy Jacques. I hope the old English pastime is not understood in these parts. Tell me how many acquaintances of yours there are in the audience. For your information, Mr Jonah Woodrose who was with us briefly has just departed, leaving his foreman behind as an observer. Who else?'

Morty looked about him. 'Wishart was here for a bit. There's an odd little bird in a shiny blue suit called Hamilton Dashwood standing on your left, beyond the green tent. He's only here at weekends as a rule. Constable Simmonds has just arrived on his bicycle. The two men in sweaters row fresh vegetables out to the ships at anchor and do a bit of fishing. The fat dame in the apron is supposed to have been a girl friend of Teague's in the days gone by, but a lot of the ladies have that reputation. The semi-dwarf is called Alan Sullivan. The tall guy in the dark glasses is one of the tearaway lot. They call him Moo Moo, the Dog-Faced Boy and God knows why. I thought he'd gone off with the rest of them and he's certainly no friend of mine. He's the guy I put on his back in The Demon. That's the lot and you still haven't answered my question.'

Mr Campion took him by the arm. 'Time for a quiet stroll before lunch,' he murmured. 'These technical birds are here at my request and if you want a share in the fun and games you must play along with me. I am hoping to exorcise the Demon of Mob's Bowl once and for all. Mossy Ling said he saw a ghost, but my private bet is that the ghost was very substantial and when the old man looked like saying too much he was literally shaken to death. I think, in fact, that he recognised somebody. It wouldn't take much to kill anyone in his condition and no doctor would be any wiser. It's not my business to say who killed Hector Askew, but I'd prefer it if there weren't any more silver bullets flying around. Even stones flung at the weathercock are disturbing to the peace.'

'You're still being goddam mysterious. Do you get a kick out of it?'

They were beyond the cottages now and the narrow strip of road to Forty Angels twisted ahead of them. Mr Campion turned aside so that he could lean over a gate and survey the inland hamlet.

'My dear chap,' he said. 'I am only vague because I should hate to be wrong. If you want a share in the proceedings you'll be more than welcome but it's fair to say that they may be rather protracted and unpleasant, nine parts boredom to one part terror—a very usual formula. You might catch nothing more than a common cold.'

'Include me in. What about Dido?'

Mr Campion sighed. 'I have failed in my efforts to persuade my hostess to get back to London,' he admitted. 'But at least she has agreed to keep out of danger. I hope she intends to keep her word. If you care to risk your own skin, there is a place for you in the ranks of the brave.'

'Just what are you up to?'

'You could say I am tethering a goat in the hope of enticing a dangerous animal. Tomorrow afternoon the hunt will shift to the copse beside The Hollies. The boys with their paraphernalia will do some preliminary research there. Then they'll call it a day and pack up, leaving a clear field. After that, because you know the whole terrain you could be very useful.'

He gave precise instructions.

Sergeant Throstle was not the happiest of men. He had worked until he was exhausted, missed a long promised day at Lords watching his favourite County play Middlesex and had achieved very little beyond a mass of detail about the private lives of a dozen women with peccadilloes to conceal who had not hesitated to show resentment at the intrusion. He sat in Inspector Branch's office and envied the local man his new uncluttered desk and his impending retirement.

'A powerful lot of trouble adding up to a gale of wind that wouldn't blow a paper boat across a bath.' The old man's summing up was cheerfully delivered but it did not make pleasant hearing. 'Ain't you got nothing else, boy?'

'Precious little. There are two items of interest but I don't see where they lead. Old Miss Kytie knew Teague quite well. He was some sort of pet of hers.'

Branch shook his head: he was not impressed. 'I don't doubt it. A wonderful lot of women fancied Jim Teague one way or another. None of them, that old girl included, could resist a rogue with a smooth tongue and a bit of real devil in him. Maybe she mended his socks and maybe she did it to spite the vicar or put her friends' noses out of joint. Maybe he brought her a bottle or two when he pulled off a smart trick. You could say the same of forty women up and down the coast.'

Throstle frowned. 'Back to Askew then. He seems to have been disliked by a lot of people, respectable and otherwise. But not deeply hated. As I see him he was a very minor sort of blackguard living under his father's thumb, which explains why he wasn't married. His girl friends seem to have left him of their own accord and without regrets as far as I can discover. The other item of interest is that he too knew Teague, and Burrows as well, come to that.'

'Couldn't have been more than a baby, could he? Do you reckon anything to it?'

'Hector Askew was thirty-eight this year. Looked a lot younger, so I'm told. He had an adventure of sorts with them in the summer before the war, when he was about nine years old. He went for a trip with them in an old sea going lugger they owned. The engine broke down when they were half way to Dieppe and they went missing for a couple of days. I don't know if it means anything.'

Branch chuckled reminiscently. 'That old hulk. A thirty-five foot gaff rigged cutter doing six or seven knots. The *Saltey Siren* she used to be called. Got around to a lot of highly remarkable places, if I remember aright. But I doubt those two would be up to anything special with a bit of a boy on board. Still, it might be a pointer.'

'Teague killed a man once because he was recognised. It could have happened again. If Askew spotted either of those two hanging round The Hollies he'd very likely have known who they were. That's how my mind's running.'

'Back to the pirates, eh? Well now, it so happens I can show you a properly strange little masterpiece.'

Inspector Branch slid open a drawer and produced a booklet which he pushed across the table. 'You recall mentioning an old friend, name of Dashwood? I took the trouble to look him over again since you brought him to mind. He works for Belcher's Novelties of Ipswich and gets around quite a bit to dance halls, piers, pleasure arcades and the like. The boys are giving him a little attention but I thought perhaps I'd keep a tab on him myself. This is his firm's catalogue. Just you run your eye over it, mister, there's a mint of good reading there.'

Throstle complied. Belcher's Novelties covered a very wide range of aids to public and private amusement from streamers, crackers, whistles, false noses and conjuring tricks to seaside souvenirs and dribble glasses. Small illustrations made the pages as crowded as an Edwardian draper's shop.

A cross in red pencil caught his eye and he began to read aloud:

'Hiroshima Demon Masks. The very latest, directly imported from Japan. Surprise your friends with this unique and humorous spine-chiller. Trimmed with genuine goat's hair. A real wham for any party.'

'Recognise it?'

Throstle snorted. 'So that's where they came from. A very tasteful item as you say. It may help the Narcotics boys in some way but I don't see that it does us much good. Dashwood could be a pedlar—he'd have plenty of opportunity and a very good cover story—but it doesn't quite relate him to Hector Askew. Or have I missed something?'

'You have, you know. Here, give me the book.'

The old man retrieved the list, flicked through the pages and pressed one open with a heavy thumb. Again a scarlet cross pointed the way.

'The Gresham Super-Improved Catapult. In heavy all-aluminium frame with leather pocket and new (patent applied for) sighting adjuster. Powerful square-cut heavy duty rubber cord gives great range and accuracy. Not a toy but a true sportsman's instrument. Kills birds, vermin, etc. at long range.'

'A true sportsman's instrument, Mr Throstle. That's what it says. Now I wouldn't know about that, but it does so happen that I've got one of these little old play things right here in this office and it might just give you an idea. An offensive weapon we called it when we took it off a boy who was doing a wonderfully mischievous bit of damage to windows in the Nine Ash Primary. Seeing it in that list and remembering the trouble we had gave me a sort of an idea.'

He re-opened the drawer and produced a modern and vicious version of the ancient device. The Y-fork was of metal and the leather centre-piece, shaped to hold the missile, had a flange which could be gripped so that aiming it became remarkably simple. The window of the office faced into the yard and the old man opened it wide.

'I've been hankering to do this all day,' he admitted. 'Picked up a couple or three likely stones out of my garden this morning in case you dropped by.' He fitted a pebble carefully into the socket and took aim towards the opposite roof. 'We don't run to a weathercock so a chimneypot will have to do duty.'

The clang of stone on metal cowling announced a direct hit and Branch closed the window guiltily. 'Makes you think, doesn't it?' he said and laughed so that the years dropped away from him. 'Powerful smart, I call that. Target couldn't have done better himself.'

'Throstle took the weapon from the old man and stretched the thick black rubber tentatively.

'Ought to have seen that one coming,' he said at last and swore gently to himself. 'A ruddy catapult—a toy a child could use. Anyone could have been scaring the pants off Saltey by this trick—Dashwood or any man, woman, or child in the place. Bang goes Target Burrows.'

The Inspector was still laughing. 'You don't want to be so sure of that. I doubt Target's good eye would be so clear now as it was twenty odd years back. But he was a smart old boy in some ways and up to any trick he could lay his hands on. He could have bought one of these things for himself if he'd a mind to. Had you thought of that now?'

Morty reached the first point in his journey after a three mile detour. At eleven o'clock on Wednesday night he had retired to his bedroom at The Demon, keeping his lamp burning for another half hour in case his movements were attracting attention. Then he escaped from the silent inn into a night that was chilly and dark; for the moon was hidden behind the banks of low cloud and the scurrying wind coming in from the sea carried a threat of rain in the salt.

He was wearing a dark green pullover with his most sombre trousers and carrying a long torch more for protection than use. He moved quietly along the sea wall beyond the Bowl and then struck inland picking his way cautiously beside wide ditches where water sucked and reeds hissed and rustled together.

A dog at Cheffin's Farm heard him over a distance of three fields and made a surly complaint about the trespasser but no light appeared in the house. Still by way of fields he passed the unwelcoming bulk of barns and outbuildings which marked the corner of the road into Saltey. Presently he arrived at the hump backed bridge which crossed the narrow Rattey river before it finally emerged above the Bowl. This was his turning point and here he was to wait, if necessary until dawn.

An open fronted cart shed whose pantiled roof was dangerously decayed provided a little shelter and he sat for some time listening to the faint lap of the stream punctured by the hunting call of brown owls in the elms which bordered the road.

In the half hour before one in the morning, two cars passed him heading for Firestone, their headlights blazing strange traceries through the gaps in the weatherboarding, but a third beam suddenly faded as it approached, though an engine continued to purr. The car halted on the road within a few yards of him and above the throb he heard the click of a gate which creaked as it swung back and scuffed the ground in its path. A door closed and the car rustled slowly into the field.

Morty followed cautiously through the opening, judging his distance by his ears. The grass track over the water meadows followed the turns of the river and three more gates were opened before the engine spluttered into silence. He knew now that the car had two occupants for both doors opened and closed. Footsteps in long grass whispered for a moment and were swallowed into the night.

To his right the ground rose slightly. Beyond this field lay the copse which marked the boundary of The Hollies property: an overgrown thicket where limes, chestnuts and thorns fought dourly for survival. He reached the outlying bushes and paused to listen.

Ahead of him a twig cracked and another. He was closer than he had guessed, but the quarry was still moving. A sapling whipped him sharply across the face and for a moment he floundered nearly off balance. Brambles clawed at his ankles: a terrified rabbit darted between his feet and was gone.

Above his head there was a sudden clatter of wings as a pair of ring doves wheeled away into the leaden sky and he took advantage of the commotion to get clear of his entanglements and edge his way towards a track which he knew must lie very near. There was a clearing beyond him centring on a Victorian summerhouse, a Gothic-rustic affair of split logs with stained glass windows and a conical roof and he crept towards it feeling his way, pace by pace, to defeat the traitorous undergrowth.

Ahead the footsteps continued, less cautious and more purposeful now. He was very close, too close for safety and he waited to give them time to reach the clearing. A half fallen branch barred his way and he stepped crabwise towards the trunk of the tree to avoid the obstacle.

For a minute he waited, straining his ears and eyes. The copse had settled into silence. Again a snapping twig ahead of him brought a respite. He took a long pace, recovered his balance and halted in mid stride. Someone, an arm's length from him, was leaning against the tree.

Almost in the same second he knew that it was Dido. The uncomplicated flower scent which she used so sparingly came clearly into his nostrils betraying her as vividly as if she had spoken. He had only to put out his hand to touch her.

The thought that to do so might make her cry out held him back; even a whisper could bring its terror. He waited scarcely breathing. A pencil of light flickered in the clearing, distorting shapes, shadows and silhouettes, bringing into sudden brightness a meaningless glimpse which was so vivid that it lingered on the retina as his eyes blinked.

Dido stiffened and began to walk steadily towards the blackness where the gleam had been. Following her, he began to count the paces. Seven, eight, nine, ten.

A torch in her hand sprang into life to show two faceless black figures frozen for a second by the glare.

'What are you doing on my property?' said Doctor Jones. 'I don't like trespassers.'

The moment of hesitation passed. The taller of the two bounded beyond the circle of light and crashed wildly into the undergrowth, but the other turned slowly, almost imperceptibly and looked straight into the beam, so that the distortion of features covered by a silk stocking was grotesquely emphasised.

A knife glinted like a diamond as the figure crouched, gathered strength and leapt forward bearing Dido to the ground.

Morty flung himself at the creature, grasping wildly at whatever his fingers touched. Suddenly there were lights from four directions, the rush of feet, a young excited voice and the struggle was over.

Dido held out a hand to Morty and he pulled her gently to her feet.

'I—I'm all right,' she said. 'Just a bit winded. What a melodramatic lot you are.' She swayed uncertainly and Morty's arm tightened about her waist. 'I am all right—really I am. No cuts or broken bones. Now, who or what is this thing on the ground?'

The figure had not moved since the tussle had ended. It lay spreadeagled, face downwards, pinned out by a tow headed young man in a disreputable jacket. He picked himself up without releasing his grip, dragging his capture with him.

Mr Campion emerged quietly from the ring of torches and taking hold of the silken mask slipped it swiftly over the dark head.

'Meet Miss Doll Jensen,' he said. 'Her other claim to fame is that she is the daughter of James Teague.'

19

Death of a Legend

A SERIES of crashes in the undergrowth followed by a cheerful shout in a strong Cockney accent made the group in the clearing turn their heads.

'Charlee-ee.... Got him.'

The tow-haired youth who had led the party of surveyors continued his grip on the girl and lifted his voice in answer.

'Don't make such a row about it. People sleep here, you know.' To Campion he said: 'Silly bastard. That's Wonderboy —I told him to keep his trap shut. Does it matter now?'

The thin man did not reply for a moment but focused the beam of his torch so that it made a tunnel of bright green along twenty yards of the track. At the far end two figures in denims emerged grasping a third between them, a black leather clad bundle limp as a roll of carpet. They halted as the light caught them and Mr Campion turned to Lugg who had been standing behind him.

'Nip down and see what they've got. If it's the one called Moo Moo, just see him off the premises.'

'Letting 'im off the 'ook, are you? Thousands wouldn't.'

'He's just a stooge and the lady had several more young things like him who do little services for her. Charlie, would you mind running your hands over Miss Jensen in case she is carrying a gun as well as a pocket knife?'

For the first time the girl flared into life.

'I've got no bloody gun. Keep your lousy hands off me.'

Charlie's delighted grin suggested he had enjoyed himself. 'I frisked her just now. Just a flick knife and a torch. That's the lot, isn't it, darling? What shall we do with her?'

'In that case you can relax your grip. She won't run away

because we have something she particularly wants to see.' Mr Campion's tone was as conversational as an invitation to a tea party. 'Perhaps we should go into the house. It's a trifle chilly out here.'

The garden room at The Hollies had undergone a remarkable change since Morty had last seen it. The two glass walls had been covered with dusty black curtain material stretched over wooden frames, evidently a survival of wartime blackout arrangements, and shades which he had not noticed before had been drawn to ensure that no light escaped from the roof. He led Dido to the big cane chair and sat on its broad arm, his right hand still caressing her shoulder. In the more normal lighting he could see Doll Jensen's face very white beneath the mop of tight coarse curls. She was breathing rapidly, her teeth clenched as if to prevent them from chattering.

She hesitated in the doorway, her eyes wide with excitement and curiosity, took in the scene and walked deliberately to a corner where a slatted bench for potted plants offered a seat. She sat very still, her head bowed and her hands gripping the wooden edge.

Mr Campion leaned over a ladderback chair at the head of the table, awaiting the return of the rest of the party. In the minute of stilted silence the senior surveyor pulled out a packet of cigarettes, offered them without success and finally lit one for himself.

When the group was complete Mr Campion addressed himself directly to the four young men who were staring at the girl on the bench with uninhibited curiosity.

'You haven't met our guest before, so it might be as well to put you in the picture. I doubt if she'll confirm the details for us and one or two of them only came in this afternoon. If she takes my advice she won't bother with protests because nothing she can say now is any business of ours.

'Her full name is Dorothy Marilyn Jensen. Her mother was Jane Felgate who was born just up the road and who married a Norwegian sailor before the war. He was killed in 1942.

There's not much doubt about who her real father is for the excellent reason that she takes after him in more ways than one and is proud of the fact. The physical likeness is very strong.

'An old man called Mossy Ling spotted it and was silly enough to say he'd seen a ghost. She frightened him to death, in my opinion. Hector Askew probably let on that he recognised the likeness when he caught her exploring in this house.'

Morty leaned forward. 'Are you saying that this ... that Doll ... killed Askew?'

The girl in the corner raised her head to Campion in a long straight glare of speculative venom. When she turned to Morty her voice became urgent and intimate. 'It's a bloody silly lie. You know it's not true—it couldn't be. The first time I ever clapped eyes on you was when you were coming down here with your godalmighty girl friend—just as I was. I ran into all that glass only just ahead of you. I was never in the blasted house until this minute. You know that. You'll tell them if you've got the guts of a louse. The police aren't bloody fools— they know I couldn't have done it. You're listening to a raving nut who fancies himself as some sort of private dick. Be your age. He's round the bend!'

Mr Campion intervened. 'Fortunately for us all I don't have to prove my theory about her guilt. But this afternoon I performed an experiment for my private satisfaction. I walked from here through the copse and along the meadows to the bridge by the same route that the trespassers used tonight and drove from there to the corner by Ponder's Farm. It took twenty minutes. I allowed myself another twenty in which to smash bottles, had I been in the mood for it. A total of forty minutes and it could have been done in under half an hour. I'm afraid Miss Jensen's alibi doesn't exist.'

The girl was still prepared to fight. She opened her mouth as if to speak but waited, angry and watchful.

'Dislike of being recognised runs in the family. Jonah

Woodrose found that out, but he has a guilty conscience about smuggling so it was easier to stop him talking.

'There is a very good reason for her to be sensitive on the subject and it goes back a very long way. I think Miss Jensen was brought up on a legend, the legend of James Teague, the great lover, the great pirate, the hero who was her true father. There are two nights in his final adventure which are not accounted for. I think he spent them in Harwich with Jane Felgate and her daughter who must have been about a year old. He probably gave a pretty colourful but not necessarily truthful account of his exploits and I expect he boasted of his adventures, implying that he had hidden a fortune somewhere in Saltey and told them that when the storm blew over they would all be richer than Croesus. Unfortunately for them he was caught.

'I think that mother and daughter talked and dreamed about that boast to the exclusion of everything else in the world. They moved from town to town over the years so that they could never be traced, waiting for the great moment when their hero was free.

'In the mean time a lot of people suspected that Teague had come ashore from the barge *Blossom* that night and had hidden something in Saltey—possibly at The Hollies. Jonah Woodrose and Wishart for example.

'The only person who refused to share in the dream was Teague himself, once he was arrested. Every sort of pressure was put upon him but he never spoke.

'Jane Felgate died but her daughter watched and waited. She refused to believe that her father would keep his secret once he was free. She arranged for him to disappear as soon as he came out and paid for his board with a woman called Medway, who is the mother's half-sister, by the way.'

The girl was now crouching on the bench so that only the swarthy curls at the nape of her neck were visible. Again she flung up her head as if she were about to protest but her breath caught in her throat and no words came.

Mr Campion's diffident murmur continued.

'I think I should explain that Miss Jensen is not short of money. How her income is made is not my business but I suspect that the police are investigating it rather carefully and her time is running short. A man called Dashwood has been arrested and they are looking for the woman he worked with. When they discover, as they will, who she is, they are bound to make other deductions about Askew's death. But what matters to us now is the sequence of events.

'Miss Kytie's death and her unexpected bequest to Dido upset everyone's calculations. It seems she was a mischievous old thing and it's on the cards that she may have had a shrewd suspicion that something had been hidden at The Hollies. She had a curious sort of aunt-and-nephew relationship with Teague. He did odd jobs for her and gave her presents. In return she may have turned a blind eye to any use he made of the house when she left it untenanted. It might—just might—explain why she decided to put everyone's nose out of joint and leave the place to a stranger. Villagers have very long memories and I think half the population of Saltey was waiting for her to die so that the house could be forced to give up its secret—if it had one.'

He turned to Dido.

'This is where you came into the picture. When the news about the will got around, Jonah Woodrose had the idea of scaring you off by getting Wishart to write those letters, hoping you'd sell out without a fight and he could get his hands on the property.

'Miss Jensen also began to take an interest in the new owner. She even got herself a part-time job in the Swallow Café so that she could keep an eye on your movements. Do you recognise her, now?'

Dido surveyed her coldly.

'Ye-es,' she said at last. 'I do now. She was a rotten waitress. I often wondered why she never smiled and generally kept her back to me. How did you find that out?'

'I didn't,' said Mr Campion, modestly. 'It was simply a logical guess. The woman who ran the café was talking about useless part-timers when I went there.

'The real upset to her plans came when Teague was released. This must have been quite a shock. Remember, she'd never seen him except possibly in an old photograph. I think they were in touch with each other in a cautious furtive way after her mother died, but she had no idea of what he was really like. Instead of a hero there was nothing but a broken, frightened old man, a poor chap who wanted only peace and quiet— no more secrets, no more adventures.

'Miss Jensen had to do some sharp re-thinking. She may have been baulked for a little, but she certainly wasn't stupid.

'Her idea, in fact, was remarkably ingenious. Both Teague and Burrows had what you might call trade marks which were well known here in Saltey—a silver bullet, a trick with a stone and a patched eye. She set out very successfully to establish a reign of terror by suggesting that they were both back and looking for trouble. By conjuring up the impression that they were around she drew everyone's attention in the wrong direction. She knew her father would be suspected, but even if he were winkled out of his hiding place he would have no difficulty in proving his innocence.

'In the meantime he provided the perfect bogey man to scare anyone who knew more than was good for him into making a move. She started the trail by leaving his pocket book at the café to make sure that the police got the message. She had a lot of willing help of course, from her tearaway friends though I very much doubt if they knew quite how they were being used, even when they were beating up Jonah and the unfortunate man Sibling.'

He turned to Morty. 'The chap who raised a bruise on your head—Moo Moo, I expect—was probably acting without instructions, paying off a score on his own behalf. But it all helped the illusion. Burrows got the credit for that one.

'This whole exercise failed because nobody in fact had very much to conceal. Like Miss Jensen they were waiting for a cat who refused to jump. That didn't deter the lady: she and her friends raided and smashed every smugglers' hideaway in the place and broke into all the secret stores and bolt holes she'd learned about from her mother's knee.

'Only The Hollies remained. On the short list now, and when our boys began to turn their surveying instruments on to the grounds she couldn't resist coming back for a final search. Not the neatest of traps, perhaps, but it worked.'

Morty straightened his back.

'You took a chance,' he said. 'Dido might have been hurt.'

'She wasn't part of the plan.' Mr Campion was apologetic. 'I'm afraid she wasn't deceived by our apparently off-handed behaviour. She made her own investigations.'

Dido looked up and for the first time placed a hand over Morty's.

'It doesn't matter any longer,' she said. 'The important thing is the reason for all this trouble. Albert, do you know the answer?'

He paused before replying as if he was re-considering a difficult decision.

'Yes,' he said, finally. 'Yes, I do. The question is really one for Miss Jensen and she may not like the truth when she sees it.'

He turned to the girl. 'You've come a long way to satisfy your curiosity. It might be wiser, even now, to leave well alone. You could walk right out of this room and as far as we are concerned no one will follow you.'

She shook her head without looking up. Her hands remained clenched, the knuckles white with tension. It was some time before she answered, speaking quietly and slowly, almost to herself.

'Anything hidden here belongs to my father. He fought for it. He did time for it. He's paid for it. It's nothing to do with anybody else. It's his.'

Mr Campion sighed and pulled back the chair he had been leaning on.

'As you wish,' he said. wearily. 'In a way it does belong to your father. Charlie, will you keep an eye on the lady? I want to move the table first.'

Morty jumped to his feet, pulling Dido after him. 'Do you mean to say it's here—right under our feet?'

'Right under our feet. It's as simple as that.'

A dusty space was cleared in the centre of the room. Beneath the threadbare turkey carpet there was a large rectangular cast iron grid which fitted flush with the yellow and red tiles of the floor. Its fellows could be found in the aisle of any Victorian church.

Lugg had provided himself with a small crowbar and with the aid of one of the surveyors he prised the diamond patterned screen from its socket. The cavity beneath contained two heavy, cast iron pipes, running from end to end, a part of the heating arrangements for the conservatory.

'Ingenious,' said Mr Campion. 'You could pass a mine detector over this without discovering anything remarkable though I doubt if James Teague thought of that one. Even the police had it up when they were looking for a gun. Evidently there wasn't a gardener or plumber in the search party, which is just as well.

Dido peered into the cavity.

'What did they miss?'

'The real pipes don't come this way at all. They run round the walls and are heated by a stove on the other side of the wall. This was James Teague's private store cupboard built out of what used to be a pool for watering flowers. There is an old photograph of it on my bedroom wall showing a draining table above it covered with prize begonias. These pipes are just intelligent camouflage fixed to a false floor. Even the hooks to lift the whole thing out have been standing in a corner for twenty years.'

He looked around him.

'This is the moment of truth.'

Morty and Dido stood very close to each other, their arms linked. Slowly Lugg and his helper lifted the pipes and the floor beneath them in one piece until they were level with the tiles. Slowly they dragged the burden to one side exposing a deeper cavity flanked by grey concrete walls.

The hanging lamp shone directly upon the thing that lay in the pit: a sprawling wreck, half skeleton, half mummy which had once been a man. Wisps of rotting blue clothing clung to the bones and heavy seaboots covered the feet but the skull from which the jaw still hung was parchment yellow and naked.

The shocking quality of the sight was emphasised by the reactions of everyone in the room. Death had come violently and suddenly to this stranger, blotting him out like a fly on a windscreen. It did not matter if he had died yesterday or lain there for a century: the impact of sudden irrevocable finality filled the room. The young men looked down, absorbed the shock, looked away, then returned to stare curiously. Morty held Dido back, his arm about her shoulder. Mr Campion alone watched Doll Jensen, his eyes cold and speculative.

Her voice, strangled to a whisper broke the petrifying silence.

'Christ,' she muttered. 'He's looking at me. He's not dead.'

Mr Campion shook his head. 'I'm afraid he's very dead indeed. You are looking at the body of Thomas Alfred Burrows and somewhere in his rib cage you'll no doubt find a silver bullet. He was wearing his glass eye when he was killed. His trademark has outlived his body.'

The girl stepped closer to bend over the pit. The vivid blue eyeball stared back from its socket giving the bones an expression of suspended life, a leering secretive grimace which changed oddly to simple astonishment as the light caught it. She straightened herself and began to laugh in a high pitched, mirthless wail which was more frightening than the thing beneath her feet.

Dido considered her coldly for a moment and then, releasing

Morty's arm she moved round the cavity. Two smart slaps across the face with a left and a right, rocked the dark curls backwards and silenced the screams. Charlie, standing behind Doll, caught her by the shoulders and shook her.

'That's enough of that. Here, sit down. Put your head between your legs, if you feel faint.'

He lifted her off her feet, dropped her on to a chair and tried to bend her forward. She thrust him away and began to sob quietly and uncontrollably, hugging herself and weaving her body from side to side.

Dido eyed her professionally but without pity.

'There's very little wrong with her. She's had a shock—haven't we all?—but she's as tough as nails. The question is, what do we do with her?'

'The answer to that,' said Mr Campion, 'is simple and uncharitable. We do nothing. We're none of us policemen. A good counsel could probably demolish my theories even if they resulted in a charge. My responsibilities here are to the living, to the future.'

The sobbing had stopped and as he turned to the girl she raised a blotched white face, streaked with mascara. She was still frightened, still choked with shock, but an instinct for self preservation flickered in her eyes.

'I think you must go now. I think you must go right away—indeed you would be remarkably foolish if you ever tried to come back. I hope you understand that?'

She nodded almost imperceptibly, glancing from one face to the next, making certain that he spoke for them all.

'What about that—that thing?'

Campion waited before answering.

'That thing, as you call it, is your father's secret. As far as you are concerned it must stay that way. You should be on your way.'

She stood up and shook herself, straightening her shoulders as if she had been freed from carrying a heavy knapsack and sidled carefully round the dark hole in the centre. Lugg opened the door into the garden and stood back for her to pass but on the threshold she hesitated and turned directly to Morty.

'You wouldn't...?' she said and paused. The question answered itself. 'No, you wouldn't.'

When she reached the far end of the lawn she began to run.

20

Cargo of Eagles

A S Lugg closed the door the remainder of the group turned to Campion. He was sitting forward in a chair, his hands clasped between his knees, staring absently into the cavity in front of him.

'What now?' said Morty. 'Is this the end of the whole goddamned business? Is this what the entire shooting match was about? A matelot who was murdered twenty years back?'

The thin man looked up as if he found the question surprising. 'Oh, no. Not the end. In a sense it is only the beginning. Dr Jones, speaking professionally, would you prescribe tea at this moment? I'm afraid the dawn is going to sneak up on us very soon. Lugg can arrange it if you agree?'

The tension had broken and Dido gave a sigh of weariness and relief.

'Speaking professionally,' she said, 'I prescribe Farmer's tea, thick, hot and strong. But for the love of mike anywhere else but here—the kitchen, perhaps. I'll give him a hand.'

Mr Campion rose to his feet.

'Charlie and the boys,' he said, 'have a rather tricky job ahead of them. They are about to compound a felony and we are all, I suppose, accessories before the fact. But Burrows has served his purpose and I think his remains should be discreetly removed. If you and Morty agree, he can be transferred very efficiently into oblivion.'

He turned to the leader of the surveyors.

'You know what to do. Could you be ready and move in half an hour?'

Charlie grinned. 'We can fix our own tea break.'

Mr Lugg had worked miracles with unpromising material in

the kitchen for the room had a stone flagged floor, an ancient black oven and an air of hard working austerity. It was now warm, polished and glowing with a bright scarlet and white chequered tablecloth as the centre piece. Hot amber tea laced with whisky appeared within minutes and the reviving benison was sipped in silence.

Morty broke the spell by thumping the table. 'The loot,' he said explosively. 'The pirates' hoard that's driven Saltey round the bend for all these years. Was it just another myth, an inflated nonsense like the Demon— did it ever exist?'

Mr Campion surveyed him over his glasses.

'Oh yes. It certainly existed.' He stood up and crossed the room to a cupboard beneath a dresser. From it he produced a dark green metal box about eighteen inches square and four inches deep, a solid unattractive object which might have been designed to hold ammunition. He placed it carefully on the table for it was clearly heavy.

'A treasure chest. Or part of it.' He patted it gently before continuing. 'This is the real object of the exercise. It weighs fifty pounds and there are ten of them. Until two nights ago when Lugg and I found them they were lying beneath the body of Target Burrows but it seemed best to satisfy Miss Jensen's curiosity by allowing her to know only half the story.'

He pressed a spring catch and raised the lid. Inside lay a row of cylinders each wrapped in discoloured paper which had once been white, fitting closly into grooves. He prized one free with a kitchen knife and unwrapped it methodically, balancing it in his hand. The column swayed in the air and broke, splaying a yellow cascade over the table. On the chequered cloth the coins made a gay modern design in red, white and gold.

'Double Eagles,' he said. 'Twenty dollar gold pieces. Pirate gold—fairy gold—a king's ransom. It depends how you look at them.'

The steaming drink provided an essential pause. The bright coins glistened on the table between the tea cups and it was some time before Morty picked one of them up, holding it gingerly between finger and thumb.

'Give me a minute to get my breath,' he said. 'I've never seen one before except on a bandleader's watchchain. They must be worth a fortune.'

Mr Campion sipped his tea thoughtfully before producing a slip of paper from his wallet.

'According to my Bank Manager, who says he is not really used to this sort of enquiry, the Double Eagle is worth £15 and weighs 0.967501 of a fine ounce. Today's price for bullion gold is £11.11.9 an ounce. Mathematics is not my strong point but I make the grand total around £100,000. Quite a haul, even for a modern pirate.'

'How much did Doll really know of this?' Dido's voice had the trace of an edge. 'Or was she guessing hopefully in her little dream world?'

Mr Campion shook his head. 'She didn't know anything. All she had to go on was the vague boast repeated by her mother. Teague only opened his mouth once and as soon as he was caught he thought better of it. He had killed two men to keep his secret and in a way, three. But twenty years is a long time to think over one's sins especially if not all of them have been found out. There's no statute of limitations for murder, you know, and he dared not face the chance of a second charge when he was old and broken. When I saw him it occurred to me that he'd had some sort of mild stroke. He...'

Morty interrupted. 'You said he killed two men and possibly three. Who was the third?'

'The third death was Matt Parsley, the undertaker. I don't think Teague killed him but he was certainly morally responsible. On that particular night the 26th of March, 1946, when the barge *Blossom* lay off the Bowl, Teague and Burrows took their cargo ashore. It was stowed in champagne cases which fitted the boxes very neatly, two to a case.

'Matt Parsley was an old villian who knew all about smuggling and had certainly helped them many times before, and his workshop was very close to the quay. They loaded the stuff on to his barrow, probably putting most of it into a coffin, in case anyone noticed them going up the road to Forty Angels. Teague had his hideaway here at The Hollies, a cache he'd built long before the war for hiding contraband. Miss Kytie was away all that spring and the house was empty.

'What happened in the garden room that night is a matter of pure guess work. My guess is that Matt Parsley, who was a fat, asthmatic old man with a weak heart, had an attack, perhaps brought on by lifting heavy weights, I think he died in this room, but quite unexpectedly—leaving only Teague and Burrows. They may have quarrelled and had a fight for Teague may have killed his partner in cold blood. Again Burrows may have been killed first and the shock was too much for Matt Parsley. Remember, there was the very devil of a row about the piracy when it became known. On the night the *Blossom* lay off Saltey a description of the two men was broadcast, with particular emphasis on Burrows' glass eye, which made him very easy to recognise. They had to hide the loot and they certainly didn't trust each other enough to lie low separately until things quietened down. Teague was the brains of the act and he probably realised that as long as Burrows was anywhere near him, his chances of being recognised and caught were more than doubled. He was a calculating killer and the idea could have been in his mind all along. He is the only man who knows the truth and he is pretty certain to die with his secret.

'What I am sure he did was to put Matt Parsley's body into the coffin and trundle it back to the shed, where he abandoned it in a rather spectacular way.'

Mr Lugg lifted one of the curtains and looked out. 'Dawn coming up,' he said. 'I'll take the boys a drop and see how they're gettin' on with the packin'.'

Morty was still playing with the golden array on the table.

'Who owns this stuff? What happens to it now?'

'Two very good questions,' said Mr Campion. 'And the first

one isn't so simple to answer. Strictly speaking it belongs to the Treasury but that is not quite where it is going.'

He drew his chair closer to the table and began to arrange the coins in a pile.

'This is the whole story. I couldn't tell it before and for reasons you'll understand it must never be told again.

'At the end of the War I was with a man called L. C. Corkran—you spotted him the other day in Killowen Square, Morty—doing one of those hush-hush jobs in France.

'I'm afraid a lot of bribery and corruption came into it and the only reliable currency was gold. In the Middle East they used British sovereigns but in the Resistance business it was best to pay in twenty dollar gold pieces. When the show closed down the remainder of the cash, all this pirate's hoard, among a lot of other items which we didn't want to explain to the French Government, had to be brought home. At that point it had to be got away very quickly. Not all the people we dealt with were noble souls. They knew we had big money available. An ocean going yacht, the *Clymene*, which belonged to the Greek millionaire Christoff, a chap very much on our side, seemed the ideal transport. He had diplomatic immunity and so far as customs were concerned the yacht could get into any port in England with no questions asked. Our little outfit was so secret that no one was allowed to know about us but the fact must be faced that we weren't secret enough. Somewhere along the line there was a leak. Teague and his pal Burrows who'd spent the War in the Merchant Navy were hanging around Marseilles, up to no good and looking for trouble. They had a couple of other thugs in tow, Goddard and Hunter and between them they ran a profitable line in smuggling and probably gun running between the Riviera and Algiers.

'It looks as if they had a longer trip chasing the *Clymene* than they'd expected or they'd have headed back for an African port once they'd got what they wanted. As it was they were probably running short of fuel so they had to make a dash for the Hamble river and abandon the pirate craft.

'But Christoff's cargo was certainly hi-jacked in a big way and the really valuable part of it vanished without trace. To complicate matters there couldn't be a full scale official enquiry because officially the cargo didn't exist.

'Christoff got most of his own property back and was compensated for the rest because he was a very wily bird and heavily insured. The Eagles were never mentioned. After the trial—when it was clear that Teague had no intention of speaking—the loss had to be placed very regretfully in the just-too-bad section, and filed for reference.'

'Written off?'

'The Department,' said Mr Campion formally, 'never explains its budget, but it has to ask for it just the same. Unfortunately, this does not mean that the funds are liberal—in fact the place is run on the well known shoe string. Things were getting pretty tight when I left them at the end of 1946 and I gather that they've got progressively worse since then. No more golden gifts to keep the natives friendly and precious little sugar for the weekly issue of office tea.

'The Eagles may have been written off, but they weren't forgotten. From then on any really big expenditure had to have sanction from Whitehall. Two months ago a situation arose in which a big sum of money—in Eagles, incidentally—was urgently needed. A British Agent, a woman, had been arrested in an area which is virtually behind the Iron Curtain, even if it pretends not to be. She wasn't charged, but just held and questioned, probably very unpleasantly. It doesn't look as if the people concerned were quite sure of what they'd got hold of, but they were prepared to take a long time finding out, using any methods they pleased.

'Now in the ordinary way of business if a really valuable agent is caught and sentenced an exchange is arranged—it's part of the game and very well understood by both sides. But this case is rather different because as yet they are uncertain if she really is what they suspect. To offer an exchange now, or at any other time come to that, is to admit the woman's guilt and to damn everyone faintly connected with her. Break one link and a whole length of chain goes along with it. Corkran has his human side where his own people are concerned but an admission of that sort would endanger a lot of lives and destroy a whole network.'

He paused to empty his cup. 'There was—there still is—an alternative. Really a very simple one if you know that part of the world. Bribery. A well greased palm for politican and policeman alike. A lot of money, a cargo of Eagles distributed judiciously very near the top, would open any prison in the country.'

'Lovely work if you can get it.' Mr Lugg's throaty tones brought the party back to immediate considerations. 'More tea, one and all?'

'The problem,' continued Mr Campion, 'might be summed up as "First catch your Eagle". Corkran's overtures to the money boys at the Treasury met with a remarkably frigid reception. In fact he was turned down at every level and finally right at the very top. But he had one shot left in the locker. If he could recover the cash which had been written off twenty years back—even if it was technically no longer his to dispose of—he need do no explaining or pleading to anyone.'

He turned to Dido. 'You don't know the old boy, I suppose? Very few people do. He's theoretically too dyed-in-the-wool to thumb his nose at Authority when it's entrenched against him but the idea appeals to him all the same. A lot of his success had been built on it and now that he's retiring he's less respectful than ever.

'In this case he said nothing to his colleagues in the department but called back a member of the firm who had left the business just after the war. Since I had no official standing no one could ask awkward questions. "Who owns that bag of gold you happen to be carrying?": "The Treasury, I suppose, but we have other plans for it".'

'That situation had to be dodged. I'm afraid my efforts have caused you a lot of trouble.'

Dido shook her immaculate head.

'You laid the ghost for me,' she said. 'No one else could have removed Doll Jensen and her friends. Where is all the money, by the way—the rest of it. I mean? Somehow I don't feel it would be safe in a kitchen cupboard, even now.'

Mr Campion's diffident smile broadened. 'If you look in your cellar,' he murmured, 'you'll find seventy-two bottles of excellent champagne. A very good year—I chose it myself. The cases are missing because they are on their way to foreign parts under a diplomatic seal. You can guess the contents. As for the specimens on the table, they will travel to London with the surveyors. All except two, which will never be accounted for.'

He passed one across the table to Dido and another to Morty.

'Just the thing for a watch chain.'

Mr Lugg cocked his head to one side at a sound from above their heads.

'Your refined Ding Dong,' he said. "Orrible friends you've got, ringing up at this time in the morning. As soon as I've packed this lot up I'm ex-communicating meself until late luncheon.'

When Mr Campion returned to the kitchen the old man had disappeared and light was streaming through the curtains. The dawn chorus was reaching a crescendo and the table in the centre of the room was empty.

Dido and Morty who were standing very close to each other by the open window did not hear his arrival and after a few moments he coughed discreetly. They turned towards him and he noticed with a flicker of amusement that Dido's hair had lost its flawless perfection.

'What was all that about?' said Morty.

Mr Campion surveyed them benevolently from over his glasses before he answered. 'A chap from the Department. He rang to say "Mission accomplished".'